Praise for Christian Baines

For *The Arcadia Trust* series

"Baines' brave new underworld is well devised, multi-layered, and dense with political and personal agendas—and it's frightening: so much so that I found myself looking over my shoulder more than once at night." FELICE PICANO, author of *Like People in History*

"Baines has a gift for twisted psyches, playing the supernatural to expose the human evils at play, and a talent for turns of phrases that leave you shuddering even as you turn the page." 'NATHAN BURGOINE, author of *Light*

"I love the world created here. It has the same feel as Laurel K. Hamilton's Anita Blake Series, with a little more grit, and of course, the added m/m element. There is plenty of paranormal elements involved, some more gruesome than others, but it is a very colorful and interesting story." JUSTJEN, *The Blogger Girls*

"Just fantastic! I'm just amazed by the imagination the author put into this, from the culprit to the resolution I just couldn't put it down." SARINA, *Love Bytes Reviews*

"A wickedly subversive wit." JEFFERY ROUND, author of *The Dan Sharp Mysteries*

"I really enjoyed this book and have great admiration for Baines' literary skill. My reaction to *The Orchard of Flesh* is that it's something of a mashup of Clive Barker and Noel Coward." ULYSSES, *Prism Book Alliance*

For other works

"Christian Baines is a writer with a bold, original vision, a vision not beholden to the limits of conventional genre tropes. This is a writer who knows his own voice, and a writer to watch." MICHAEL ROWE, author of *Enter, Night*

BY CHRISTIAN BAINES

THE ARCADIA TRUST *series:*
The Beast Without
The Orchard of Flesh
Sins of the Son

Other books:
Puppet Boy
Skin

CHRISTIAN BAINES

THE BEAST WITHOUT

Christian Baines has written on travel, theatre, film, television, and various aspects of gay life, factual and fictional. Some of his stranger thoughts have spawned novels, including queer urban fantasy series *The Arcadia Trust*, the horror novella *Skin*, and *Puppet Boy*, which was a finalist for the 2016 Saints and Sinners Emerging Writer Award.

Born in Australia, he now travels the world whenever possible, living, writing, and shivering in Toronto, Canada.

Acknowledgements

Thanks to Stuart, Shane, Conrad, Chris, Mark, Tina, Yaniv, Adrian, and others who gave freely their time, feedback, encouragement and love in realising this book. To Bern, whose three printers gave their lives for subsequent rewrites.

To my family, especially the most generous and supportive mother I know. We've come a long way since 'I'm not sure how I feel about reading sex scenes written by my son!'

To David Reiter and IP team for shepherding the book's journey so far and introducing Reylan to the world. Special thanks to my editor Lauren Daniels, who assessed my first manuscript and has been tireless in her perfectionism and encouragement ever since.

To my writing mentors, tutors and workshop partners, particularly Jean Bedford and Anthony Macris. To writing colleagues and booksellers who've championed this novel and subsequent adventures since its publication.

Very special thanks to Cameron, for opening the door onto this world, then believing in, loving and exploring it with me.

THE BEAST WITHOUT

By Christian Baines

CHAPTER ONE

On any given night, in any city in the world, somebody will die before sunrise and most of them will die alone. I speak, not of the peaceful, 'tucked up in bed' deaths, which mark the passing of the fortunate, but rather the deaths that go unseen and often unmourned. The lost soul who climbed a bridge one night and thought the water below might be hiding what remained of his dreams. Or perhaps the one who picked up the wrong one-nighter in some bar. One way to avoid the 'alone' part, I suppose.

Most humans put this sobering thought out of their little heads while they're out on the town. After all, it's not going to happen to them, is it? The nearest to death they'll get on their big night out is a splitting hangover, come morning.

I'm not human, but even so, this is a reality I can't ignore. If I'm not careful when I feed, when I take my fill of blood, I can quickly become the wrong one-nighter.

I'll thank you not to use the 'v' word.

Given my proximity to Oxford Street, the sleazy, pulsing artery of Sydney's nightclub district where I've lived for the better part of thirty years, I try not to visit any club twice in the same week. It's safer that way, particularly for a man whose lifestyle depends on discretion. Barely two nights ago, I'd graced Fantasy, a club full of pretty, if flighty young things—some gay, some straight, most happily open minded on the subject. So, the following night's destination was Blaze, a club currently serving as de facto cathedral to the Church of Saint Muscle Mary, where the buff and beautiful took time out of their forty hour a week gym schedules to model, preen and occasionally dance the night away for the slack-jawed ogling pleasure of curious onlookers.

For hunting clothes, I chose a pair of tight leather trousers, an equally tight lycra vest and a silver-studded belt. A little attractive, a little sexual, and a little ridiculous. The perfect human mix I'd developed over the years. Not the epitome of modern style, but on a healthy twenty-four-year-old man, which is what I appear to be, it did say 'come hither and bed me,' which was the whole point.

Then, there was the pill. I rarely use them, but if options are lacking and I get too impatient, a little chemistry in a capsule can seal the sumptuous fate of any prospective companion. You needn't judge me. You do a lot worse to your food. Besides, it's not as if I've had to use it—recently.

I finally mussed my hair into a high swept fringe that resembled the current trends. There. Reylan had arrived. And so, the hunt commenced.

* * *

If Fantasy was an over-priced showcase of Sydney's most precious 'see or be seen' crowd then Blaze was a stream of hedonistic delights, corrupted further by a tacky West Hollywood sheen, as imagined by a designer who'd had never been within a hundred miles of the place. The neon show was frightening—more Hong Kong than California—turning its lobby into a maw of the throbbing techno-driven beast that lay beyond its doors. Still, there were the delicious beasts within that beast. The elite bodies of Blaze. The blood bags of Blaze. Shallow though it may have been, this was a club not without its advantages.

Flashing the bouncer a smile, I was admitted with a polite flourish. I'm pretty, after all, and pretty's good for business. In front of me, two epicene boys, barely old enough to enter, strutted around with... glitter. Glitter, plastered over their faces and arms, their hair styled up and cemented in place like ghastly exotic birds. Escapees from Fantasy, perhaps? Show cockatiels belong in cages, children.

I quickly turned my attention to the chiselled beauties of mankind that crowded the room. Physically flawless—the pesky confines of mortality notwithstanding. It was rare to find half a brain between them, but for blood that sweet, I was willing to forgo intelligent conversation. Then, there was the ever-present smattering of fine looking women, mingled throughout the posers and their admirers.

Decisions, decisions.

Seduction remains, without doubt, one of the safest forms of feeding available to our kind. I have taken to my bed women, men, white, black, Asian, young, old, fat, thin, muscular... any creed, colour, sexuality or physical type you care to nominate. It is only the taste of the blood that varies.

For example, men taste harder, bolder and fuller in flavour than women. This doesn't necessarily make their blood better, and I've nothing in the world against women. But over decades of hunting, I have found the blood of men much easier to attain. Men are confident to go home with a stranger for a night of rough passion while women tend to balk at the prospect, an unchanging observation for as long as I've depended on their blood. Women are perceptive. Men are dumb—many adorably so.

Like the one who caught my eye, leaning on the bar just a few metres away, swilling expensive beer from a thin bottle.

His short blonde hair shone immaculately in the pulsing lights. His legs snugly filled out dark blue jeans and his black shirt was tucked into a leather belt, laying bare his muscular chest and strong back. I could tell by the bored, lazy expression in his eyes. An easy, tasty meal. A meal named Rory, as a smile and quick introduction soon revealed.

I take great pride in my ability to summarise people at a glance, and Rory was more or less as he appeared. He was twenty-seven, infatuated with the gym, loved to party and knew none of the authors, musicians, or artists that I longed to speak of.

On the bright side, our lack of common interests allowed me to hand out half answers while I focused on what was important, the veins, rising deliciously from his forearm to his shoulder. As I looked deeper, I could almost feel the warmth of his blood, unpolluted with drugs, save the little beer he was drinking. That body, lean, athletic and well kept, was a brilliant store of health. Enough to last me two nights, if I was careful.

Now, do you understand why I love Blaze?

After a half hour's 'conversation', I was actually starting to enjoy Rory. He had a hearty laugh that matched his physical appeal and occasionally caught my attention with flashes of keen intelligence. A law graduate, completing his thesis at Macquarie, he was trying hard not to bore me with details, despite the best pleas of my glazed over expression. Anything but the blow-by-blow description of some fitness class he taught. Please, I beg you. Make it stop!

Before the boxercise-induced aneurism could take hold completely, the blood flowing beneath his smooth flesh glowed hotter, and he put his beer down on the table. Before I could move—not that I tried—he leaned down and kissed me.

It is one thing to be kissed as a human, by someone gifted in the act. But for one of my kind, being kissed is a far more revealing experience. In that brief moment of intimacy, we can sample a mortal's blood without drawing a single drop. We can know their health, their quality and breeding, their nature and mood... anything that may affect the blood's flavour, but remains invisible.

As long as his lips were against mine, Rory was happy to be explored. The aroma of his blood was so sweet I had to fight the temptation to bite his tongue right there and drain him. His hard, smooth body, damp with the sweat of dancing, slid over my lycra vest as he pushed deeper. He put a hand on my back and worked his way down, somehow forcing his fingers inside my unyielding pants, gently kneading the smooth cleft of my behind. Not wishing to seem frigid, I began a little exploration of my own, slipping a hand inside his belt.

"Ahem." The bartender winked at us. It was one of the modern club scene's most elegant phrases summed up in a very simple act.

Time to get a room. Mine.

*   *   *

Rory made a striking figure, striding along Oxford Street towards my home, now wearing the black singlet that had hung from his belt inside the club.

I cut a nice figure myself, letting a little of my gifts pervade the air around us. In the pursuit of companions, one's appearance prior to the 'change' matters very little. It's a sly benefit, brought on by centuries of rapid evolution. Once our predatory nature takes hold, it radiates with sexual magnetism. A lure, if you will. What's the use of eternal youth if you can't convince the world you're irresistible, after all?

As we weaved through the crowd at Taylor Square and met the privacy of Darlinghurst's darkened streets, I felt Rory throw a heavy arm over my shoulder. I hoped the man wasn't going to play clingy. I don't play well with clingy, no matter how beautiful–or drunk–it is.

My companion had no way to detect the sudden stillness of the night air, his already limited human senses dulled by liquor. But I knew. I knew it was too still.

"Rory…"

"Mmm?" The man's pace never slowed.

I softened my steps, acute ears reaching out for anything nearby. Something accustomed to hiding, something that didn't want to be seen.

Perhaps, something like me?

"This way." I eased Rory towards a side street that took us off the main road and out of public view. I could partly cloak both of us, even from the prying eyes of another of my kind, but not for long. This enviable specimen of humanity was mine, damn it. I had seduced him, I would drink from him, and I was not inclined to share.

"Hey," my lunch called.

I swear my fangs flashed as I rounded on Rory with a furious glare. He was too drunk to notice. Idiot. You don't 'Hey' our kind when we're nervous. The consequences are typically… unpleasant.

"You want to have some fun with me?" he teased.

"Yes, but we've got to keep moving." I sniffed the air. No scent. No sound anymore, either. Had we lost whatever I thought I'd heard in the dark? I took Rory's hand again and tried to lead him away.

The man just smiled. "Why not here?"

I stared at him. "What? No!" This was the last thing I needed, a drunken exhibitionist.

"Come on, man. There's nobody watching. It'll be hot."

I could barely contain my annoyance behind clenched teeth as Rory pawed at my shirt, his warm fingers dancing over the cool flesh of my waist. I tried to push him away, careful not to use my full preternatural strength. If I was already facing some rival predator, lurking in the dark, I didn't need the complication of accidentally breaking my companion's ribs.

I gasped as Rory slid a hand inside my 'impenetrably' tight trousers and kissed me. I let him nuzzle me a moment, then forced him to break. "Not here. Not now."

Mumbling what sounded like an obscene description of precisely what he hoped to do to me 'here and now,' Rory grabbed my vest and yanked it up, his tongue cutting a low, sensual dance down my chest. I shivered as cold air hit the pale, moistened skin. My companion lapped at my abs with warm, open kisses as he pulled open my belt and pants. He wasn't taking no for an answer.

I listened for the intruder once more, trying to shut out the mortal's lustful sighs as he explored me. Still nothing.

Perhaps I'd imagined it, or 'it' had lost us. In any case, I'd soon lose my prey if I didn't get back into character. I closed my eyes and tried to relax.

"That's better." Rory grinned as he took me in his mouth.

I wasn't convinced we were out of danger yet. With a sniff of the air, I was certain. Yes, something was out here now, and it was close. At least Rory was distracted. I shuddered as he yanked down my trousers, grabbing my backside with strong hands, pulling me deeper as his fingers teased me.

I ran an appreciative caress over his biceps, shoulders and neck. Then, in the dark, I saw the intruder's outline. He was roughly my height, but slouched, his manner almost tentative as he watched us. I tapped Rory's arm to get his attention, nodding at the intruder. "Excuse me, do you mind?"

No answer.

Rory quickly turned and shouted as I redressed, "Hey, are you deaf, mate? Piss off, will you?"

Still nothing.

Rory glanced back at me with a grin. "I think somebody wants to party with us."

This, I sincerely doubted.

My companion turned back to the figure with a cocky swagger. "Show us what you got, then."

A young man stepped tentatively from the darkness. The stench of cheap cigarettes hung from his clothes. His jeans were ripped, and he wore a stained and faded jacket that at one time had been blue. His hair was a mess of dark brown locks. The kid's face had been unshaven for just over a day, and his tongue bled from an accidental bite. I could smell it.

Rory shook his head, putting an arm around me again.

"Jesus. You into rough trade, Rey?"

"Shut up!" the kid barked.

We startled as he waved a flick-knife at us. Still, I was relieved. I'd had every nerve and fibre primed, ready to fight for my prey, yet my nemesis had turned out to be some unkempt delinquent too gutless to hold up a convenience store. He couldn't have been much more than twenty, probably still living with his parents in some suburban backwater in the outer west.

I almost pitied him.

"Your wallets, fags. Now!" He flashed the knife at Rory and tried to look intimidating. This was no easy feat, for while the mugger was almost six foot tall, Rory was several inches clear of that benchmark and almost as broad around the chest.

"Okay." Rory eased off of me and took out his wallet. Any trace of the drunk, muscle-bound horn dog, who moments before had been so focused on the worship of my flesh, was now gone as the situation sank in. "Just relax. It's okay, you can have it. Just be cool, all right?"

I had to admit, the man's calm confidence impressed me. Ego and alcohol were, just occasionally, a useful mix.

"I said now! You too." This time, the bastard pointed the knife at me.

I slowly took out my wallet, the focus of my curiosity shifting from companion to thug. Surely, Rory wasn't intimidated? One swipe of those big hands and this discussion would be over. Hell, I wasn't bound by human limits. One punch from me would achieve the same outcome. But that was out of the question in front of the human. Plus, there was every chance the thief would remember it when he woke up. If he woke up.

But something was different now. Too different. The mugger was flinching, like a dog taking fright.

"Rory, get behind me and get ready to run," I said, backing away. It's not always gratifying to have one's first instincts confirmed.

"Shut up!" The thief lunged at Rory with the knife, striking a deep cut to the man's wrist.

The aroma of sweet blood swirled around me as it spilled out over his flesh and dripped to the street. God, I didn't need that distraction. More blood spilled as the muscles in Rory's arm tensed. He grabbed the kid's jacket, lifted him high off the ground and shoved him against the wall. The thug swore in defiance, but Rory was firm.

"What's your problem?" Rory yelled, his hands scrunching the young tough's shirt in a hold so tight, the knife clattered to the ground.

"Get off me, faggot!" The boy spat in Rory's face, but the crude gesture only angered my companion more. The thief convulsed under the impact as Rory threw him against the wall again.

"Rory, drop him and follow me, quickly."

The air had changed. A musky odour now wafted through it, and it was coming from our would-be mugger. The boy's shirt had ridden up as Rory gripped it, exposing his belly. I could swear it was a lot hairier than it had been when the man had first picked him up. That was bad. Very bad.

"Rory!"

With one final push, my companion threw the kid back, letting his head hit the wall and his body slide to the ground with a pained groan.

"Nasty little punk." Rory lifted his singlet to wipe the sweat from his brow. Blood still seeped from his wrist.

I backed away, beckoning my companion to hurry up.

Rory shrugged, grinning at me. "I don't think he'll be doing much—"

A long, hollow howl cut him off mid-sentence. I'd only heard that sound two, perhaps three times before. But I'd never forgotten it.

There comes a point where a prudent predator severs ties to his prey, and that point was now. Rory ran toward me, but it was too late. The werewolf brought down its claws and grabbed his midsection. My companion's screams echoed around the street as his stomach was ripped open. But they were soon silenced as he lost consciousness, and the beast bit into his leg, tearing it off.

I could have intervened. Rory was still alive, though barely, and I could have distracted the creature. Used my own powers and forced it to leave the mortal alone. I appreciate that some may have been horrified by my inaction.

But, hello? Werewolf?

Popular fiction would have us believe them inherently spiritual creatures. At one with the call of nature, their social rituals governed by centuries of pack tradition and worship of the moon, Gaia, and all that's good in the realm of night.

All this, I call bullshit.

What I know is that they grow to over nine foot tall after full transformation, with teeth and claws capable of tearing prey apart within seconds. And if their 'society' is one governed by spiritual discipline, this one seemed lapsed, at best. My kind hunts for food by necessity. Werewolves kill for sport. We're predators, they're monsters. That's the difference.

Rory was lost to this beast. There was little I could do now but slink back to the shadows and return to one of the clubs for another companion, getting hungrier by the minute. And no, I did not consider feeding from the werewolf. Would you?

My better sense compromised by panic, I clean forgot that my kind were not the only supernaturals with enhanced senses. The monster looked up and sniffed the air. I ducked as Rory's body was tossed to the ground, his blood soiling my clothes and bare arms. I licked away the few specks that had spattered across my mouth. A fine vintage of man, and I couldn't abide waste.

I tried to run, but there was nowhere to go. Was I mad? If Rory's screams hadn't attracted enough attention, luring a fully changed werewolf into the open street was just begging for more trouble. One human death was already too many.

If I couldn't run out of the maze of colonial laneways, behind the empty terraces and warehouses of Darlinghurst, my only option was to lead the beast into it. My shaking limbs strained against hunger as I tried to bolt past the creature. I'd barely gotten more than a few steps when a weighty paw scraped down my back, knocking me to the pavement.

As I struggled to my feet, it came down again, picking me up, claws now digging deep into my leg. The monster's terrible breath swirled around me as it prepared itself for meat far sweeter than any mortal.

Damn it! I'd lived three human lifetimes and it couldn't end there. Not consumed by some young beast that tore men's limbs off before tossing them aside like broken toys. I wouldn't accept it!

I did the only thing possible, and can now say with certainty that werewolf blood tastes foul. My teeth, quite capable of puncturing plate glass if necessary, neatly pierced his thick, leathery flesh. I could scarcely begin to describe the awful sensation that flooded me.

Was it even blood? It tasted more like a liquefied pulp of rotting meat, streaking the brown, matted fur as it erupted from the vein. The beast howled as it tried to shake me loose.

I felt the crushing blow of a brick wall against my back and dropped to the street. My vision swayed. I couldn't focus. What was wrong with me? I hadn't had a concussion since… I'd never had a concussion. I wasn't human, for Christ's sake!

I staggered to my feet, steadying myself against the wall. As I watched, the werewolf began to yell, not in pain, but frustration. Its incomprehensible yelps gradually began to form words as the fur retracted and his body shrank.

"No! Not now!" He fixed on me with murderous eyes, unable to move as he caught his breath.

I took my chance, lurching toward the now weakened and naked young man as the last traces of fur shrank from his body. I snatched hold of his throat.

"I'm going to enjoy this, you—" Before I could finish, the nausea returned. I lost my grip on the thug's throat, and a great stream of vomited blood spewed from my mouth. Werewolf blood. Not just vile to the taste, but completely poisonous.

The punk shrieked as the blood, his own blood, spewed over his feet. "You're sick!"

The irony of the statement wasn't lost on me. Nor was how ridiculous he looked, standing there, trying to shake vomited blood from his bare feet and shaking his fist at me. I couldn't kill him now. Not like this. I was a better man than that, or so I liked to think. I picked up a piece of the jacket he'd worn, which now lay ruined on the ground from his transformation. I gingerly wiped my face and arms and threw it back at him.

"Hey!"

As the nausea left me, I took a moment to look at the wolf's scruffy human shell. He wasn't a pretty, or even handsome boy in the traditional sense. He was well built across the chest, a little too much so for his height, with a lack of body hair that surprised me. Just a light trail on his stomach, belying his true nature. Captivating my attention though, were the tattoos. Intricate and complex, they adorned both his arms, yet by far the most striking was a sizeable tiger, which wrapped itself over his left shoulder, arcing down to its fearsome face, expertly etched into his chest. A beast to guard the beast within. It seemed both poetic and pretentious. It almost seemed to stalk the faux silver ring mounted on his left nipple. At least, I assumed it was a fake, in deference to werewolf myth.

"Hope you're happy, vampire."

The air instantly chilled around me. I could feel it. A reflection of my own heart. "What did you say?"

"You heard me, vampire!" He drew closer, his demeanour still not entirely free of the wolf that had possessed him.

That did it.

I took him by the throat again, throwing his human body against the wall and pinning him there, my fingers closing around his neck like iron bolts.

"Hey!" He tried with futility to pry me loose. "Jesus, man!"

"Do you enjoy having a tongue, wolf man?" I asked, keeping my voice level, a counterpoint to the violence of my hands.

"Fuck you, bloodsucker!" he choked out, each syllable audibly more pained than the last. "Let me... argh! I can't—"

"Because if you wish to keep it, you will never, ever use that word again." I gave him an emphatic shake, cracking his head against the wall. The impact cut him and I felt warm blood trickle down over my fingers. I was beyond hungry by this point, but not for this bastard. I wasn't putting my body through that again. "Now, tell me you're sorry,"

The boy hissed and I squeezed again, wringing another pained yelp from him.

"What's your name, wolf man?"

"Piss off!"

"Your name?"

Whoever he was, he was now going the most alarming shade of orange about the ears, among other places.

"Jorgas," he got out. "It's Jorgas, now put me—"

I silenced him with another jolt against the wall. "Hello, Jorgas. I'm Reylan. And when meeting a stranger for the first time, it is customary in polite societies to introduce oneself before becoming a hideous cretin of the night and threatening to kill said stranger. Are we clear? Now, tell me you're sorry."

He squirmed under my grip, the tiger twisting on the flesh of his chest with such vigour that I half expected it to snarl.

"Jorgas?"

"I'm sorry, okay? I'm sorry!"

"Have a good evening." I withdrew my hand with such speed that Jorgas instantly dropped to the ground, twisting his ankle as he went down. He coughed and spluttered, ignoring the thin trail of blood down his back as he fell to his knees in front of me. I smiled, noting that the tiger's tail went halfway down, until its black tip neatly crossed his spine. Fine work, indeed.

Call it a fetish if you like such blatant terms, but tattoos fascinate me. For one thing, my species can't have them. Within hours, our bodies reject the ink like venom, expelling it through the skin—a rather painful process, or so I've heard. Secondly, there's the art and symbology behind them. Though I doubted I'd get a stimulating story out of this one.

"I'm going to kill you, vam…"

My foot stopped two inches short of delivering a sharp kick to his face.

He snarled at me, teeth glistening in the dark, as I hauled him to his feet and pushed him away. His naked form limped up the street, clutching at the scraps of his clothes.

I sighed in silent relief that he hadn't changed again. I could never have lasted another round with his beast form. But there was one more thing he needed to know.

"Jorgas," I called, astonished when he actually looked back at me. "You killed a mortal tonight. There are penalties for that."

The boy didn't move. He just stood there, staring at me. Even my sharpened vision struggled to see detail in the dark. But Jorgas' eyes never left me, like tenacious shadows, piercing me from their owner's pale, frozen face, until he vanished up the street.

An involuntary shudder took me as I surveyed the carnage left behind. Rory's severed leg lay on the ground, still wrapped in bloodied and ripped blue jeans. I carefully picked it up, wrapped it in some industrial plastic from a nearby bin and dumped it inside.

It had all been too easy. Jorgas had killed Rory in less than a minute, and should have killed me soon after, but he'd lost the change. He couldn't control his transformations. That young man was wandering around, a mindless, volatile thug in his human form, shifting into werewolf form with neither warning, nor any means to control it.

And I'd let him go.

I kicked the bin, crying out in frustration at my own stupidity. All for pride and some misguided sense of mercy.

Stupid!

But as my cry echoed off the surrounding buildings, I caught hold of my senses again, scanning the nearby streets for passers-by. Plenty of dark corners, but they were all empty.

Likewise, it seemed our screams and shouts had attracted no attention at all. But that was Darlinghurst, little changed since my first visit to Sydney in the early eighties.

It had been love at first sight.

Witness to countless murders and debaucheries throughout their history, the secluded streets and colonial stone cottages of Darlinghurst now served as a haven for many of the city's guppies—gay yuppies, that is—most of whom were not only fond of a night out on the town, but were blessed with the uncanny sense to look the other way in the event of seeing something they ought not. This discretion typically allows me the opportunity to enjoy companions in private when I don't have a 'home' available.

It's a style of hunting not without challenges, of course. Competition from others like myself included, though the human population hadn't quite abandoned the murderous habits of its past either. Good for us. Not so good for the humans who lived here, but very good when one of them needed to disappear, or when their horrified screams needed everyday dismissal.

"Reylan?"

I almost leapt out of my ageless skin. The sound was barely audible. Mortal ears could never have picked it up, a hoarse whisper coming from the ground on the other side of the street.

"Reylan… where…"

Rory. I couldn't believe he was still alive! Blood poured from the stump where his leg had been. His clothing and the flesh of his stomach were in tatters and he was covered in his own blood. But he was alive and conscious. I hushed him quiet and laid a hand on his chest, my other hand under his head, imploring him to lie still.

"My legs are freezing."

Clinically speaking, this was probably true. I thought it best to omit the fact that they were no longer attached.

"Don't move. I'm here."

The mortal tilted his head, and a trickle of blood flowed from his mouth over my wrist. Fragrant, life-giving blood, now wasted as it ran to the cold pavement.

"What... how—"

"You were attacked." I brushed a gentle hand over his hair, trying to soothe him as I lifted what was left of his shirt and examined his injuries. His insides had been ripped out and hung limp from his wounds.

Rory's voice was no more than a whisper and blood ran from his mouth. "You... you called him 'wolf man.' What was he?"

What did our secrets matter? It was too late now, and the only thing I could give Rory was the truth.

"That was a werewolf. You were attacked by a werewolf."

Rory's lips turned up in a smile. "Fuck."

A fat drop of blood spat out over the street. He'd had more to drink than I'd thought. Not only was the alcohol dulling his pain, he actually believed me.

"And he called you a vampire?" He smiled weakly as he gazed into my eyes. I winced at the word, but I could hardly force the point now.

"Yes, I'm... what you'd call a vampire."

"Is that why you picked me up? Were you going to kill me, Reylan?"

"Shhhh." It would have done him no favour to try and explain. How was I meant to articulate to a dying drunk man the finer points of blood-drinking morality? I ran a calming hand over his chest, wiping the blood off and feeling the pulse of his heart as it struggled beneath his breast.

As Rory's eyes closed for the last time, I leaned down and kissed him. He tried to return the kiss, swirling his tongue in my mouth as I gently sucked the blood from it. I licked his mouth clean, kissing his forehead as I withdrew.

He knew we existed, and that others existed. He would lie there, in that knowledge, crying in pain until he died. Unless someone found him and got him to medical care, where he'd surely relate his experiences and be condemned as a madman. I could have hypnotised him. Wiped his memory. It would have taken just one look into his eyes. But Rory was a fitness freak. In this state, what could remain of the things that had brought him happiness? Even if human medicine saved what was left of his body… I couldn't bear the thought.

The decision was fast being made for me as his heart slowed. I thought of taking what blood he had left. It would at least give him an exquisite and beautiful end, an end only my kiss could bring.

I lay down next to the man, holding what remained of his body against mine. The sweet smell of blood drove me mad with hunger as it overpowered the stench of the street beneath us. Then a hand–Rory's hand–reached for mine and squeezed it. I couldn't take him like that. I've been many unpleasant things, but never a vulture.

"Sleep well."

All I could do was make sure he didn't die alone. With one swift movement, I took his tender chin in my hands and ended it.

CHAPTER TWO

At a touch under one hundred and fifty years old–or a touch over, depending on who's asking–I'd like to think my existence fairly well-ordered. Nights like this one spoiled this illusion, but the night didn't end with Rory's demise.

After doing my best to ease my companion's untimely shuffle from the mortal coil, I disposed of his corpse as best I could and set off on the uncomfortable walk home. My clothes were caked in spattered blood. I couldn't see it against the black vest, but I could smell it. Feel it. The sticky, bloodied cloth clung to my skin. Over the years, certain scholars come gossips have alleged that our kind enjoys the occasional bath drawn of blood, only to be shown just why we find the notion so unappealing. I don't believe they drowned for their misjudgement.

Blood-soaked or not, chance was on my side as I caught sight of a young drunk in the back street. The boy was barely coherent as he pissed away a night's liquor against the wall, just out of sight from the main strip.

"Be there in a minute," he called.

The silent lack of reply spoke volumes of his friends' patience. I let him button his pants before offering my introduction, staying in the shadows as he–Simon–drew closer. I hoped he was too drunk to notice the stench of stale blood.

But in the dark, his hungry smile reassured me, as did the glint of cocky desire in his eye. I beckoned him closer and slipped an arm around his shoulders, ensuring those eyes met mine. Within seconds, any chance that he'd notice the stains on my vest was gone.

That night, I'd brought comfort to a mortal in his darkest moment. How good of fate, to repay my kindness in the form of Simon.

*   *   *

Simon proved to be impressively acrobatic company as the night went on, and while I hated to think ill of the dead, his flavour was an improvement, even on Rory's. One might say I'd traded up for the evening. I wouldn't, of course. I'm not that callous.

Through the early hours of the morning, I lay there patiently as the boy slept, turning Jorgas' bungled attack and Rory's senseless death over in my mind. Jorgas had seen my face, heard my voice. I'd even introduced myself. Whatever had possessed me to give him my name? I'd nothing to gain by proving alpha male dominance to a werewolf.

Having Simon's head nestled under my arm brought a strange comfort—a clarity to my mind. My breath was gentle as his hand slid over my chest, down the curve of my stomach.

Oh yes, I breathe. Contrary to popular legend, I'm not 'undead'. I wasn't turned this way by some dark master of the night draining my blood and replacing it with his own. I was born to and raised by human parents, only to become aware of my... difference, in my early twenties. Ours is a dormant condition that emerges in a family line every few generations, granting immortality and agelessness once the change takes hold. I don't know if the conceit that a corpse may rise to drink the blood of the living is testament to human imagination or sheer narcissism. Probably both.

Werewolves, to my understanding, emerged through a similar mutation. Jorgas was probably a recent change, perhaps no more than a few weeks old. A rank amateur of any species, unchecked, violent and ill-tempered around the Darlinghurst clubs, was something I didn't need.

I checked the clock. Just past four in the morning, though the gently changing light could have told me that. The blue of pre-dawn remains one of my favourite colours. The light seems so pure at that hour, spilling out to fill the night sky, like the blood of angels, or so I've heard it called.

If I was to enjoy the blood of angels, then Simon was certainly not among them. Our small talk had raised the topic of his church, Saint Barnabas. It was one of the Pope's more influential institutions in Sydney, less known for its service to God than for the behaviour of its spoiled clique of 'only children,' which included the boy in my bed. 'The Brats of Saint Barnie's', some pompous ass on talkback radio had called them. The name had stuck. Still, so long as Simon was a pleasing companion, and he'd certainly been that, he was welcome to remain.

The young man pressed his body against me, and I could feel his hot breath wash over my chest, raising gooseflesh as he stirred under the covers, still asleep. Such a sensual boy, wasted, you could say, on a creature for whom sexual sensation meant nothing. I'd taken him to my bed only to feed, yet I'd pushed his ecstasy to climax, three, maybe four times. I wasn't sure. To be young, stupid and oversexed again. A fine fantasy, I thought.

Another hour, we lay there, until the first lip of sunrise broke the horizon. I felt my skin tingle as the moonlight was replaced.

My kind's sensitivity to sunlight has been somewhat exaggerated over the years, but it has basis in fact. Even reflected off the walls of a dwelling, the day's light does my skin no favours, and a short burst of direct sunlight will tear through it like a razor.

Easing Simon off me, I closed the blinds, pulled on a pair of cheap, figureless pants and went to the kitchen. Loss of blood or not, Simon would wake soon enough and he'd need nourishment.

The contents of my refrigerator were a glaring testament to the one constant crack in my mortal facade. I never remember to shop. A pair of eggs—whose age I couldn't remember, but which fell somewhere between fresh this week and a borderline Chinese delicacy—and a block of butter that looked more likely to have come from a building site than a supermarket. Well done, Reylan. Drain the boy, then make him starve. Idiot!

I winced as a loud rapping on my front door broke the silence. Only one person had the nerve to knock before six in the morning. Christ, not today. No lectures, please.

"Morning, Dorotha." I grimaced, remaining in the shadows and squinting, as though it could somehow dim the sun. It didn't. "What can I do for you?"

The small Polish woman, my tenant, whose formidably matriarchal presence and lifetime's collection of antiquated worldly possessions occupied the small apartment upstairs, stood primly on my doorstep, a tartan shawl wrapped over her shoulders. It teased the lowest point of the tight, ashen grey bun she considered a hairstyle. She clutched a handful of envelopes as she examined my shirtless, yawning form.

"You not wear pyjamas? Something warm? But is winter, Mister Raymond. You catch your death of cold!"

"I don't feel the cold, Dorotha. We've discussed this. Is that my mail?"

"Yes, it is. I thought I would catch you before bedtime. You and your odd hours! So much time at those nightclubs. All that doof-doof music and drinking? It not do you any good!"

I ignored her advice and accepted the envelopes gratefully, skimming through. Internet bill, gas bill and a letter from my financial planner, upping his fees, no doubt. All mine. I hated it when they were all mine. The tedious expenses of inner-city human living, all addressed to Raymond Wilde, my assumed name when dealing with mortal authority. Cardinal rule of supernatural anonymity? Names that sound cool and sophisticated are great for picking up in the clubs. Not so hot on your mortgage application.

"Thank you, Doro—"

I didn't get to finish before she made a break for my kitchen.

"Dorotha, this really isn't a good time for a tea!" I'd invited the old woman inside my home only once. Once. Since then, she'd considered our arrangement 'open house,' a trick I had thought exclusive to our kind. That's another myth, by the way. A rather quaint one, to my mind. If I ask for an invitation into your home, I'm really just being polite.

"Look, I hate to be rude, but I've had a very big night."

The old woman was hunched over in my kitchen, inspecting my fridge. Ugh. Here we go…

"You lie to me, Mister Raymond! Every time I come visit, you promise me you eat! I know you fairy boys like your diets, but this is madness!"

"I've been eating very well, I assure you." Very well.

Don't wake up. Please, Simon, don't—

"Hey, Rey! Where's your bathroom again?"

Curse you, Barnie's brat!

"To your left as you come out," I called, ignoring Dorotha's frigid glare.

"Another gentleman caller? Is the third one this week?"

That she knew of.

"I get lonely," I smirked.

She closed the fridge and poked me–actually poked me–hard and sharp in the shoulder.

"Ow!"

"You not be lonely if you ask that nice Italian boy to move in with you."

"I assure you, that won't be happening." I was fighting a losing battle, to the great amusement of Ross, the 'nice Italian boy' in question. That reminded me. I was supposed to be meeting him at Valia's on Goulburn in fourteen hours. Somewhere in that time, I needed to sleep. Now, if only my guests would take the hint.

"He very good to you," Dorotha continued, "and very handsome."

"Rey?" Simon emerged, standing in the entryway to the kitchen, a scrunched t-shirt in his hands, jeans low on his hips, still unbuttoned. He quickly fastened them closed and threw on his crumpled shirt as Dorotha fixed him with a look.

"You too skinny too," she snapped.

"Simon," I muttered, "this is Dorotha."

"Hello. Nice to meet you." So, the boy could turn on North-shore Catholic manners, after all. I was impressed.

Dorotha snorted indignantly. "You both come upstairs. I make you nalesniki."

I sighed. "Look, Dorotha, I'm really tired."

"Hah, I shouldn't wonder!"

"Umm, I should go." Simon quickly stepped forward and kissed my cheek. "Text me, yeah?"

"Sure." I squeezed his waist, letting my cool fingers tease the small of his back as I let him go. His eyes met mine just long enough for me to wipe his memory of the evening. Not immediately, of course, but within the hour, he'd remember nothing. A fine boy, who'd no doubt make some man—or woman, for who was I to presume—very happy one day. If ever I chose to break my rule of not feeding from the same human twice, he'd have been a more than worthy candidate.

My affectionate gestures didn't escape Dorotha's notice.

"Thanks for the breakfast offer." Simon shot her an apologetic smile. "Maybe next time."

She mumbled something in Polish as Simon scurried out, then returned her attention to me. "He not good for you, Mister Raymond. Too young. No discipline."

Right. Because the other men in my life of late had been all about discipline! The sudden appearance of my cat on the kitchen bench brought a welcome end to the discussion.

"Demetrius, get down!" I snapped.

"Pooska!" More words followed in Polish, which my cat apparently understood, as he hopped down immediately.

I fumbled in one of the kitchen drawers for Demetrius' favourite toy, an expensive ball of silver twine. Real silver, mind you. Fibres tougher than nylon, coated in genuine silver, sold at a small occult shop I'd once visited in Bratislava, for the specific purpose of binding captured werewolves.

I'd bought it almost as a joke. Yet in over seventy years, the twine had never aged or weakened. After last night, I was tempted to start carrying it as a matter of course. I tossed the shiny 'toy' out of the kitchen and up the hall, watching the cat bounce off walls as he scrambled after it. The animal didn't need a ball of string. He preferred to try and pull mine.

"He eat better than you," Dorotha mumbled. Was she calling my cat fat? "You come up for nalesniki?"

"I'm afraid I have another appointment this evening, with Ross."

She looked up at me with a smile that was far too conspiratorial. "Oh, all right then, Mister Raymond. You get some sleep." She finally left me in peace. Thank you, Ross, my former protégé, closest friend, and get-out-of-conversation free card with Dorotha Malinowska.

And before a meeting with Ross, I needed sleep.

I really needed sleep.

* * *

"You survived a werewolf attack?" Ross' eyes were wide, his red lips tilted in a typically unshakeable grin that belied his question.

"Others have survived. You've just never met them." Not that I'd met them myself. I could be so full of it when it suited me.

"Do you think he knew what he was?" Ross took another sip of the 'tea' specially brewed by Deborah, our waitress at Valia's, and the only mortal we trusted with knowledge of our nature. Slipping just a few drops into each pot, she always kept her blood so pure for us, bless her heart.

"Knew his way around claws well enough, at my companion's expense, I'm afraid."

"Your companion?"

"Gym junkie. Bright for his type. I did, however, run into a very nice young man on the way…" I trailed off. Ross had levelled his eyes with mine. No, wait… between mine. It somehow itched. "What?"

"Reylan, when was the last time you drank from a woman?"

I lifted up the cup of blooded tea.

"Other than Deborah," Ross qualified.

"Men have a stronger flavour. You'll learn to appreciate it one day, I'm sure." Was this peculiar change of topic for my benefit?

Ross shook his head, laughing. "But women are so much sweeter. Gentler—"

"And you're implying I'm chauvinistic?"

"I didn't mean—"

"Women are perfectly fine, until you crave something bolder, more aggressive."

"The blood of men, you mean?"

"Modern, sophisticated men in particular. Repressed aggression, the urges of a hunter, all bubbling just below the surface. The skills may be lapsed, but they're still within the blood. That potency? Exquisite."

"So, you've sworn off women completely?"

"Oh, come now. Abstinence? That's your upbringing talking."

Ross smirked as he took another sip of tea. Glancing over, I saw Deborah, smiling from the corner of her mouth. She'd seen this discussion play out many nights before. I wondered how much of the conversation she'd overheard.

"More tea, gentlemen?" she called from the counter.

I nodded. It was easy to see how Ross had been such a rogue in mortal life. Six foot two, his body was tanned and athletic. His curly black hair was cut short and perfectly shaped to frame his firm set olive complexion and deep brown eyes. I would have been fascinated to know him before his change; the handsome young Italian medical student and womaniser. But I doubted even the most attractive man would have interested Ross. Now, he was nineteen forever, having changed several years earlier than most.

Of course, he hadn't aged a bit in twenty years, physically, emotionally, or mentally. At least his English had evolved to sound natural.

"Well," Ross smiled, "I might not technically be 'straight' anymore, but—"

"You're still binding yourself to limited, human terms. All I'm saying is men are a stronger taste. They're also safer to feed from than women, in terms of attachment."

"I'm hearing this from a virgin?" Ross chided.

"I've witnessed three lifetimes worth of relationships. My choice not to pick up that particular snake has not left me ignorant of its bite."

He was right, of course. As a young mortal, I'd never known true physical intimacy. With the façade of sexual magnetism obscuring my body's natural disinterest, I typically managed four, sometimes five 'guests' a week, which probably made me a man-whore by contemporary standards. But no guest had ever been invited to return or stay. It wasn't that I'd never given thought to finding a nice human with whom I could explore something deeper–a kinship, if you will–but the requirements of my lifestyle hardly lent themselves to such openness. Even with Ross, or my first protégé, Isobel, any conjugal union would have been impossible. 'Till death do us part?' Please. There's a fine line between commitment and cruelty.

"I'm not disputing your wisdom," Ross continued as tea arrived. "It's just you've never experienced lust, so how can you—"

"Ross, in case you'd forgotten," I began, switching to Italian in light of Deborah's sudden proximity. "I was attacked last night by a werewolf. You'll forgive me if my non-existent sex life is not of primary concern right—"

"Werewolf?" Deborah asked. "Seriously?"

Damn you.

"You never told us you could speak Italian," Ross observed, slurping his tea.

"You never asked," she replied with a shrug. "I grew up in Leichhardt, remember? When your first boss barely speaks English, you learn fast."

Ross and I exchanged awkward glances. She was hovering now, in that uncomfortably deliberate manner.

"My dear," I began, "whatever you think you heard—"

"Do you think I'm stupid?"

"I never said that."

"No, you said 'werewolf'. As in an actual werewolf? Here in Sydney?"

I was tempted to wipe her memory of the discussion, but it seemed pointless—and just a little rude. "Yes."

Deborah's interrogative gaze softened as she mopped tea off the pot's lip. "Dangerous?"

"He might be."

"And will he be coming in here too?"

"I doubt that."

"Good." Our host's cheery demeanour returned. "Because if I lose any customers over this, you're all banned. Werewolves, fairies, you lot... all of you. Out. Is that clear?"

She was gone before either of us could answer, returning to the counter with that unmistakeable bounce in her step that went all the way up to her old-fashioned auburn bob-cut.

Fairies? Just who else was she serving in here?

"Have I mentioned how much I like her? I've always liked her."

"Ross..."

"Fine. So, what are you going to do if you see it again?"

"What?"

"The werewolf, Reylan."

I lowered my voice, determined to keep my irritability in check. "Whatever he is, in human form he's young, weak and stupid."

"So, he has no control?"

"Not enough. Far as I can tell, his shifts are aggravated by mood. But if he shifts in the wrong place, in front of the wrong people? Even if the media ignores it, it only takes one sighting for every zealot, holy warrior and hunter in the country to declare open season."

"You're saying he has to die?"

"Preferably."

"So, are we going hunting?"

"No, we are not. If I see him again in human form, I'll tear out the bastard's throat. But if he's in beast form, I'm not staying for the trisection." I found a curious confidence in my own words. The reality seemed so simple. Kill the unstable delinquent or stay out of the wolf's way. Or just never cross paths with either one again. I wasn't some newly changed amateur. I could handle this.

Ross cracked a wry smile I wasn't sure I liked. "So... not going to get the House involved, then?"

There it was. The inevitable political implication I'd so wanted to avoid. The House of Blood claims all of our kind as members, along with any others 'touched by immortality,' a broad definition that includes fairies and various minor deities. In Europe or the Americas, this probably would have been House business. But a supernatural in Sydney was expected to fix his own problems, before his peers fixed him. Besides, Jorgas was a werewolf, which technically put him within the House of Magick's domain. Talking to them meant talking to the witches, and I'd neither the patience, nor tolerance for their trademark condescension.

"I'm going to take that silence as a no," Ross muttered, taking out his wallet. Was he going to pay for tea? No, that was impossible. Instead, he took out a small business card and tossed it to the table.

"What's this?" I asked.

"Someone who can probably help catch wolf boy, if that's what you want."

"Hunters?" I snapped, rejecting the card without so much as a glance. "Have you completely lost your mind?"

"Calm down," Ross pushed the card straight back. "It's a... kind of network for people like us. I've been a regular there for the past year or so. Just a suggestion, if you don't want to involve the Houses."

I picked up the eggshell-coloured card, now curious as I read its gold lettering. "The Arcadia Trust. Ross, what in the hell…?"

"A safe haven, not just to protect us but to seek us out, nurture us and help us blend into society."

Deborah looked up, startled as my laughter rang out inside the café. Fortunately, we were the sole patrons at that time of night. Most mortals are horrified when one of us gets the giggles.

"I knew you'd be like this," Ross grumbled. "Why do you always have to be so damn cynical? Jesus!"

I stifled my laughter. "I'm sorry, but what, for the love of God makes them think… makes you think, that this is worthwhile or necessary? We're independent creatures, Ross. We choose our own friends, make our own way, and just occasionally, take another under our wing to teach them how it's done."

"I know all that," Ross said, knowing he'd been the subject of my last remark. "But a lot's changed since you took your first blood. Even since I took mine. There's a lot more supernatural activity, especially in Australia."

"New arrivals, you mean? That's inevitable, Ross."

"Sydney's becoming what LA was in the thirties. Plenty of food, no old-world politics. It's attractive. But the way we do things is too random. One slip-up too many and humans are going to start asking questions."

"Need I remind you that Isobel and I were part of that migration to Los Angeles? California had its problems. It grew up, as will Australia." I reread the expensive lettering on the card. "The Arcadia Trust? What is that even supposed to mean?"

"Arcadia was the legendary home to the temples of Zeus and Hera. The true realm of gods and monsters—"

"Thank you, Ernest Thesiger. I'm familiar with the word itself. It still tells me nothing."

"Will you at least think about it? The Trust is there to help people like us. They might even help you with your werewolf problem, if you let them."

"Wonderful, so I can pop in for blood tea and crumpets while they hunt down this creature? Aren't we lucky, to have such proactive, gregarious individuals in the supernatural community?"

"If you don't want to call, then don't. You don't have to be so sarcastic."

I restrained myself when I saw genuine hurt in Ross' eyes. I hadn't been there when he'd first come to this existence, but I had been his tutor in the laws of the night. I'd thought it best, given I'd initially found him staked out for the sunrise by his own family. 'The Scimitar of Light' they called themselves, an organisation of fundamentalist humans from supernatural family lines, who felt bound to destroy the bodies of their non-human offspring to 'save their souls'. The Scimitar had come to Sydney to straighten out their prodigal son's hedonistic ways, only to find he was no longer quite the same noble defender of the faith they'd raised. The results had been... unfortunate.

"If it pleases you, I'll call this 'Trust.'"

Ross looked up in surprise. "You're serious?"

"You've intrigued me." I gave Ross' judgment more credit than to dismiss them out of hand. "I may go there tomorrow evening."

Ross managed to smile. "Promise me you'll behave?"

"No."

"Fine, then don't say you know me."

"And who said martyrdom was dead?"

"Reylan, I think if Isobel can give it a fair shot—"

"Isobel? Isobel is in on this little venture too?" I don't know why it surprised me. Ever the socialite, Isobel had been my pupil and travel companion for several decades until we parted ways. When she'd finally grown tired of globe-trotting, she'd sought me out and settled in Sydney, where she had wasted no time establishing herself as an immortal of some note, or notoriety, depending on who you asked.

"Anything else, gents?" Deborah called. "I'll be closing in a few."

I shook my head as we got up from the table, taking out enough cash to settle the bill with a moderate tip, about five hundred or so. A fair payment, for such a precious resource, I thought. "No thank you, my dear. Can't have you collapsing on the job, can we?"

"If you want that much, you'd better be ready to transfuse me," she smirked. "Happy hunting, Reylan. I mean that. I won't have any trouble in here, werewolf or otherwise. Understood?"

"You have my word."

She smiled sweetly and kissed us both on the cheek.

"Good night, Deborah." Ross gave her a slight bow.

I'd so implored my friend to be more imaginative when choosing his worldly alias, but in fairness, it takes a couple of alter egos to get it right. Our names last about thirty years before they need to be refreshed, meaning 'Ross' would be dead soon enough, and a new man of the night would be born.

Don't ask what my first alias was. I'd really prefer to not talk about it.

*   *   *

We went on to the Alberta, a Canadian themed bar on the edge of King's Cross, with an appallingly overstated sense of rustic charm. Worse still, it tried to carry itself as off a sports

33

bar, missing the wilderness appeal of its namesake entirely. This was one of Ross' preferred haunts. I found the tedium set in after the third or so time you had to duck under the fake moose head on the wall. At least the irredeemably Aussie-accented bartenders had given up the shtick of tacking 'eh?' onto the end of every sentence.

Arriving early, we took up an enviable vantage point opposite the bar, with two large glasses of virtually untouched, rapidly warming beer between us for show. Ross, for his part, managed to steer the conversation clear of werewolves, this 'Arcadia Trust,' or my long forgotten non-sex life. After an hour or more I actually began to relax, even allowing myself a smirk at the latest poor dote to run afoul of the low-hanging moose.

"Tye, look out!" the size six, bottled-blonde girl on his arm shrieked.

I nodded at them to prompt Ross' attention, realising my mistake only when his lips spread into a broad grin. I knew what that look meant. Prey.

"No," I muttered.

"No?"

"You know perfectly well what I mean."

"Reylan, she's hot, and I'm hungry," Ross protested.

"So am I. Do we need to discuss the difference between hungry and desperate?"

Ross still didn't take his eyes off the girl, as she led Tye up to the bar and snapped her fingers for the bartender's attention.

"Come on, Reylan. She's a total—"

"Like, total plastic in need of a lobotomy?" I winced as a Valley Girl squeal peppered my words. Too much time in Los Angeles. "Besides, she's taken."

"So?"

I narrowed my eyes as the girl tried to wipe beer from Tye's shirt. "So, you can have any companion you want." I tried shaking Ross' wrist to regain his attention. "Now can we please go find you a companion who doesn't redefine the term 'classless society?'"

But when I glanced back at his prey, I knew it was too late. She was smiling at us—at Ross. Tye also turned to see what had so caught his lady friend's attention. Then, he too began to smile. That wasn't natural; he'd met Ross' eyes.

"Ross, stop it. Stop it right now," I growled, keeping my voice low to avoid a scene.

"Come on, Reylan. I'll take her. You take him.

"They're two bags of pure, undiluted... what is the Australian word? Bogan. That's it."

"Don't be a snob. I've seen you with worse."

"That's not the point, and how dare you!"

My protests were useless. Ross had his prey now, and apparently, so did I. Brilliant.

Within minutes, it was clear that Tye and Shontel—correct spelling, for I glimpsed her driver's licence—were the fast food of haemoglobin-based cuisine. Still, Ross knew his assets, and played them to full strength. So it came as no surprise when he bowed to kiss Shontel's hand. The chivalrous gesture prompted an ear bleeding giggle and a look of bemusement from Tye, who proceeded to talk up a storm about his championship title at the local gun club.

"You ever try your hand at marksmanship, Reylan?" he asked me mid-spiel.

"No, but you're tempting me to go out and buy a gun as we speak." I ignored Ross' glare. If he was going to drag me into this stupid game, he could hardly expect me to suffer his dredging of the human blood pool without having a little fun. Besides, if all went to plan, I'd be feeding on Tye before the night's end. Most men taste better with their tempers wound up.

I must have been hungry. The man was starting to look almost… appetising. I could feel the anger and confusion rising in his blood as his fiancée became more and more rapt with the beautiful Italian boy entertaining her.

She passed Ross her phone to photograph them, and while Shontel made the obligatory duck face, I watched Tye's mouth flatten into a tight grimace, his fists clenching and releasing as he watched Ross. To his credit, the man kept his cool. He even answered the odd comment or question Ross tossed him, like a dog licking up scraps of attention. I almost felt for the guy. Ross was premium, fat free steak while Tye was bulk buy mince, and Shontel knew it.

"Let me get you a drink, Tye." I guided him away, allowing Ross to finish the charade. I was bored and could no longer suffer the temptation; the tantalising red flush beneath the man's skin. I looked back in time to see Ross' hand on Shontel's thigh. Was that wise, given the trigger-happy company kept by his prey?

"She's lucky to have you," I offered, buying Tye a beer.

"Yeah, maybe. I think I'm the lucky one."

They always say that. Why do humans always say that? It's no wonder they struggle with self-esteem.

I smiled at him. "I mean, you're obviously not the jealous type. You give her plenty of freedom?"

Tye eyed Shontel suspiciously as Ross continued entertaining her. "Hey, maybe I've had a few too many, but is he—"

"Ross? He's harmless."

Then, Tye saw Shontel running a hand through Ross' curly black hair as she leaned in to kiss him. And so, it began.

The next few moments were a flurry, and to describe the events blow by blow would nary do them justice. I do, however, remember Tye clumsily throwing punches in Ross' direction, only to have them effortlessly dodged or deflected, Ross saying something about inbreeding affecting hand/eye coordination, along with Shontel being called a slut, whore, and other more profane, if unimaginative sexist slurs. This carried on for several minutes until the manager, a stout, balding man with uneven tufts of white hair, none of which was atop his head, and a cigarette hanging from his jaw, asked in so many words if we'd mind pissing off. Ross took Shontel one way up the street, while I took her enraged partner the other.

"This is the last time for that slut!" he barked.

Heads were turning, but I didn't look back.

"And your mate, who does he think he is?"

As the rant continued, I led Tye into an unseen side street, then deeper into the narrow laneways until the lights of upstairs windows were out of sight. Here, he could shout his anger out, though I hoped he'd have at least some fight left in him. Enough to keep a certain spice to his blood, at least. Tye wasn't much to look at, but he'd get me through until morning. There was plenty of nutrition in that body. Plenty of rage too.

"Just try to relax. I know it's hard…"

"What do you know? You got a girl?"

"No, I don't, but I've been where you are." I laid a hand on each of his shoulders and got exactly the response I'd hoped for.

"Don't you bloody touch me! I'll glass you, faggot!" He shook me off and went to raise a punch to my face.

I grabbed the opportunity to bring my own fist up under his chin, snapping his head back and leaving his throat wide open.

Perfect.

I threw myself against him, pinning him to the wall. He screeched in pain and fury as I bit into him. Holding his body against mine, I felt every muscle tense as his blood surged to the tiny punctures I'd made, the bloody stream flowing eagerly to my hungry mouth. Tye's heartbeat slowed to perfect unison with my own. I can barely describe the beauty of that experience. To feel so close to another being that their life force pulsates in tandem with yours. Also, when I say his muscles tensed, I do mean every muscle. He thrashed in protest, but the limits of his petty, human sexuality were soon swept away as my hands wrapped around his head, holding him closer as I imbibed his sweet juice. I felt his weakened fingers grab my shirt, pulling it up as he clawed at the skin beneath, Shontel forgotten. For the moment, he belonged to me.

I strengthened my hold, pushing his face away as he tried to kiss me. I checked up and down the alley for any casual observers. Not that they'd see anything more than two guys having a good time, which wasn't an unusual sight in this part of the city. But we were alone, and I was almost done. Just a few sips more and I'd have to release him before he died. Beyond Tye's ecstatic moans and the steady rhythm of our hearts, the night air around us was perfectly silent, offering no sign that we were being watched, until the shot rang out and the bullet exploded into my back.

I cried out in pain, spraying a geyser of blood across the wall. My hold on him broken, Tye screamed and ran, clutching his neck. I risked a glance into the shadows and seeing only darkness, leaped on my companion. He wasn't going anywhere, not with his memory still intact.

The pain of singed, broken flesh tore at my back like a half dozen cutthroat razors. I screamed again as another bullet grazed my shoulder. I'd taken gunshots before. They couldn't kill me, but they hurt like a bitch.

Tye kicked and screamed as we wrestled on the filthy street. He tried to push me away, but even with a burning bullet in my back, I had at least three times his strength.

With an agonising lurch, I licked closed the wounds on Tye's neck. His eyes met my own, until he finally threw me off and ran up the street, screaming. I felt like death, but the man's wounds were sealed, and within minutes, he'd remember nothing.

Summoning what speed and strength I had left, I slipped back into the shadows. If I couldn't see this bastard, I could at least put him at the same disadvantage. A sound theory, thought, until I felt a cold pressure against my chest.

The final shot was louder still. The sting of sharpened wood pierced my body, and the world collapsed to blessed sleep.

CHAPTER THREE

When my eyelids peeled open, one after the other, the world seemed a blur of vague, muted colours. My head throbbed as the blood began flowing to my thirsty brain. My legs and arms felt as if they'd been weighted with lead. They too, struggled for blood flow as my heart resumed beating, dragging back to its familiar rhythm over a few moments that felt like eternity.

I'd been staked.

I felt a tingling as blood returned to my fingers and I was able to flex them again. My vision had partly cleared, and though it still had ways to go, it was just strong enough to make out… yes, most of the room was blue. My favourite blue in fact, the blue just before dawn. How pretty. And I was helpless, unable to move. Shit!

"Reylan, you're awake!"

I turned my head to see the vaguest outline of a man standing beside me. A lithe, athletic Italian man, with a familiar, foolish grin.

"Ross…"

"It's me. Sorry, old man. Kelvin gets a bit eager. He… shot a stake into you."

"Kelvin?"

"Whoa, lie still." Ross put a cold hand on my cheek.

Feeling had finally returned to my legs, as they soaked up the red elixir that struggled to bring me back. My shirt had been removed and the staking injury over my heart had healed.

"Where am I?"

"This is the Arcadia Trust. Hell of a way to make an entrance, buddy."

The Arcadia Trust?

"This… Kelvin is an associate of yours?" I asked.

"Well, kind of."

I beckoned Ross closer with a finger, then shot out a hand and grabbed his throat.

"Hey! What are you doing?"

"Ross, listen to me closely. We have been friends for a very long time and I really, really don't want to hurt you. But unless you very quickly come up with a damn good explanation for this outrage, I may remove your oesophagus, then tear a hole in your chest, remove your heart and eat it. Is there any reason I should not do these awful things to you?"

Ross choked again, unable to speak, and I assure you, those of our condition do need to breathe.

"Is there?" I hissed.

"Reylan, Let him go."

The no nonsense voice had come from somewhere beyond my feet, past the limit of my vision. My grip on Ross' throat loosened just enough to give him air. He still strained to force my hands away, but his strength was pitiful compared to mine.

"And why would I do that? I was almost killed by his 'associate' tonight. That is what you called him, isn't it, Ross?"

A small, middle-aged woman wearing a flowing, full-length white gown and a severe, tightly cropped blonde hairdo emerged gracefully from the darkness and offered herself for my inspection. "Aside from the fact that he is your friend, physical violence does not become a man of your breeding."

I wasn't sure if she was being ironic, but her flattery only fanned my anger further. She was right, of course. I wasn't prone to threatening friends. But if the Arcadia Trust's idea of an introduction was to bring my immortal existence perilously close to an all too mortal end, they could hardly be counted among them. And if, after all we'd shared, after all I'd done for him, he associated with such an organisation so freely, dismissed their actions so casually... could Ross?

I let out a low growl as my grip on him tightened once more. He choked out a small gasp as the blood flushed to his face, turning him an alarming shade of pink.

"If you do not, we will have no option but to destroy you," the woman continued. "I will not allow those under the Trust's protection to be threatened, even by another we seek to assist. Is that clear?"

Fine. If this went badly, I'd tear them both apart. Ross' arm cracked hard against the floor as I pushed him away. I could tell by the sound that it hadn't been broken, though if I knew Ross, that would surely become the 'official' version of the story.

"What the hell is wrong with you, Reylan?" he screamed, clutching his arm and staggering to his feet. "You think I put Kelvin up to this? I've been here for hours, patching you up!"

"Ross," the woman snapped. "Your tone is offensive. Leave us."

Ross scowled as he hurried from the room. The woman turned to me. She didn't smile, but there was an apologetic softness in her eyes.

"You have him quite broken in, I see." I sat up to face her, a cold breeze sweeping over my bare chest as I glanced at the moonlight's source; two bay windows, wide open, their curtains billowing.

As my eyes adjusted to the light, the room seemed almost like an empty blue void. No books lined the walls, just a couple of paintings. I smiled. German Expressionism, from the Weimar era. Those seven years living in Berlin had been among the happiest—and most decadent—of my life. It was a happiness the artists clearly had not shared. I couldn't make out detail, but the works were filled with dark shadows surrounding pale, bleak, human figures. One painting loomed large on the room's back wall, like some gaping portal to the artist's anguished imagination. But elsewhere in the room, there seemed so little. The white piano against the wall remained closed and silent. A porcelain doll sat in the corner, long neglected, with a missing eye and dirty white dress.

The room looked like some dark hybrid between a long-neglected ballroom and an old-world nursery, with perhaps a touch more of the latter.

"Ross is not mine to command," the woman said. "I ask only that he respect my wishes whilst in my house. I expect the same of you."

"And I expect you to keep the way to your nearest exit clear and pray that I never, ever have to come back."

"You are not a prisoner, Reylan. I would thank you to put aside such thoughts."

"So, you send hunters to stake us and bring us back here, only to patch us up and let us go for fun? Or research perhaps? If I've been micro-chipped, I assure you, you'd best tell me now."

"Our intent is neither hostile nor scholarly in nature, and I do apologise for Kelvin's rash actions. He is… overly eager, and particularly mistrustful of Blood Shades."

The use of the term grabbed my attention immediately.

"What did you say?"

She knew. Whoever this woman was, she knew the correct term for our kind.

"Your species? Blood Shade, I believe is the preferred name. Or vampire, to the ignorant. I understand believers in the scientific community use *homo vampirus*, though I doubt very much I'd find the term in any textbook. Let us stick to your preferred title, as a show of respect, perhaps?"

I blinked a few times, something I rarely do. I hated to admit it, but something fascinated me about this woman.

"You might consider me a scholar of Blood Shades," she explained, "along with other supernatural beings born into this world. And others, created outside the purview of nature. Composites, for instance."

Composites. Creatures fashioned from natural or artificial materials and given life by science. I knew little more. Only that such dubious alchemy had once been considered heretical and was now rarely shared.

"And this 'Kelvin?'"

"A Cloak Walker. Again, I pray you, accept my sincere apologies."

Cloak Walkers, I genuinely pitied. They too were born human, only to vanish when they came of age, lost to their families and friends for the rest of their lives. Blood Shades are fortunate, in a way. We can maintain the human illusion for several years after our change. But the few Cloak Walkers I'd known had simply vanished, without a chance to prepare or say goodbye. It was when they started extending their condition to inanimate objects—like weapons—that I got testy.

"And werewolves?" I asked. "You've one or two of them as well, I shouldn't wonder?"

"We do not use that term here, any more than 'vampire.' Flesh Masters is preferred."

I rolled my eyes. "It sounds almost... pornographic."

The woman raised an eyebrow. Though the thought had probably never crossed her mind, I could tell she didn't entirely disagree. The name was just like the lycanthropes, pretentious, self-adulating, brutish and vulgar.

"And you would be?" I asked.

"Human and mortal, I assure you."

This was going to take time.

"Perhaps we should start with an easier question, like your name?" Cheeky of me, but I couldn't allow myself to be outdone by a mere human's boldness. There was a hierarchy.

"Sister Patricia Bakker. Formerly of the Order of St Francis in Prague, and numerous appointments before that."

In other circumstances, it might have bothered me that Ross and I had thrown such a violent spat in front of a nun. As things were, it didn't.

"Very well then, Sister Bakker. May I bother you for the top half of my clothing?"

"Your clothes are being mended and cleaned as we speak. They will be returned to you in pristine condition as soon as they are finished."

"I'm sorry, mended by whom?"

"One of the Shapers kindly offered—"

"Oh, wonderful. Shapers! Absolutely spiffy! Not only do you collect supernatural beings, you keep a boarding house for witches."

My host sighed. "Reylan, that is hardly an appropriate or polite descrip—"

"As I would hope you're aware, Sister, witches and Blood Shades, are not what you'd call the closest of bedfellows. So, I will ask you only once. Is this little zoo of supernatural activity you profess to run endorsed by the House of Magick? Yes or no?"

"It most certainly is not."

"I see. Despite the presence of witches?"

"That's right."

"You know, I remember a time when people of your religious beliefs would much sooner have had them burned?"

"How very droll. However, I know that you do not."

"I beg your pardon?" Her rebuttal had been just a little too confident for my liking.

"You don't remember a time when the church burned 'witches,' or Shapers, for that matter. You're only one hundred and fifty-three years old, as I understand?"

"Close enough," I muttered. She didn't have to be quite so damn specific.

"That would put you several centuries short."

"I see the art of hair-splitting is alive and well. All right then, exactly what am I supposed to wear while Dolce and Gabbana are being occulted to within an inch of their lives?"

"I'd be quite content for you to run around naked. However, I felt retaining your pants would help ease the shock of your surroundings."

"Naked? You're not one of those nuns, are you?" I smirked, waving a finger at her.

Rather than humour me with a response, Bakker momentarily left my side, returning with a black t-shirt, which I slipped over my bare chest.

"I'm not a nun anymore, Reylan."

"Oh really, what did you do? Lose your virtue to a Blood Shade?"

Her fiery blue eyes levelled on me, her mouth a steely line, perhaps the closest to a scowl I would see. "It's difficult to lose one's virtue to an impotent being, Reylan."

"Madam, you wound me!"

"Ah, yes. What is it the children say? If you can't take it...?"

Terrific. I was being held captive by the Mother Superior to the Sisters of Sass.

"And your family is Dutch?"

"Very good, Reylan. Might I enquire—"

"Bakker, an extremely common Dutch name," I explained.

"That it is, and you were born…?"

"The usual way, head first."

She nodded. "You wish to protect the secrets of your past. I can respect that."

"So why are you no longer a nun then?"

"I too value the privacy of my past, Reylan, though I should have thought it at least a little obvious. Daemonology is not a field of study approved by the church." Her eyes softened a touch, as she became almost reflective. "The House of Magick has been good to me in aiding continuation of that study. But the Trust is not their invention. It is entirely my own."

I gave a silent nod and decided not to press her further—on that subject, anyway.

"But Ross recommends you highly," she continued, the warmth in her eyes now replaced by the officiousness of her introduction. "We've known of you for quite some time, keeping a respectful distance, of course."

"The zoo analogy draws distressingly close, Patricia."

"Reylan, I'll say this only once more. I keep no one here. I merely welcome those beyond human to my house, provided they behave themselves. The Arcadia Trust is a safe space to meet with others of their kind."

"So, I'm to interpret the attempt on my life as, what? A rite of initiation?"

My host was unamused. "Kelvin has difficulty understanding interspecies cooperation. His parents were killed by Blood Shades."

"Is that the best sob story he could give you? The man shot a stake into me, Sister, and you're telling me it was an accident?"

Her head tilted sympathetically. "An unfortunate product of ignorance. Your existence is not widely known within the Trust. There's your privacy to consider, after all. Kelvin came across you feeding on that man in public."

"The back streets of Darlinghurst are hardly public," I objected.

"Be that as it may, Kelvin errs on the side of—"

"Violence?"

"—caution. He incapacitated you and brought you back here for examination. I contacted Ross as soon as I realised. He's been here for several hours, taking care of you, feeding you blood and so on."

Great. That was going to be an awkward apology. Still, it was nice to know Ross was not in league with plotting my untimely demise.

"So, I suppose you're going to show me around now? Show me the wonders of the Arcadia Trust and make me the obligatory offer of a lifetime?"

"No. I most certainly am not."

"Pardon?"

"Reylan, you appear to have mistaken this for a recruitment drive. The key word here is trust. You, sir, are rude, quick to anger, dangerously independent and arrogant beyond description. I am not about to show you my facility or introduce you to those I assist. I don't trust you."

"Nor should you!" I snapped, tired of her posturing. "Have you even the slightest concept of what you're undertaking? A human? Managing cross-species relations? Dear God. You're talking about some secret brotherhood of supernatural beings in the heart of the city. It's naïve and it's ludicrous."

"That's enough, Reylan. It's clear you've no wish to understand what we're attempting here. No matter. You are not welcome to join the Trust at this time, and when our task is done, I should be glad never to see you again."

"What task?"

"You were attacked last night, by a Flesh Master. Is that correct?"

"The term is 'werewolf,' Patricia, and yes, I was. Did Ross tell you that?"

"It is at his request that we are offering our assistance."

Oh good, more humility, ahoy.

"Patricia, don't think me ungrateful, but I doubt that will be necessary. If I see this creature again, I will deal with it. If not, that's even better. Now, thanking you very much for your hospitality, please have my clothes brought to the front door, ready or not. I'm going home."

It was hard to ignore the one-eyed stare of that neglected doll.

Patricia stepped out of the way as I headed for the door. She deliberately waited until I'd almost left the room and said, "Of course, if he changes again at random, in front of mortals, before we can find him..." She was starting to annoy me again. "As you can see, Reylan, the world of the supernatural does not revolve solely around you. You're the first person we've encountered who has met this individual."

"Jorgas," I interrupted. "He calls himself Jorgas. Early twenties, not too fond of the gays, might even be found tearing into a few of the boys near Blaze. Has a taste for petty theft, without the talent to achieve much by it. That's your wolfie bastard. Glad to be of service. Good evening." I turned and made my way down the hall.

Patricia didn't stop me this time, though a young woman carrying my shirt and jacket met me part way. I took the clothes from her and held them up to the light for inspection.

"I'm sorry your garments took so long," the woman smiled. "You Blood Shades leave quite a mess, I'm afraid."

"So next time, don't stake me."

There wasn't the slightest hint of damage or wear on the clothes. They looked fresh off the rack, not a trace of blood or a stitch out of place.

"You know," I muttered, "if I didn't know better, I'd say witches repaired this."

"We prefer Shapers, Reylan. We use our abilities to shape reality—"

"I know damn well what you are and what you'd prefer, my dear." The comment was gruffer than intended, but I'd never much tried to hide my disdain for witches. There was nothing magical about their practice. It was all science. Science they wouldn't share, from simple parlour tricks to the creation of Composites. They weren't supernaturals, just damn cocky humans. Unfortunately for the rest of us, they had the talents to support their overblown egos. I looked down at the witch, and saw her blood glow with embarrassment and a little resentment. "However, I must compliment you. These look better than when I put them on."

"Yes, I know." She turned her back to me and strolled up the corridor. "You know your way out."

"I expect I'll find it."

"That wasn't a question."

Before I could respond, she was gone. It seemed Kelvin wasn't the only one of Patricia's lackeys uninterested in making friends. Fair enough. I'd hardly been Mister Congeniality myself.

Patricia, for all her pretence, kept an immaculate home. Whether it was her own, or simply a house used by this 'Trust', I couldn't tell. But the furnishings of the main hall were very different to the stark, almost empty ballroom. They were borderline Victorian, the doorways lined in gilt paint, perfectly maintained. Nothing had been allowed to peel or suffer the weight of years. The carpet looked new, but the patterning was ornate, as though it had been laid many years prior.

Of course, with witches in the house, no level of restoration or maintenance was impossible. That made the ballroom even more curious. It seemed so... neglected, by comparison. Overall, the house seemed cosy, and though clearly of a time long passed, felt like it belonged in the here and now. Perhaps the ballroom, or nursery, or whatever it had once been, was used as a lab or simply a medical bay of some kind, and decoration, of this classic, Victorian flavour at least, was redundant.

I sniffed the air carefully, in case the over-zealous Kelvin was keeping a cautious eye on me. It's said, perhaps cruelly, that you can smell a Cloak Walker long before you hear him, such is the inevitable toll of invisibility on personal hygiene. It's even been claimed that the condition brings on leprosy, and that a Cloak Walker may be tracked by the body parts he leaves behind. I find what this theory lacks in credence, it makes up for in originality.

I opened the front door and greeted the night.

"Well, if it isn't my own personal open-heart surgeon." Ross' sarcastic tones sank my steadily recovering mood. I would have preferred time to rehearse this moment.

"How did you think I would react?" I asked. "A chest full of wood, then waking up with you standing over me, saying you knew the creature responsible."

"Okay, so maybe that wasn't a good look," Ross admitted, "but how could you even think I'd set you up like that? I mean, getting you staked? Me?"

"You don't get to my age without a certain level of healthy paranoia."

"Healthy paranoia? More like—"

"Don't push me, Ross."

"You threatened to tear out my heart and eat it!"

I sighed. This wasn't helping. "You're right. That was a slight over-reaction. I apologise."

Ross just stared out into the night. What was he hoping for? A bouquet and chocolates?

"Where's Shontel?" I asked.

"How should I know? I was done with her before I heard about you and Kelvin." Ross shifted his weight to one leg, his arms folded. "Just out of curiosity, did Patricia invite you into the Trust?"

"No, she did not."

"I'm not surprised."

I stared at him with suspicion. "Why did you tell them about the werewolf attack? It's none of their business."

"I beg to differ. He can't control himself and at least one mortal's already died for it. That's everybody's business."

"Right. So do all of Patricia's little sideshow know about this incident?"

"What do you think?"

"I think I should have choked you. What were you thinking?"

"Reylan, work with me here. Rogue werewolf?"

"Fine." I stepped down off the porch, walking towards the street. "If you really think you can do something useful, by all means, have fun."

"Knew you'd see things our way, old man."

I could feel his self-satisfied grin burn into the back of my skull. "That's enough from you. You're not too old to be put over my knee." A faint smile crept across my face, as he hopped down from the porch and caught up to me.

"Almost four. You need a ride home?" he asked.

"Where are we?"

"Paddington."

"Ross, it's a twenty minute walk," I laughed.

"So? You're not going to get fat, are you?" Ross was smiling, but it was a smile that masked fear. Or possibly anger, I couldn't be sure. He didn't stop to kiss me before going to his car, and male or female, close or casual, Ross always kissed his friends goodbye.

I took one last look at the building, then began the short walk home. Full credit to the Arcadia Trust, Paddington was an excellent locale to hide the dubious nature of their work. Old, sophisticated, and expensive, lined with some of Sydney's prettiest terrace houses, interspersed with the occasional gothic behemoth that somehow managed to swallow a half-block of land, without overwhelming its terrace neighbours.

The Arcadia Trust had taken up residence in one of these giants, a colonial, stone-wash and brick manor house, tucked behind looming jacaranda trees. Now, two hours before dawn, the cool, perfectly still air of the night radiated through those trees, channelling the moonlight to the pavement, where it illuminated the crushed purple petals that fell under my shadow.

How I'd wanted one of these houses when I'd first arrived in Sydney—and how I'd almost died upon seeing the price tag. Gentrification was one thing, and had secured its hold on Paddington long before my arrival, but I refused on principle to pay more for a property in Australia than I'd paid for comparable homes in Paris and Los Angeles combined, though in fairness, those had been purchased in 1904 and 1947 respectively. I needed to get both reappraised.

As I rounded a few more streets back into Darlinghurst, the smell of human industry hit me in a wave, the stench of a newly swept street, counteracted by the sickly sweet aroma of fresh roasted coffee. The city's concrete monuments to ugliness soon surrounded me, and the harsh lights of the developed world shone down, quickly swallowing the light of the moon.

I felt a familiar twitching within me, the first pangs of hunger. Of course, I'd been staked. Any sustenance I'd gained from Tye, or been fed by Ross had been spent waking up from that misadventure. Damn it. Two hours before dawn was a bad time to get peckish.

CHAPTER FOUR

I checked every side street on the way home, determined to find some lost soul either coming off a night on the booze, or with no place to go, looking for someone to take away the pain. Soon enough, I realised that I was being stalked. Faint, awkward footsteps, failing dismally in their attempt to remain silent. That at least ruled out the Cloak Walker, who'd never have been so careless. I slowed a little to inspect the streets around me, but it was mainly for show. The footsteps were clearly behind me, and they'd gotten louder.

Then came the subtle, familiar odour of that greasy hair. I couldn't believe it.

Jorgas screeched as I rounded on him and pinned his human body against the wall. His clothes were fresher this time and he smelled marginally better, but there was no hiding that obnoxious sneer.

"Problem, bloodsucker?" he hissed at me, trying with futility to push my hand away from his neck. Strong as he was, without his wolf form, his strength was only human, and that, I could handle.

I shoved him back harder against the wall, just to drive the point home. "You've got a lot of nerve, trying to hunt me. Do you know that?" This was my opportunity. I didn't care how he tasted, or how I'd feel the next night. I was going to enjoy this.

Again, Jorgas screamed, a long, deep cry of powerlessness and ecstasy as I pushed my body against him and buried my face in his neck, opening those two little holes and drawing deeply. His low, angry moans faded as the blood began to flow faster.

He tasted… good.

In human form, his blood tasted fine—better than fine. It was somehow stronger, sharper and more potent. I recognised the vague hint of cheap scotch drunk hours earlier, and the smoky strain of even cheaper cigarettes that he'd been smoking. I found myself utterly intoxicated, despite his monstrosity as the blood surged through me. I gripped his writhing young body tighter, sucking the tender flesh surrounding his wound clean as I siphoned his blood.

This would end now, if I had to drain the murderous bastard dry and dump his shrivelled corpse with Rory's.

He grabbed at my shoulders and tried to pull me off his neck, but quickly surrendered to my thirst as the erotic thrill surged through him. The thin jacket slid off his shoulders, revealing part of the tiger tattoo, its head and claws hidden only by the stained white singlet that clung to his body. I could feel the jewellery on his chest press against me as he pulled closer, nuzzling my throat as eagerly as I did his.

Then, he seized the scruff of my neck and broke my hold.

Blood spurted from his wound as I cried out in shock. But he didn't hit me. He just let go of my hair and stared into my eyes, the base of his neck, bloody and bruised from the battle between my hunger and his flesh. I licked a spot of blood from my lips, watching him as my breath slowly returned. In that moment, I almost forgot who he was. Before me was an athletic, even handsome young man. A faint red glow tinted his dark eyes, catching the reflection of the blood across his shoulder that now marked him as mine. I owned his body. I owned his blood.

Before I could move, he grabbed my collar, pulled me close and kissed me. His tongue pushed through my jaws, lapping the blood–his own blood–from my lips as he held me fast. The wounds in his neck spurted blood over us both as he kept on kissing, the sensual warmth of sweat, breath and blood filling the air as I pulled him closer still. It wasn't until I'd pushed deep into his kiss that I realised what I was doing.

I felt sick.

I quickly pulled away as he tried to grab me. His mouth was wet with blood and he stared at me, eyes full of wonder, perhaps fear, or raw hatred. I couldn't tell which.

I felt the sting of incipient claws as he hit me across the face. He'd begun to change.

He bounded up the street, his speed already enhanced, as the first fibres of the monster took hold. Still stunned, I struggled to keep up, managing to keep him just in sight as he rounded back streets he'd obviously worked many times before. I couldn't let him go, with my body so weakened. If he came back for me, the fight would be over before it began.

My exhausted legs screamed for blood as I lurched clumsily after my slowly changing prey. A cat hissed as I leaped over it, careful not to send it flying with a misplaced foot. Even like this, I couldn't bear the thought of feeding from animals. Besides, any delay could be just the chance Jorgas needed to escape. He had to die and it had to happen before he changed again. I'd make sure of it. I followed him around one more turn and saw the wall ahead. A dead end, or so I thought.

With a single, mighty leap, Jorgas grabbed hold of a fire escape ladder that was a clear eight feet above his head. Then another, across to the scaffolding of an adjacent building, then from wall to wall, until he grabbed the lip of the rooftop and disappeared over with a canine snarl.

"You have got to be kidding me." I was in no mood for this asinine urban free styling. It was a waste of what little energy I had left. The cold ladder stung as my hands reached it, and each time I extended my nails to keep a grip on the brickwork, jumping from wall to wall, it felt as though my fingers were being torn from their joints. But I couldn't afford to lose him. Not now.

With a final groan of frustration, I dragged myself over the threshold, and slumped to the filthy rooftop that my prey had reached moments before. I tried to regain some feeling in my tortured hands as I panted for air and looked around the roof, piercing the dark with every sensory gift I had. No sign of Jorgas anywhere.

How dare he touch me! And kissing me? What the hell had he been thinking? I knew werewolves were beasts, lost to their passions, but I'd made no secret of my intent to kill him. Beyond stupid, was he quite mad?

Yet as he'd kissed me, I'd enjoyed it, hadn't I? No, that was impossible! I'd enjoyed the potency, the sweetness of his blood. Nothing more.

In the dark, my eyes made out a small structure on the other side of the roof. A tool or maintenance shed perhaps, certainly big enough to hide my prey. I should have been more careful, but all I could think of was finding the boy before he changed again. My thoughts came too late. Those terrible claws came down across my head and knocked me to the ground.

As if Jorgas' blow hadn't been hard enough, my skull cracked against the concrete roof and set me bleeding again. A wave of nausea swept over me and I barely managed to turn onto my knees, forcing myself to keep down what little blood I had left. But I couldn't move or get up. It was an effort to even breathe.

I tensed, bracing myself for another swipe of claws. My body shivered as it tried to cough up blood, pink tears welling in my eyes as my back and shoulders ached. The pain so gripped me that it took me a moment to realise, no werewolf claws had come down to finish the job. Instead, I heard Jorgas' increasingly shrill cries as his flesh reshaped itself back into human form. I watched in morbid fascination as the monster shrank back inside, its hair evaporating into his skin, its claws retracting, as his bestial body betrayed him. In that moment, I realised the wolf was not his weapon to command. Not yet. It sought only to control him, governed purely by vicious impulse.

His human side however, had a fury all its own. He grabbed my jacket with rough hands and threw me up against the shed. I heard the loud clang of the cage door on my back, a strong wire mesh gate, serving as the shed's fourth wall.

Still groggy, unable to fight, I looked at Jorgas. He stood naked again, holding me firm against the metal gate. His eyes pierced me with the same furious glare he'd given me in the alley. I grimaced as he pushed me tight against the gate. His eyes softened a little, though his grip remained firm. Whether his strength was fuelled by werewolf genes or rage, I couldn't tell.

"I don't want to kill you," he murmured, more to himself than to me.

He startled as my laughter ripped through the air.

"I'm touched but that's not a sentiment I share."

The pain tore through my body as Jorgas threw me against the gate again. With surprising grace, he pushed me out of the way and forced it open, throwing my limp body inside the shed. I sprang to my feet and ran at him but I was too slow. The gate clanged shut and bolted as Jorgas closed a padlock over it. I screamed, bashing the door of my new prison as

Jorgas backed away, his face a strange blend of satisfaction and… no, that couldn't be regret, could it?

"You're not sharing anything," he said. "See you round. Hope you like the sun."

So much for regret. He pulled on a jacket I recognised–that was my jacket! He'd slipped it off me while I was stunned. But as I watched him walk away, I realised I had bigger problems. The exposed mesh gate faced the east, and it was barely an hour before dawn.

Oh yes, I was definitely going to kill the bastard.

*   *   *

The hours from pre-dawn to mid-morning were a torment I'd not wish on anyone. Not like this. The blue light of evening drained away as I sat there, watching from the shadows as the instrument of my death emerged from the horizon. I watched, helpless as the sun's poisonous kiss cracked open the city sprawled beneath. On how many streets had Arthur Stace scratched his futile gospel warning of 'Eternity'? How little he'd understood the gravity of that word. Hell wasn't some realm of everlasting suffering for the damned after death. Hell was waiting for death.

I wanted to phone Ross, but my mobile lay in shattered pieces on the rooftop, glistening in the sun's first rays. It would just be me and my oblivious executioner, rising high above its worshippers, as had been its place for centuries, to countless human cultures. These religions had not been far wrong. The monster gave life and took it just as quickly. What made a god, if not that?

Another hour passed, and I huddled in the corner of my flimsy shelter. My body was numb from throwing myself against the gate, attempting to break the lock. Eventually, my muscles had refused to lift my weight any more.

"Been an exciting night for you, mate." The voice came from somewhere close.

I flinched, searching in earnest for the speaker. My first instinct was to have his blood. Rude, perhaps, but understandable. I was weak and hungry. Yet, I saw no one there.

"Aren't you going to answer me?"

"Show yourself then!"

"Sorry, can't do that."

"Now you listen to me," I growled. "I am extremely hungry and beyond aggravated. If you've nothing better to do than taunt me, I will quite happily hunt you down and show you your own spleen. Am I making myself clear?"

"Ooooh, he threatens me. Sorry Reylan, I meant what I said. I really can't do that."

I paused for a moment. If he really couldn't let me see him, then… "You have me at a disadvantage."

"We've met before. The name's Kelvin. I'd say it's nice to meet you, but the fact is I don't give a shit. They just told me to look out for you, like I'm a fucking babysitter."

There are times I hate being right.

"I owe you a lump of wood through the heart." I rose to my feet and glowered at the empty space. "Rest assured it'll do far more to you than me."

"Look, we can keep this line of threats up all day if you want, but Patricia wants me to let you out of here."

"Releasing me is fine," I laughed. "But in case you've been misinformed, my skin doesn't much care for sunny days outside. How exactly are you planning to—"

"In a minute. First, I'm gonna make this worth my while. Don't worry, I just want a chat. You like to chat, don't you?"

"Not with you."

"Yeah? Too bad. But you look famished and apparently I'm supposed to do something about that."

I looked up, realising too late I'd made a tactical error. How weak I must have appeared to my gloating rescuer. How hungry. A bag of blood was tossed at me, landing just inches out of the sunlight. I'd been too slow to see its point of origin. I carefully picked it up, punctured the bag with my teeth and sniffed the flowing red juice.

"Oh for God's sake, just drink it. It's good stuff. I mean, if you like that kind of thing. I haven't poisoned it, and trust me, I gave that some serious thought. Now, drink up."

Satisfied with my own risk assessment, and sick of Kelvin's voice, I licked the bag clean and raised it to my lips, taking a long drink. I pulled it away a second later, spilling and spitting foul blood as I stared at the bag with disgust. "What the—"

"What? You don't like horse?"

"Horse? I'm trapped here, possibly dying, and you bring me—"

"I'm not giving you human blood. Forget it, pretty boy. You want to butcher the norms? Do it on your own time."

I squared my shoulders angrily. "I've never tried Cloak Walker. Now, where are you?"

"Oh please, you couldn't even find where to stick the curly straw."

My mouth lifted into a half smile before I could stop it. I reluctantly returned the awful bag to my lips and finished it, fighting the urge to gag.

"There, that wasn't so bad, was it?" Kelvin goaded.

"Horrible. I owe you for making me drink that."

"Bring it, leech boy," he teased. "But I want to get some answers about you."

"Really not feeling autobiographical today, Kelvin."

"That's okay, I can wait. I've waited two hours already. Thing is, can you?"

My eyes widened. Two hours?

"Did you really think Patricia wasn't going to have you followed? I've been in here with you from the moment Jorgas locked you up."

"And you said nothing until now, why?" I asked.

"To see you squirm."

I rolled my eyes. "You stake me without having the slightest idea who I am, and now this? Tell me, were you born a psychopath? Or is this something that develops slowly in Cloak Walkers over time? I haven't known many, so do feel free to enlighten me."

"Why are you so interested in this guy?" Kelvin asked, ignoring me.

"Guy?"

"The street trash wolf man, like you didn't know. Why's he so important to you?"

"He's not. But he's too dangerous to leave running around, so—"

"Save that shit for your autobiography. I saw you feeding on him. Thought you were going to finish the job right then and there. Ross says you're a cold bastard when you want to be, Reylan."

"He does, does he?" I growled.

"I think it's more than that. I think you've got a mean streak a mile wide, and I saw it when you fed off that kid. Your eyes? That was personal."

"Now, see here—"

"Hey, I'm not judging. If the son of a bitch can't control himself, he needs to be put down. I just want to know why you're so fascinated by him."

How was I supposed to answer that? As infuriating as he was, Kelvin had a point. I honestly had no answer. Damn it. I had better things to do than be psychoanalysed by a Cloak Walker. "The same reason you're so fascinated by me."

"Am I, really?"

I peered as close to the lip of sunlight as I was safely able. "My parents were torn apart by werewolves and now I can't rest my immortal soul until every last one of these abominations burns in Hell."

My sarcastic melodrama was met by the sharp sting of a fist hitting my jaw. I stumbled back into the comfort of the shadows, smiling.

"Vampires," Kelvin muttered. "And you wonder why everyone hates you?"

I ignored his use of the heinous word. With the threat of encroaching sunlight, I was in no position to take an invisible enemy in a fight. "Not everyone hates us. Just you."

"And who told you that?"

"Your beloved Sister of monstrous charity, Patricia."

Silence.

I pulled back another inch into the safety of the shadows. When Kelvin did speak, his voice was shaking. Whatever nerve I'd struck, I'd ripped all the sneering confidence out of him.

"I have asked Patricia not to talk about that." He hissed the words with such venom, I tensed. If he grabbed me, or hauled me out into the light…

But I couldn't show weakness. Not now. "Do you really think your parents were the first killed by Blood Shades? We try to avoid it, but it happens. We're predators, humans are prey. If the predator gets careless, the prey dies. It sucks. I'm sorry for your loss, now get over it."

"That's not what happened. I don't know where she came up with that story but I'll speak for myself." His voice was low, almost a whisper.

"So, speak for yourself! How about a deal? A little more about you buys a little more about me and so on."

"How about you get off my back or I'll tie you to the gate and take photos for that wolf while you burn?"

"And to think, you were doing so well." I smiled.

"Well at what?"

"Proving you might be worth my time."

I heard Kelvin's breath grow heavier. No mean feat. As I understood it, Cloak Walkers wasted no time in learning to keep their breath silent after their change. Undetectable. If Kelvin's was audible, he was riled. Had I pushed too far?

"You're lucky Patricia would rip me a new one if I didn't help you," he conceded.

"I'll include those words in the card I send."

I felt the heavy flop of cloth impact my skin, like a thick blanket of some kind. A moment later, the padlock outside the cage sprang open.

"Put that over your head. Its cloak should work for another hour or so, but I could be wrong, so I'd go straight home if I were you. If the cloak fails before you get there, you'll be walking around with a very obvious blanket over your head. Could be... awkward."

"Umm, thanks." I stood up and put the blanket on, balanced as I could manage, hoping it covered any exposed skin. "Kelvin, I swear to you, if this doesn't work—"

"This is what I do. Do I try to tell you what type A negative tastes like? Or do I have to get behind you and push?"

"Try it, and you're a dea—"

"Just get on with it."

Cautious as I'd ever been, I eased a shoe-enclosed foot into the sunlight. Then, holding my breath, I jumped into the light proper, feeling my body spasm as the sun's warmth hit it for the first time in over one hundred and twenty years. It was sickening, that awful heat drenching every square inch of my vulnerable form. The sudden burst of warmth swelled into my stomach, up through my heart and lungs, wrapping itself round around my chest and arms. My eyes! How they lied to me, a kaleidoscope of bursting colours and shapes, radiant and vivid beyond all reason as the light battered my acute, nocturnal view. I near threw the damn blanket away before catching myself mid-panic. Strange though it felt, I wasn't burning. Kelvin had been telling the truth.

"I wish you could see yourself," he laughed. "That cloak will fool you and anyone who sees you. But you can still feel heat, because the sun knows better. And, ah… so will any animals that see you, so don't go pissing off dog-walkers in Hyde Park."

"Got it. Look, don't think me ungrateful, but wouldn't it have been easier just to bring me a big hat?"

"You want me to go back to the Trust and pick you out a hat?"

I considered the possibility. "No. Absolutely not."

"Alright then," he grinned. "I think you'll find the cloak's much better protection anyway. And I like to show off. That a problem for you?"

I supposed not, and somehow, it didn't surprise me. God, I felt sick. I swallowed, composing myself as I tried to ignore the heat. I wasn't far from home. I could do this.

"So, what are you going to do about this obsession then?" Kelvin asked.

"You idiot. There is no obsession. He's a beast, a wild animal who needs to be dealt with. My relationship with him ends there."

"I wasn't talking about your obsession. I was talking about his obsession, with you."

"What do you mean by that?"

Silence.

"Answer me!"

But that was all Kelvin was going to say, if he was still there at all. Only a small, fresh envelope hinted at where he might have been. I carefully bent down to pick it up, turning it over before taking out the paper inside. Threaded parchment,

Indian in origin, if I wasn't mistaken, with delicate, coloured fibres baked throughout the paper.

Reylan,

Please accept my apologies for illustrating our point in such crude terms, and of course, for Kelvin's manners. I pray that you make it home before his cloak fails. If you are reading this, I assume my suspicions have been realised, and our young Flesh Master has taken a personal interest in you. I hope you will now recognise the need for our assistance. You will meet me at The Black Soul this evening at eleven o'clock sharp, where our discussion will continue.

Yours in good faith,
Patricia

The Arcadia Trust deserved credit for their persistence, but now they were irritating me. And why choose such a god-awful venue? The Black Soul was the goth club that real goths avoided, kept alive by emo posers who savoured angst and despair over absinthe and Diet Coke. This was the club where no Sydney supernatural with any sense of social pride or status would stand to be seen. Trashy and commercial, it was an insulting freak show, designed for those who couldn't be freaks for real.

I simply had to know why Patricia Bakker wanted to meet there.

CHAPTER FIVE

The Black Soul was a relative newcomer to the less fashionable end of Oxford Street, just off Hyde Park. It had started its life as the latest place to be seen in Enmore, the centre of Sydney's goth scene. But within a month, the goths had given it the official black-nailed thumbs down, effectively closing its doors. A year later, it found a new lease of life, as a small upstairs emo club that opened early and traded till well past dawn. I had to wonder how it kept a turnover in those hours, given its theme and crowd. Unknowing, late-night club-goers, perhaps? Stumbling in during the wee hours, pissed as newts and immune to the Soul's black cloud? It was as good a theory as any.

I'd been there only twice. The first time, to the original Enmore venue for its opening weekend. The goths and I, all bored out of our skulls. The second time had been soon after the reopening on Oxford Street, when Ross, who'd been in Japan for the duration of the club's failed Enmore venture, had begged me incessantly. He'd lasted twenty minutes before coming down with a severe bout of self-pity and leaving with a sudden headache. Isobel knew better. She wouldn't be caught dead in the place.

My stomach turned as I trod up the stairs to the thrashing, white rap metal sounds above.

"Whoa, hold on there," the bouncer said, blocking the entrance. "Costume party tonight. Not much of a costume there, buddy."

Oh, terrific. As if to compound the humiliation of being seen in this dump, I was now expected to play fancy dress. I'd chosen my best black silk shirt and figure-hugging black jeans, too. Hell, I hadn't eaten properly since Tye, and no matter what club I was forced to endure, I intended to catch some refreshment.

"Sorry, but do you want to leave? You're holding us up," the bouncer continued.

I regarded the bleak faces behind me, all painted deathly white with black nails. Fancy dress, indeed!

"Look, I'm not going to say it again—"

Before the bouncer could finish, I rolled up the sleeve of my shirt, bared my fangs and ripped a gash in my forearm, seven inches long. With a flick of my arm, I sent a spattering of blood over the wooden floor. The gawkers behind me jumped back to avoid the red shower. The bouncer trembled as I looked up at him, my mouth glowing with fresh blood and my fangs exposed with a campy fervour that would have done Aunt Christopher proud. Christopher Lee, that is. There's a story behind that, but it's an inside joke. No really, forget it. It's a Blood Shade thing.

The bouncer blinked, his eyes bulging as I locked them to mine and licked the blood from my lips. My natural, pleasant expression slowly returned.

"Awesome costume, mate. Go right ahead." The bouncer hurriedly stepped out of my way.

I smiled, sweeping past and quickly checking to ensure I'd no lingering audience. I licked the gash closed, pulling the sleeve back down to cover my now perfectly healed skin.

Only at The Black Soul could you get away with theatrics like that. I just had to keep that arm covered for the night. No scar, no make-up, and most importantly, no questions.

A menagerie of every horror cliché you could imagine met my eyes as I scanned the room. Though in fairness, what many of the costumes lacked in originality, they made up for in craftsmanship. No common, store-bought Halloween trash. These people knew their genre and lavished it with sincere affection. There was a Pinhead, crafted with painstaking accuracy, who had struck up conversation with two other nameless, Barker-inspired abominations. There were a number of imitation Blood Shades, some of whom had even done well enough to leave the Stoker and Rice imagery behind. I allowed myself a satisfied smirk until I saw... Ugh. There had to be one. No more than a teenager. His skin, sparkling as it caught the club's pulsing lights.

Don't. Start. Me.

Away from the pop culture front, even I was impressed when the headless body of a man excused himself, and looking down I saw the missing head. That of a woman. It seemed... cute, if not particularly innovative. I expected neither quality from The Black Soul's crowd. Of course, all these monuments to macabre creativity weren't The Black Soul's crowd. I knew this because most of them were actually smiling. Perhaps the club had advertised in the student press again. The place seemed almost... tolerable, though it still didn't explain why Patricia wanted to meet here.

There were, of course, those I took to be regulars. I winced at the emos who'd invaded the tiny dance floor. Their idea of costuming was benign and tacky, plastic knives through the head, faces bloodied beyond recognition. Had one of them dressed as Carrie, would anyone have known?

It was twenty minutes before eleven. Later than I would have liked, but I could find an acceptable meal in twenty minutes. Probably.

Scanning the bar, pickings were slim. Nothing compared to Fantasy or Blaze. But he was there. About twenty-five. A short scruff of black hair atop his naturally pale face. Tall, but not overbearing. His expression suggested a disinterest in the place to rival my own. Not to mention a growing impatience, evidenced by the swiftness with which he upended his drink.

The black denim jacket he wore was decorated with silver chains–quite a lot of chains, in fact–stylishly clipped into buckles all over the garment. A number of them extended to his handcuffed wrists, but the links between the cuffs were broken in the middle. No make-up ruined his firm, square features and despite his pale complexion, the blood flowed rich under his skin. Why, hello there, my ghostly, chain-laden, young friend.

"Waiting for someone?" I asked, pulling up a chair next to him.

"No."

Despite the dismissive–and pointedly untrue–reply, he smiled at me before returning to his near empty glass.

I'm not being conceited. I'm a Blood Shade, and therefore impossible for most humans to resist.

"Can I get you another?" I asked.

Truthfully, you'd be hard pressed to find a genuine, goth styled Blood Shade anywhere in the world. It's such a tiresome cliché, isn't it? Yet I've always enjoyed the company of humans who've embraced the style. Not the emos, but the grown-ups who'd made it a conscious, fashionable lifestyle choice. This one was smiling at me now. Like many on the goth scene, he went from morbid to quite handsome when he smiled, and without make-up, his face made it seem all the more real.

"If you want."

I ordered another screwdriver, having caught the fresh smell of the last one on his breath, and passed it across to him.

"Thanks."

"So what're you supposed to be?"

"The self-liberated condemned man."

I balked at the apparent contradiction. It made sense on some level. I was just too hungry to work it out.

"It's my metaphysical comment on the essence of pain," he explained. "Or... something like that."

I smiled at him. Just smile and nod, as the humans say. "Looks good on you anyway."

"Thanks. Hey listen, I don't want to waste your time, so... I like girls. Only girls. Plus, I just got out of a relationship, so I'm not really... you know." He threw back the fresh screwdriver with the speed and confidence of a man whose liver was either made of steel or resigned to a state of apathetic surrender.

I laughed at him. "What's your name?"

"Brett."

"Presumptuous one, aren't you, Brett?"

"Dude, we're in a club. You bought me a drink—"

"If I had any intention of sleeping with you, we'd be halfway to my place right now." I'm nothing if not truthful. "Please, try to relax."

He looked away apologetically. "Sorry man, I just remember seeing you at Fantasy a few nights ago."

"You go to Fantasy?"

'Only girls', indeed!

"I meet my dealer there. It's safe. You got any by the way? I can pay you."

Before I could answer, a short emo girl barged between us, cash in hand, launching her ample body at the bar.

"Suzette?" the bartender gruffed, apparently recognising her.

"Get me another Slit Karma," she whined.

The girl couldn't have been more than eighteen, and her eyes–or at least the parts her black make-up hadn't smudged– were red with crying. She was taking far too much interest in the two of us as the bartender fixed her drink. Or more accurately, she vastly overestimated our interest in her.

"You guys get it, right? He dumped me via VidVoo! Angel dumped me on VidVoo! I mean, who does that? I'm so over it!"

"Despite all evidence to the contrary?" I asked, wondering what the hell a VidVoo was.

If Suzette had heard me, she didn't show it "He didn't even send me a message. He just… put it right out there and boom! Six thousand views. It's viral. He dumps me and it goes fucking viral! Are you kidding? Oh my god! I don't even know what I'm doing here by myself!"

"Hey, don't worry about it" Brett mumbled. "It's not so bad."

"Not so bad?" the girl asked. "Were you even listening? He broke—"

"Yeah, six thousand?" Brett continued. "That's nothing. Worry when it gets to a hundred."

"What?" the girl shrieked.

"Hey, calm down," I said. "There's plenty of other… Angels, or VidVoos, or whoever. Go have a good night, okay? I'm sure somebody else is lonely like you and will talk to you."

Suzette was too drunk to hear condescension, and stumbled off, leaving her drink on the bar.

"Dude, they all come here."

"So, why do you come here?"

"Blind date," he said, downing more of his drink.

"I thought you just got out of—"

"I know. Stupid, huh?"

"My condolences."

"You find ways to deal, yeah?" The boy leaned closer to me with a smirk I found oddly endearing. "So... got anything fun?"

Ah, yes. As a matter of fact, I did. The question was whether to use it. I glanced at the time. Not long before my meeting with Patricia, and possibly not long enough to broaden Brett's mind about his choice of potential bedfellows. I checked the pill in my pocket, wondering if deploying it twice in a year would really put that many black stains on my karma. It was certainly handy, but more than a little unethical, and worst of all, highly unpredictable. If Brett was stable enough, he would quickly surrender to the ecstasy of my feeding, and leave none the wiser. But if anything went wrong...

Why not? Brett seemed stable, compared to my other options, at least. And with less than ten minutes before Patricia's arrival, I'd little choice. I took out the small packet and discretely showed him the product.

"E?" he asked.

I wasn't sure how to answer. I'd never actually wondered what went into these pills. Judging by the effects, I guessed a little E, a little Viagra, just a little Rohypnol, and a hell of a good time.

"That's right," I said. "Highest grade. Shouldn't mess with your drink, either."

"I don't know. E kind of gets me horny."

"Is that a problem for you?"

"You're bad," he grinned, shaking his head. "How much?"

Good question. Money really wasn't the issue here. "Forty?"

Brett's face lowered as he reached for a wallet that was no longer there. "Shit! I've been lifted! Fuck, man!"

"Sssh, calm down. We can work something out." I put a hand on his arm.

He watched that hand with suspicion at first, then looked me straight in the eye. I had him.

"Haven't you and your dealer ever made other arrangements? Let me get you another drink." I felt his leg move against mine as I ordered for him again. So tentative in its curious exploration. Sweet, in a way. I kept my gaze fixed on him, his strong countenance now broken.

The screwdriver arrived and I slid it over to him, avoiding the drink Suzette had left on the bar. My other hand took gentle hold of Brett's, his flesh shivering at my touch. The quiet pulse of his thumb quickened. His eyes stayed on me, unable to move as he took a sip of the new drink and began tracing the back of my hand, mapping the new terrain of my body, one intimate frontier at a time. His fingers delicately slid over my skin, like he was afraid of breaking it. I smiled at him again. He couldn't break me. He was welcome to try.

"Dude… I've never been with a guy."

I nodded patiently. "Just do what feels right. No rush, no pressure."

Brett put his drink down and slowly leaned into me, a nervous bead of sweat forming on his brow. His eyes closed as his lips touched mine. "But I'd really like to try with you. You're beautiful, man."

I allowed myself the gentlest nibble of his lower lip. It was sweet from the juice of his drink. My chest tensed as Brett slid a nervous hand between the buttons of my shirt. I returned his touch, running the back of my hand down his firm chest and belly. But I was careful not to let my fingers stray inside his clothes. Not yet. Better to let him explore first. Straight male companions exploring their 'flexibility' had to be handled with care. I grinned as his tongue danced over my lips, his cool fingers fascinated by my flat chest and the faint, delicate hairs that covered it.

"I can't believe I'm doing this," the man grinned.

"Believe it," I whispered. "You're a very special man, Brett. I hope you realise that." Well, perhaps not 'special,' but it was nice to meet a companion who didn't immediately go for my lower regions. The seduction of the right straight man had its advantages.

Though I doubted its necessity, I held the pill over Brett's drink, just in case, as my tongue broke from my lips and met his. Excited and emboldened by the taste, Brett gripped my shirt within his fingers and pulled me closer. But the second was gone when tiny hands clawed between us. Suzette pushed our bodies apart with surprising strength. Worse still, I dropped the drug in the confusion. Where it landed was anyone's guess.

"Excuse me! Sorry guys. I forgot my drink." Suzette grabbed her glass, turning to me with a smile. Unlike Brett, she wasn't attractive when she ditched the angst. Nor was she attractive with the angst. Some people are just not meant to leave the house. "You were right, you know? I said to myself 'Suzette, that guy's right. Forget the video. Just talk to somebody and see what happens,' and so I went to talk to some girls and they were, like, really nice. You're so smart, and cute. And you…!" She drove a finger against my companion. "Tara over there? She's crushed."

"Huh? I don't even know who she is!" Brett protested, his confused glare rapidly moving between Suzette and myself.

"You big silly, she's been checking you out all night. She didn't know, see? But don't stop, it's cool. Kind of hot, actually, seeing you guys together. Not that I was staring, it's just—"

"Jesus," Brett hissed, getting up. "Will you both just back off? I don't need this shit."

I watched him retreat to the stairs and disappear. There was no point following. My hold was broken. I glowered at Suzette, tempted to take her home in the hope that Jorgas did decide to cause trouble. It was freshly diced emo for the wolf pack tonight.

"Did I do something wrong?" she asked, her voice dripping with a genuine yet whiny concern that just irritated me.

"Suzette. How's the traffic at this time of night?"

"Traffic?"

"Be a good girl and find some, would you? And go play in it!"

The stunned emo's face was a mask of shock, until she finally made a noise not unlike Demetrius retching a hairball. "Rude!" she spat out, lifting her drink. "So not adding you to VidVoo now. Forget it!"

Alone at last, I scowled, scanning the bar. Patricia had already taken her seat, a glass of red wine in hand, at a table at the quieter end of the club. Her outfit, however, near floored me. A habit, modest and traditional as you could ask, slashed all over with wild, violent cuts, shredding its black material. To top it off, fake blood was visible on the defiled garment's wimple. Patricia obviously felt no great attachment to her former order.

I sensed another presence; one I knew quite well. I could smell the subtlest hint of real blood in the air. I recognised its flavour instantly, and smiled.

"Isobel, hel—" I felt the sharp sting of nails as her hand rapped over my cheek. "I suppose I deserve that?"

"You certainly do," she answered with an insufferable smile, Spanish eyes glowing from behind a black net veil. "What have I told you about stealing my prey?"

"Brett?"

"No," she laughed. "Surely you remember?"

I stared at her, as though her nails had contained some vile toxin that would render me dead within minutes if I didn't recall. "Are we having another 'I'll never forgive you for Rock Hudson' moment? Because I really think it's time you let that go."

"When we were last out? The Crystal Lounge?"

"That was… weeks ago," I protested.

"And where would I be if I let old debts slide?"

"Popular?"

"Alright, you bitch. Have you said hello yet?"

"Hello? Oh, to her, I assume?" I nodded at Patricia, who glared at us impatiently. I was prepared to wager my old friend's presence had not been part of the plan.

"Sister Trish, and you call her that at your peril." Isobel took out a man's wallet and briefly examined its contents. Brett's wallet, I assumed.

"Pickpocketing is beneath you, my dear."

"I only did it for you. I was going to give it back, until you lost him." She tucked the object away in a small black handbag. "By the way, recognise anything?"

With a quick glance, I inspected her navy-blue outfit, which, coupled with several beaded necklaces, brought an eerie, cold quality to her skin under the club's lights.

"The blazer," she muttered. "Paris, 1919."

"Oh, yes!" This, I remembered very well, the only time Isobel had let me buy her clothes without argument. "Why tonight? What are you supposed to be?"

"In mourning," she shrugged. "For the death of dignity in fashion."

I smirked at the surrounding crowd. The death of dignity, indeed. "I thought you said never again, or did some Shaper dietician put you on a strict regime of tears and ennui?"

Isobel snaked her arms around my neck and whispered in my ear, her voice like ice against my already cold skin. "I'm here to make sure everything goes smoothly between you and Patricia—and to watch you squirm. Purely for my own entertainment, you understand."

I gently pushed her away, grimacing. "I'll try not to disappoint you. I don't see how you stand her. Night in, night out at that place."

"I don't." Isobel shrugged. "None of the Blood Shades live there, dear."

"But the Shapers do? Kelvin? Patricia herself?"

"Perhaps."

"So, it is run by the House of Magick?"

"I didn't say that."

"But—"

"Darling, you will have to make up your own mind about her, and the Trust, and that's all there is to it."

I looked over at Patricia just in time to see her indicating her watch, even more pointedly. "Well, my dear, as the fates have made it painfully clear I'm going into this meeting blind and hungry, I should bid you adieu—"

"Hold on." Isobel disappeared for a moment into the crowd.

I couldn't follow her path at first. But she re-emerged soon enough, with a Vampira styled young woman in a long black dress who grinned at me. Surely this was the only night on The Black Soul's calendar where its patrons smiled at all!

"Brenda? I want you to meet my friend, Reylan," Isobel introduced with a smirk.

The woman she'd so confidently escorted warmly took my hand. It was a refreshingly human gesture, for the venue.

"Hey you," she remarked. "Nice trick at the door. Did you see that guy's face? How'd you do that?"

"An ancient family secret, to remain closely guarded for another evening, dear lady." I gently lifted her hand and kissed it. Annoyingly vague truths always sounded better with a touch of old world charm.

"Oh my God, aren't you something? 'Dear Lady'… and Reylan? Nice name." She was attractive when she smiled, which seemed to be all the time.

"Is this your first time here?" I asked.

"Yeah. Blind date. Some friends' idea of a joke."

Oops.

"I think I've been stood up."

Not exactly.

"Did they at least tell you your mystery man's name?" It seemed polite to ask. I wanted that blood, and Isobel knew it. This was just mean.

Patricia had given up urging us on, settling for piercing glares as she drank her wine in long slow gulps.

"Brett somebody," Brenda continued. "Was supposed to have some weird Frankenstein-ish thing going on, but I haven't seen anything like that here."

"I have." Isobel sighed.

"Brenda,"

"Yeah?"

"Brett's gay," I lied.

"Come on, you can't be serious?"

"If his valiant attempts to explore the inside of my trousers are any indication, I'd say he's quite serious." A little creative storytelling never hurt.

"Rock Hudson," Isobel muttered, too low for Brenda to hear.

Hmph. I'd been right, hadn't I?

"I see. So, what happened?" the human asked. "Shouldn't you be with him?"

"Sweet boy, but not really my type," I lied again.

"If you two will excuse me?" Isobel grinned and winked at me twice, meaning I now owed her two. Damn it, this was

Sydney. The *new* new world. Don't try those social etiquette games with me here, Missy. I taught them to you.

But I now had my hand on Brenda's, stroking her long, immaculately manicured black nails. Her skin was soft, beautifully maintained. It almost radiated joy, even through her miserable Vampira persona. Ross was right. It had been ages since I'd taken a woman, aside from Deborah. I mean, really taken one, and given her the full, unbridled joy of a Blood Shade's touch. More importantly, I was running out of time. Brenda would do nicely.

"Anyway, I just wanted to say hi. Hope you find a nice guy to kill the night with." Brenda started to back away politely, though there was no resistance when I pulled her closer.

"I said Brett was gay," I whispered. "I never said I was."

Her smile broadened to a mischievous grin. "That's the best news I've had all night."

*　*　*

"You're incorrigible, all of you." Patricia tried to keep anger from her voice, which only brought a prim snap to the end of her words.

"Now, now, speciesist," I scolded. "Isobel offered me a favour. How rude would I have been to refuse?" I poured her more wine from the new bottle I'd bought us. I'd grown to trust Isobel's judgment when it came to companions. Brenda had been delicious, rich and sapid, spiced with just a hint of some light, citrus inspired perfume I couldn't place. Unusual, but tasty. No doubt her next blind date would be a fortunate man.

"I've less against Blood Shades than I do against your attitude, Reylan. All I'm asking is, when is it enough? When you're not feeding—"

"Patricia, had I not wasted precious blood waking up from Kelvin's stake, and had you provided me with half decent nourishment instead of that god-awful horse juice, I could well have offered you my undivided attention this evening."

"All I am saying is that for sexless beings you seem terribly… oversexed."

"Still a Catholic at heart, then?" I mused. "Burdening yourself with other people's sexual proclivities?"

She glowered at me a moment, refusing to bite. "To business, then?"

"One more question."

"Yes?"

"Why of all places would you choose to meet here?"

"Because neither one of us would be seen here under any normal circumstance. The nightly social drama pageant of a Blood Shade forbids it, and as for a woman of my years…. well. Who would think to look? Though, those among us may turn their heads, as you've discovered. Care to draw any more attention to yourself or are you quite finished?"

"And what was Isobel doing here?" I took a sip of my wine and instantly regretted it. While I'm quite capable of drinking non-blooded fluids, the experience is often far from pleasant.

"She's here specifically and I would assume quite deliberately against my instructions. Lovely girl, but on a personal crusade to push my buttons. More wine?"

Why not? I didn't have to drink it.

Patricia refilled my glass with a steady hand, pouring only a little. How many 'meals' had she shared with Blood Shades? Enough, it seemed. "Very interesting, your encounter with Jorgas last night, don't you think?"

"So interesting in fact, your agent almost waited till Ash Wednesday to help me. I've no doubt you find this fascinating, Patricia, but—"

"Am I going to finish a sentence this evening or is this verbal pissing contest going to continue?"

I couldn't help but smile. I'd met some remarkably liberal nuns in my time but Patricia Bakker was new territory. Refreshingly new, in fact. "Please, continue."

"Reylan, I won't lie to you. I'm hardly an authority on Flesh Masters. They're aggressive people, difficult to deal with in their human form and quite impossible once the beast takes hold. A few within the Trust have a rudimentary idea of their abilities, hunting habits and so forth, but until a Flesh Master cooperates with us and shares this information first hand, it's purely academic."

I wasn't sure I liked where this was going. "Is that why you're so interested? You want to capture Jorgas? Study him? Rehabilitate him? I think it's a bit late for that."

"Reylan, we have to take him in." Patricia picked up her bag and rummaged around inside, finally throwing down several photographs and newspaper clippings.

I carefully turned them over as though they'd break apart if gripped with any force. I could barely stand to look at them. The mutilated bodies of two teenage girls and one boy filled the various photographs. One of the girls had an arm missing and her abdomen had been ripped open. The other's throat had been slashed. The boy, about sixteen or so, had been shredded up the middle, with three heavy rips up his abdomen and chest, and chunks of his flesh removed. One of his legs had been torn off, along with much of his groin area.

"My God…" I whispered, turning the images facedown so I could focus on the newspaper clippings without distraction.

They described the three killings in grisly detail, including some exaggerations I couldn't see in the photographs. The headlines, such as 'Killer Rips through Inner East Teens' and 'Tiger of the Concrete Jungle' were almost comical, though not without irony, given Jorgas' body art. It was sickening, but that was tabloid reporting for you.

"Jorgas, you think?" The crimes seemed so brutal, so beyond him. Yet in his wolf form...

"We can't be sure. But Jorgas has proven once that he's capable of killings this violent, be it consciously or through mindless instinct. Even if these deaths aren't his handiwork, something is responsible for them, and I doubt that something is human. That makes it our problem."

"How old are these murders?" I asked.

"A week or more. The last happened just five days ago. That would make your companion... what was his name?"

"Roy. No, Rory, I think."

"If we're right, he was number four."

I nodded. It was the unwritten law of both Houses—one I agreed with. Innocent, human children. Jorgas was a dead man.

"Kelvin mentioned... an obsession?" I asked. "A bit extreme, don't you think?"

Patricia's brow furrowed for a second. "I'm not sure I'd call it that, but Jorgas was waiting for you last night, and I suspect that if he finds out you survived that cage, he'll come for you again. I don't think he's remotely stable."

"Would you like a prize for that observation?"

Patricia's eyes flashed at me to be silent again. Damn, she was good. "To hazard a guess, I'd say you've awakened something within him. Something he doesn't like, or that he's afraid of. He's well aware of what he is, whether he's encountered others of his kind yet or not. He also recognises you as a Blood Shade."

"Vampire. He calls me vampire, among other things."

"He may simply be trying to insult you, but I doubt it. He needs discipline, Reylan, whatever form that may take."

"Does the House of Magick know about this?"

"The Shapers have agreed, at least officially, to not know about this, and to let us handle him without interference. To let you handle him, specifically."

"Why me? Do you think he blames me for awakening his wolf?" It seemed unlikely. The thoughts of a young, newly awakened supernatural rarely extended beyond the self-indulgent panic of 'me, me, me.'

"Not directly. If he blames you for anything, it's a kneejerk reaction, not a conscious grudge. We also don't know if he's encountered any supernaturals before you."

"When he discovered what I was, he hardly seemed surprised. It's fair to assume he's at least read about us before."

"And of course, if that's the case?" she prompted.

"Then he's a smarter boy than he's letting on." Great, my adversary had a head for research. For all the myths, legends and popular culture, real information on the preternatural was hard to find, particularly in a country as young and resistant to folklore as Australia. "I'd like to know where he found his reading material."

"He's smart, yes, but he's also scared," Patricia continued. "If he attacked you and lost; if in that moment, he saw something darker, scarier and nastier than he is—"

"Hey, steady on."

"—that would explain some of his behaviour."

"Would it?"

"If he can't control his changes, and you defeated him, frightened him, made him feel foolish, then it's not unreasonable to think he's taking his frustrations out on you when his courage allows. You've become the focus of his self-loathing, a symbol of everything he hates within himself. You're both supernaturals, and if he's afraid of the wolf inside, that would explain a certain..." She trailed off, running a bony finger over the rim of the wine glass before continuing,

"…aggression, towards similar beings. It seems you have the misfortune of being the 'closest' one."

"So, I'm his punching bag on the road to self-actualisation? Spiffy," I hissed.

"Fascinating as all this is, the immediate problem is the same," Patricia leaned forward and lowered her voice as she came to the point. "But if you are the target of some fascination on Jorgas' part, it does present us with an opportunity. If he keeps coming after you, we know where he'll be. As these photos attest, time is a limited commodity for us, Reylan."

"You're asking me to serve as both assassin and bait?"

"You have a unique edge. That's why The House of Magick has given us a free hand in the matter. I'm hardly blind to the dangers, but the Trust would be extremely grateful for your assistance."

"How grateful, exactly?"

Patricia shrugged. "We'll cover your expense account of course, free blood and medical aid as you require it for the duration of your service and if you're successful, I'll reconsider allowing you access to the Trust's resources."

I couldn't help it. The laughter rose inside me and burst across the club, earning us bewildered stares from the startled patrons. I stifled it as soon as I was able, though I still found myself giggling like a schoolgirl. "What was it Groucho Marx said about joining clubs who'd accept him as a member?"

"You'd find this less humorous if you knew the collections we hold, Reylan. Everything you'd ever want to know about the preternatural world, or your own nature. I'd give it serious consideration."

"And what, Patricia, is left after one learns everything they'd ever want to know?"

"The desire for more. I've always seen the Trust's primary goal to be research and improved understanding. If that's done by fostering cooperation with those in the so-called 'supernatural' community, then I'm happy to do so. It's the pursuit of knowledge that drives me in this venture, Reylan."

I raised a hand, stopping her before she wandered aimlessly into hyperbole. I'd heard enough. "I'll do it."

Patricia didn't even blink. She'd known I'd accept. I felt suddenly... manipulated.

"Not for you, just so we're clear. I'm doing this for me."

"Reylan, I don't care if you do it for your beloved Aunt Christopher, just do it."

"And there's one more thing."

"Yes?"

"Jorgas is a werewolf. That makes him Magick's mess, not ours." I could tell by the way Patricia's face darkened that she disliked where this was going. Too bad. "For this, the House of Magick owes me a favour."

Patricia cautiously licked a spot of wine from the edge of her mouth, then took another sip. She wasn't looking at me now. She just stared into the glass. "I can't speak for them, Reylan. You know that."

"Then you'd better speak to them, hadn't you?" I pressed. "Please don't take this the wrong way, Patricia, but I am not risking my hide for a ramble through your library and the goodwill of an organisation I know nothing about."

"I'll talk to the Shapers," she conceded. "I make no promises. And my offer still stands. Don't dismiss our records out of hand. You may find something useful there. If you're injured, let us know immediately. The same goes for needing cash or supplies. That includes weapons."

"Weapons? Like what exactly?"

"Just a few pieces I've procured over the years. Several tasers, tranquiliser darts, that sort of thing. The Shapers may even be willing to prepare a few unique items for you, though I doubt it."

"Why am I not surprised?"

"If you can bring Jorgas back to us alive, you will do so. Is that clear?"

"You expect me to bring it to you alive?"

"Reylan," she scolded. "First of all, you will refer to 'it' as 'him'. Somewhere, he has a family. If he disappears, he'll be missed. Secondly, this operation will be sanctioned by the Arcadia Trust and if you want to keep the Houses out of it, I expect you to conform to our principles for its duration, is that quite clear?"

"Abundantly." I was unable to stop the smirk crossing my lips.

Our discussion was interrupted by a loud shriek from the dance floor. Suzette had jumped onto the shoulders of a young emo boy far too thin to carry her weight, sending them both crashing to the floor. She got up with nary a second thought, leapt up onto the bar and started singing some thrashing metal song I didn't recognise, her legs kicking in the air as the bartender shouted at her to get down. When she did, she wrapped her legs around the nearest man's shoulders before falling into the crowd.

Then, she hit someone.

I escorted Patricia out of the club, hearing only the rumblings of the baby-goth brawl behind us. At least I knew where my pill had gone. It was the most life The Black Soul had seen in years.

*   *   *

Patricia and I were soaked to the skin the moment we reached the street outside. It had been impossible to hear the rain over the roar of the club, but now revellers darted from one cover to the next as the deluge pelted down, gusts of wind firing droplets of rain like bullets.

"How are you getting back to the Trust?" I shouted over the din.

"I was relying on Ross for a lift." She struggled to hold her slashed habit in place, her make-up running down the lines of her aged face like a colourful delta of paint.

"You relied on Ross?" I asked incredulously. "Never mind, come on."

I darted up next to a young drunk who was waving down a cab a little way up the street. Patricia stayed at my side, keeping up with me by sheer strength of will, though probably only the will to stay dry. We pushed the drunk out of the way just as the cab pulled up to the curb.

"Hey arsehole, this is—"

He didn't get to finish. See, as sure as I can channel the intoxicating beauty of a Blood Shade through my eyes, I can also channel the horrific beast that feeds on the life's blood of humanity. It isn't a pretty little thing either.

The man shrieked in horror as he saw me. My irises glowed red, and the jagged gold lines that now surrounded them burned so bright I could feel them, like the power of the sun behind my eyes. Glowing, hot beams in the miserable deluge, their piercing light caught on every drop of water that fell between us. Then, the hissing began. The soft, subtle hiss nobody could hear in the rain, except the poor fool standing before me. He could hear it, and then came the voices. Even Blood Shades are unsure just where these come from. In less enlightened times, they were thought to be the voices of the Devil, in his many forms. Or at least, a conspiracy of powerful demons. A cacophony of screams, moans and laughs, the laughter of a Blood Shade, unfiltered by mortal form or the manners of human society. A concerto of horrors for my target's eyes and ears alone. I've seen men slit their own throats staring into my bestial nature. Thankfully, most men of polite society were no longer in the habit of carrying blades.

More often, they ran screaming into the night, and this one was no exception.

I opened the cab door and ushered Patricia into the back seat.

"Charmed," she muttered.

CHAPTER SIX

Our driver kept his eyes on the road, head down, trying to ignore the increasingly cranky nun who sat in his back seat, trying to remove her ruined make-up. I like cab drivers who don't ask questions. I have respect for them. There's wisdom in silence, particularly when dealing with non-humans. Before long, we pulled up outside my home, just in time to see Ross making a run for his car in the pelting rain.

"Sorry. Time got away on me." He hurriedly took off his jacket and held it over Patricia as we rushed inside.

"We were forced to leave earlier than expected." Patricia shot me a knowing look.

I ushered them into my sitting room and hung the jackets up over the barren fireplace to dry. I'd deal with that in a moment, but first...

"You're not adverse to men's clothes I hope?" I asked Patricia, retreating to my bedroom.

"Anything dry will suffice. Thank you." She freed her wimple and hung it up next to the jackets.

I returned with a towel, a pair of plain grey pants from a long-ago companion that were too small for me, and one of my less flattering long sleeve t-shirts, loose enough to allow Patricia ample room. Nothing designer. She had taken a vow of poverty, after all. She accepted them gratefully and disappeared into the guest bedroom.

"No clothes for me, old man?"

Ross stood behind my couch, for all appearances, naked. His bronzed chest glistened with rain that had soaked through his shirt, and his wet hair shone under the lights.

"Exactly what do you think you're doing?" I advanced on him, droplets of water still running down my face as I brushed away my soaked fringe. "What if Patricia saw you like that?"

"Oh, she has." He laughed, stepping out from behind the couch, revealing the pants he'd graciously kept on.

I raised a playful hand to slap him, which he blocked with a broad grin. If Ross was still bothered by my outburst the previous night, he didn't show it. I pulled his body toward me and held him close. His chin rested on my shoulder.

He'd not long fed, and I'd no doubt he could sense the same change in me. His skin felt so warm to the touch, no matter how wet he'd become. The aroma was subtle and sweet. He even kissed me as he withdrew, his eyes growing wide as the smile returned to his face.

"Oh my God! Reylan, you dark horse. Was she good?"

"She was. Thank you. Now, let's get you a shirt."

"What's the matter? Homo-globin not your thing tonight?"

"It was a matter of availability at short notice, Ross. Nothing more."

"Oh come on. It's your first woman in how long? The Pope will be pleased. Oh, wait…"

I didn't bite that. Some arguments can't be won. I began stuffing the fireplace with newspaper and kindling, quite forgetting the shirt I'd planned to get Ross. But he wasn't letting me off so easily.

"Isobel. She did go tonight, didn't she? God, she's a liar!"

"She may have been there," I admitted.

"And she set you up with this… Reylan, she's not on the reunion prowl, is she?"

I lit the place up and waited for the fire to take hold. Much better. "I'll remind you that our history does not include romantic ties. Now, drop it."

Ross relented, raising his hands with a smirk. I'd little patience for one of his ponderously playful moods tonight.

Patricia rejoined us, looking decidedly boyish in her borrowed clothes and cropped hair as she struggled to pull up the shirt's overlong sleeves.

"Quite fetching on you," I observed.

"Thank you…" she paused, shooting me a worried glare. "Please tell me they're yours."

"My pants won't fit you," I pointed out. "You did say anything dry would suffice, did you not?"

"Hmm…" Patricia slowly circled the room. Sure enough, she ignored the half-dressed Ross, instead casting her eye over my bookshelves, which contained the few traces of my birthplace left in the house, and the bright, abstract paintings I kept on the wall. "All originals, I assume?" she asked.

"Local artists, mostly."

"They're very… interesting." She picked up a small metal sculpture that had been crafted into some gothic, yet chillingly mechanical interpretation of a cat arching its back.

"Is that a compliment?"

"An observation. I expected your tastes to be somewhat more… traditional."

I could have sworn I heard Ross stifle a laugh. I took the sculpture gently from her grasp and returned it to the shelf. "A personal preference. If one's been gifted with immortality, it seems foolish to spend it pining for the past, don't you think?"

"I just would have taken you for a patron of the classics," she mused. "IKEA? Really?"

"I like my guests to feel comfortable. This is a townhouse, Patricia, not a Hammer movie."

"But your books... Johannes V. Jensen? Karen Blixen? All originals too, I see."

"I didn't know you were such an authority on Danish literature."

"No, you didn't," she replied, in just slightly accented Danish. Whether I liked Bakker or not, she fascinated me still.

"The cab's still out there. What's he doing?" Ross peered behind the curtains, his body bathed in streetlight.

"That's for me," Patricia explained. "Thank you for your hospitality, Reylan, but I'm not staying."

I nodded slowly. "I expect the clothes back."

"Of course. Ross, will you bring my things next time you come by the Trust?"

"Sure."

Patricia nodded to us both and opened the door, dashing through the pelting rain. Her freshly borrowed clothes were instantly drenched.

"Ross, you know her better than I. Was there even a reason she came inside?"

Ross shrugged. "I expect she just wanted to see your home. To understand another piece of the Reylan puzzle."

"Is that what I am?"

She was the most curious woman.

Ross flopped down on my couch, picking up a yellow business envelope I hadn't yet noticed. He took out a wad of papers and tossed them to the coffee table. "I brought you presents."

I picked up the papers and winced, instantly recognising them as coroner's reports of the victims. Just what I needed to lighten my mood. Graphic descriptions of a werewolf attack and its aftermath. Gruesome details I hadn't been able to see in the photos. A leg split all the way up the middle, ankle to thigh, and worse. The boy's spine had been driven up into his brain. Then, a thin police file with a photo I recognised. A photo of Jorgas.

"William Myers?" I read aloud.

Ross nodded. "His birth name. The family's loaded too, up on the North Shore. His Dad's old Sydney money. His Mum's…Chilean or Cuban? I don't remember."

"Judith?" I read her name, frowning. "I think not."

"Adopted name. She came here young. Anyway, are you familiar with the so-called 'Brats of Saint Barnie's?'"

"Yes, the Catholic community's 'only child' wonders."

The tabloids had made a meal of them for almost two weeks. All spoiled North Shore kids with unlimited credit cards and less limited egos. I thought better of mentioning that I too, had made a meal at least one of them. Simon deserved that privacy. When I realised just where Ross was going with this, it seemed impossible. Jorgas? A Saint Barnie's brat? Not a chance! For all their faults, the brats were masters of keeping their noses clean and playing polite, and that was not the Jorgas I knew at all.

"I did some looking into the Myers family," Ross continued, handing me two more files. "Dad's a lawyer. A very successful one. That's the only reason Billy's police file is so slim. The family can't afford to lose face. But Billy's well known for his hot temper. So, the brats—"

"Didn't want him anywhere near them, in case he exploded," I murmured, spotting a particularly ugly entry on the file. It read like a sexual assault charge, but the details were too vague to be sure. The boy had been acquitted before going to trial. A list of minor charges followed. Possession, petty theft, shoplifting... Young Billy had led a full life, albeit without a single conviction.

"And now, he's a werewolf," Ross continued. "Pretty big explosion, don't you think?"

"Keeps Dad busy, I see?" I flipped through the file once more. "Jorgas... Why Jorgas? Sounds Germanic. Scandinavian, maybe. The father's family's not European, are they?"

"Not for at least four generations. But Billy's a smart kid. Smart enough to not use his real name."

"And smart enough to know what he is."

"Wait," Ross' face darkened as he realised the implication. "He knew there were others, like him?"

"Definitely. When he realised that I wasn't human? Nothing. Not a stare, not a remark. No reaction at all."

"Well, we'd better find out how! If someone out there is shooting off their big mouth—"

"Don't be a drama queen. Jorgas knew what he was looking for and he found us. That's all there is to it. If anything, I give him credit for tenacity." I tossed the file back down on the coffee table, covering my face with my hands. "I just don't know how any of this is supposed to help me find the bastard."

"I have the family's address."

Right. I could see that playing out: 'Hello, Missus Myers. Sorry to interrupt, but can Billy come out to play? I owe him a disembowelling and several severed limbs.' In any case, I doubted Jorgas would put me to so much effort. He would find me.

My smile fell away as I caught sight of Ross' face. I'd never seen him so full of doubt, so worried, even desperate. It was almost frightening. He quickly looked away. Something about these killings had upset him, more than the acts themselves.

"What is it?" I asked plainly.

"I'm... a little afraid for you, old man." He flinched as I put an arm around his shoulders.

"What?" I demanded.

"It's nothing." He shrugged off my arm, uncomfortably. Ross had never shied from my touch before. I had thought my protégé to be a better liar than this.

"Afraid for me? Or afraid of me, Ross?"

"Both."

"You know I was angry. I would never hurt you."

"Yeah, but… that's the first time, Reylan. Nearly twenty years, and that's the first time I've ever seen you really lose it. In that second, you could have killed me."

"But I didn't. I wouldn't."

"I know." He put a nervous hand on my leg. "But I'm afraid of what you might do. If this kid pushes you too hard. How it could affect you, your judgment—"

"I can handle him."

"But can you handle you? You're over a century old. What could you do to somebody if… if they…?" Ross was stammering, and for a moment, I wondered if he'd start shedding bloody, pink tears. "I… I'm sorry, I shouldn't be like this."

I put a hand over his and squeezed, gentle as I could manage. He was right, to a point. That hand could crush any part of him—or Jorgas—to bloody, splintered bone in an instant, were I sufficiently fed and riled. I'm just not a violent man, by nature. Only one human had ever died at the receiving end of my temper, and that one had attempted to run a stake through a very young and inexperienced Isobel. I considered my actions justified, in hindsight.

Ross' other hand had reached across to my arm. His body glowed hot to my touch as he leaned in to kiss me. I didn't pull away. His lips briefly met mine before his tongue shot out and licked me.

I sprang back in alarm. "Ross, what the hell?"

"Reylan, we've kissed before."

This was true, the act of kissing carrying an altogether less romantic or sexual connotation among our kind. But still…

"You don't normally stick your tongue in my mouth," I said. "What's the matter with you?"

He nodded uncomfortably. "So, it's true? What Kelvin said?"

"What did Kelvin say?"

"Jorgas? He kissed you, didn't he?"

I couldn't believe this. Violent man or not, I'd kill that invisible gossipmonger. Just see if I didn't. "Yes. What about it? He's very confused, Ross. Nothing he did would surprise me."

"I'll bet that did."

"Well… yes, yes it did. But that's fine. Better than fine. It means he's careless. He's going to make mistakes. I can use that to my advantage."

Ross nodded. "I didn't believe Kelvin at first."

"And now you do?"

"I had to kiss you to be sure."

"Twice?"

Ross shook his head. "You're right, I just… I'm not thinking straight, right now. I'm scared by this, Reylan. This thing he has for you?"

"He's only come after me once. The first time was pure chance." I sighed. "Patricia claims that in some sick way, Jorgas admires me. She could be right. For all we know, I'm the only other supernatural he's met."

Ross nodded, finally understanding, or at least pretending to. I still wasn't sure I understood things myself.

"What do you want to do about it?" I asked, tired of skirting the issue.

"I don't know. But I'm not leaving you just now."

"Ross, that's nice, but I don't need a bodyguard. I also don't need the Trust breathing down my neck every minute of this… assignment."

He nodded again, backing off slightly. "That's fine. But I'm staying here tonight, Patricia's orders."

"She has no right to give orders in my house." I'd been patient. I'd been polite. But this intrusion was more than I could stand.

The loud bang of the cat flap silenced my defiance before it began. A blurry ball of ginger shot out of the kitchen with a shrieking meow. It nimbly bounced over me and threw itself against Ross, who yelped in pain as a snarling Demetrius buried tooth and claw into his skin. I was too astonished to move. All these years, Demetrius had never attacked my friends, and he loved Ross most of all.

Ross screamed as the cat dug its claws in further, climbing over his shoulder and taking a sizeable bite out of it. "Reylan, get it off me!" He grabbed at tufts of orange and white fur with futility as he began to bleed from the punctures.

I tried to grab the cat, any part of it I could reach. But between its relentless clawing and Ross' wild thrashing, I couldn't get my hands in there. Demetrius hissed as Ross swatted him across the face. That was my chance. I grabbed the scrawny orange body and heard the tear of flesh as I ripped it away. Demetrius shot off towards my bedroom with a low growl.

I turned my attention back to Ross. None of the scratches were serious, but still, I could scarcely believe my eyes. He was bleeding all over his shoulders, chest and face. Even his neck was marked with scratches, all caused by my docile, cowardly pet cat. Ross hurriedly licked at the wounds on his chest and shoulders, looking not unlike some great cat himself as he sealed them shut. It was good to be people like us. I couldn't help but smile at his attempts to lick the scars on his back.

"Shut up, Reylan! I wouldn't be doing this, if it wasn't for your bloody cat! Now help me."

"Turn around then." I gently placed my lips to the wounds and sealed them. Then, the bloody scars around his neck, and finally the ones he'd been unable to reach on his face. Within a minute, Ross looked his old self again, if a little shaken. "How do you feel?"

"In shock… and kind of mothered."

I sniffed the air, recognising the smell of wet cat hair. Demetrius had been outside. "Come on!" I headed for the back door.

"Reylan, where are you going?"

Hurriedly working the locks, I finally forced open the door and flicked on the back porch light, squinting as my eyes tried to adjust. Nothing. Just inky blackness, shrouding the back courtyard. Surely Demetrius hadn't gone snarling mad for nothing.

"Shit!" I hissed, louder than I would have liked.

"Mister Raymond? Mister Raymond! What is it?" Dorotha's neighbourhood watch, I did not need. "What going on down there?"

Ross stared at me a moment.

"What?" I asked.

"Raymond? She thinks your name is Raymond?" He smirked.

"Leave the silly old bat alone! She can call me what she likes."

"Who's that with you? Do we have a prowler? I call the police!"

"It's all right, Dorotha! All under control." I shouted back, trying not to clench my teeth.

"The silly old bat likes you," Ross teased.

"Is that you, Mister Ross?"

Mister Ross was suddenly silent.

"She likes you." I grinned at him. "Wants to know when I'm asking 'that nice Italian boy' to move in and adopt her some great-grandchildren."

"Oh, sure. Funny."

A white flash surrounded us, accompanied by the loud snap of an expiring light.

"Nice bulbs," Ross muttered.

I peered into the impenetrable night. Only now, surrounded by the rain-soaked darkness, could I see it. The hoodie's grey shape, disappearing over the fence.

We'd been watched.

"Grab the files. Hurry!"

Before Ross had taken a step, I leaped off the porch and into the soaking night, running after the figure that had disappeared. It could simply have been one of the local housing commission kids, but I doubted it. I climbed to the top of the fence and scanned the neighbouring yards. Nothing, and it was impossible to pick up any scent in the rain. No matter. Any hint would do. The rattling of a wooden gate, the thud of a plastic recycle bin… But through the rain, I was lucky to hear anything clearly at all.

Then, I saw it. Just for an instant. A black streak disappearing over a fence, maybe three houses ahead. I bounded through the back courtyards, ignoring the lights of homes I passed. All that mattered was the shape.

I paused as I leaped atop the fourth fence, sniffing the air once more. There he was! No random housebreaker, but Jorgas. Damp, almost musty, and a little too well worn. Like the smell of shaggy, wet dog. I hesitated, my stomach tightening as I considered what now seemed certain. He'd changed again. Nobody would have heard his growls of fear or pain from shifting, buried under the percussive barrage of rain on the surrounding roofs. Or maybe he'd learned to change silently since our last encounter.

Jorgas, the whipping boy of the Saint Barnie's brats. How the hell had he found my house? Had he followed me? No, that was impossible. He couldn't have followed the cab, unless he'd been there, waiting for Patricia and I to leave The Black Soul. The possibility seemed remote.

I took another strong sniff of the air, refocusing my thoughts. Right now, the 'how' didn't matter so much as the 'where'. Where had the smell gone? Another thing I hated about werewolves; they were much better trackers than Blood Shades would ever be.

The tell-tale rattling of metal came from my right.

I bounded off the fence and into the next yard, crossing it swiftly to avoid the security light that chased me into the shadows. The smell was more pungent now, and I realised, just one fence to go. Jorgas was in the next yard. I could hear him, panting to regain his breath. One quick leap and I'd have him. One, two…

It wasn't so much the German Shepherd's barking that startled me, nor the reptilian texture of the garden as I slid down to the brick paved yard below. It wasn't even the stream of light that burrowed into my skull once the motion sensor detected me. It was the dog's wet nose, repeatedly bumping against every part of me where it wasn't welcome. That, and its sandpapery tongue, trying to lick the mud and rain from my face. A loving, endless cycle of sniffs, yaps and licks as it tried to bathe me. It was nice to know that if a band of armed and desperate lollipops tried to break into number seventeen, they wouldn't stand a chance.

Damn idiot dog!

No, I was the idiot. In my paranoid state I'd forgotten to consider the obvious, that the smell of wet dog in some neighbourhood yard would be exactly that. Were I not so embarrassed, I might have laughed. Who knew the grey hoodie's identity? Who cared? For my troubles, I was now soaked, covered in mud and dog slobber, had probably worked Ross into a panic over nothing, and now found myself trying to dismiss the affections of some hairy neighbourhood mutt.

For that matter, which mutt? The dog or Jorgas?

I hauled myself up over the fence and out of my furry rescuer's reach, sniffing the air again, just to be sure. This time, all I could smell was wet dog, and it was coming from me. That dopey creature had slobbered all over my skin and clothes, and the scent was everywhere. Demetrius was going to love me.

Scaling the fences as nimbly as I could manage, and avoiding the sight of a young couple putting a hot tub to somewhat unorthodox use in the rain, I returned to my own porch, taking a moment to brush off the excess water. This running around in the rain had to stop, before I ran out of clothes. All right, perhaps that wasn't going to happen any time this century, but still...

The door was locked shut.

"Ross?"

No reply. I could have kept hammering on it, but not without attracting unwanted attention. I could either be soaked while I fetched my spare keys, or have Dorotha come downstairs to investigate. She'd probably bring food.

Keys it was.

Some Blood Shades pride themselves on a home filled with fine artworks and classical furnishings typical of the bygone era into which they were born—a stereotype I chose not to embody, seemingly to Patricia's disappointment. That said, I've still gathered a modest collection of objects, artworks and artefacts that certain museums would kill for. Over a century's travels, one can't help but come by a few 'must-have' items.

That's what the basement is for.

A small space, perhaps three by four metres at most, neatly tucked beneath my kitchen, the basement had been a major selling point when I'd purchased the house. A rarity in old Darlinghurst townhouses, it was the perfect storage area for my acquisitions, along with my spare house keys, and before you ask, I tell no one the location of my basement key.

I squeezed the last of the water from my clothes and stepped inside, still keeping my distance from anything sensitive to water. An extensive list, in this room. From a Tibetan tapestry to letters from French resistance fighters from both world wars, to Trotsky's skull. Not the actual skull of Trotsky. Sorry to disappoint. In fact, I've no clue as to the original owner's identity. Only that it was Russian, and had the neatest of pinprick holes at its peak. For this reason, I've dubbed it Trotsky, killed with an ice pick to the skull and so on. All right, so technically it had been an ice axe, no doubt with far gorier results than a mere crack to the cranium. But why sacrifice a good story to mere detail?

As I reached into the cavity at the back of the skull and retrieved the keys, a tiny splash hit my forehead. Then another. I knew the kitchen floor wasn't properly sealed, but if water was coming through…

Another splash bounced off my lips. It felt warm as I licked it away. Not water, but blood. I closed my eyes, trying to determine its flavour and subtleties in the dark.

What blood it was! Rich and smooth. Had a mortal dropped by, unannounced? Had Ross even managed to catch the young hoodie, and bring him inside? If so, why was blood now dripping through the cracks in the floor?

Ross wasn't that sloppy.

More drops found their way to my tongue. It was better than perfect. The taste of night air, sweetened by the first thaw of Spring. A taste untouched by sunlight, yet with the vaguest spark of…

There it was. The flaw. A stale, almost coppery taste. I hadn't tasted that in years.

A few large drops splashed onto Trotsky's skull. Even in the dark, I could see the stains. But so much blood? Not from a companion, surel—

Shit!

I raced out of the basement, pounded up the stairs and immediately began fumbling with the locks, swearing under my breath.

"Ross!" I called. "Ross! Open this door, damn you!"

"Mister Raymond!"

I ignored Dorotha's scolding, ready to tear the door off its hinges. I'd just forgiven Ross for the staking incident. If he'd accidentally killed a mortal in my home...

I finally burst into the kitchen, only to see Ross, slumped against the cupboards, covered in blood, with four great gashes ripped across his abdomen. Demetrius gently pawed the wounds, lapping at the blood. I picked the cat up and put him into the lounge. No wonder the blood had tasted so fine. The blood of a Blood Shade. My friend's blood, and I had licked at it like a ravenous, primal beast.

Panic is a curious thing. My breath grew short as I tried to wake Ross. I took him by the shoulders and gently shook him, but the movement only bled him further. Blood Shades don't clot.

I tried to lick the wounds at least partly closed, but my tongue just lapped more blood. I spat out as much as I could, fighting the temptation to gulp it down. So horribly addictive, despite everything I knew, everything I believed, telling me to resist, the blood still called. I could taste its sweet burn on the back of my tongue again, longing for more, just a few drops.

No! Even tainted with the stench of death, there was no disguising that flavour. Idiot! I should have realised it when the first drop hit my lips.

I forced myself away, catching sight of myself in the hall mirror–yes, we can be seen in mirrors. The first thing I saw was my red mouth, dripping with Ross' blood, smeared over my face like the war paint of some wicked cannibal tribe.

This was ridiculous. I was Reylan, and I could fix this.

Ross couldn't be dead. He may have looked horrendous with his flesh carved up, his eyes so dark they were little more than tiny glints in two vast black pools, and his skin, that deathly shade of enamel white. He couldn't talk, or even move. But he was there. Paralysed, perhaps, but not lost to me.

A mortal ambulance was out of the question. I grabbed my phone and took the Arcadia Trust's business card from my wallet. Within minutes of ending the call, a car arrived out front.

I ran a hand down Ross' arm, taking gentle hold of his fingers. "You'll be fine," I whispered, not knowing if he could hear. A gentle squeeze told me he had.

In my panic, I'd barely noticed that despite my friend's injuries, the kitchen itself was largely undamaged. Jorgas had entered the place in human form. What's more, there were no signs of a struggle, which meant Ross had been taken by surprise. The Scimitar of Light trained all its children to fight from an early age, in preparation for their joining the 'holy' cause in killing supernaturals. An unfortunate scheme, particularly when one of them, like Ross, not only turned, but accepted their true, adult nature. My friend could more than handle himself in a fight, but Jorgas hadn't given him that chance.

A pair of Shapers, a man and a woman, passed through my wall, leaving only a faint ripple of energy in their wake. A little disturbing in hindsight, but I had more important things on my mind. The woman took an empty plastic blood bag from her pocket and raised a hand, pointing to the blood on the floor. There were no words, just an elegant spout of blood, sweeping upwards to pour itself into the open bag. Within seconds, the floor was clean, save for Ross' body. The witch ran her fingers over the bag's lip to seal it.

I stared, fascinated as each Shaper reached out a bony hand, levitating Ross from the floor and gently glided him out of the room. Medically skilled Shapers were the best doctors money couldn't buy.

"Reylan, we need you to come with us, at least to answer some questions," the man called.

"Oh, I'm not leaving him," I assured them, stopping only to pick up the files for closer study. Suddenly, the disembowelling of William Myers didn't seem like a bad idea at all.

CHAPTER SEVEN

I took a long draw of my cigarette, generously donated by Isobel before she'd quickly departed. I hardly blamed her. She and Ross weren't exactly close, for all their similarities.

She'd offered the cigarettes with a pitcher of fresh blood, which I'd now almost finished out of sheer nervous hunger. It tasted horrible. Dog, if I recognised it. But nothing would keep me from Ross, not until I could be sure of his recovery.

The Arcadia Trust ran an impressive operation in tending their wounded. Within seconds of our arrival, Ross had been rushed with surprising gentleness to a room to which I'd been forbidden access, despite my vociferous protest. Apparently the 'magic' of the Shapers was to remain a mystery for another night. I was curious as to what they considered 'medical treatment'. Perhaps they'd developed a cure for our aversion to sunlight or a means to slow our need for blood? The possibilities were enough to make a Blood Shade's mouth water, and that, I feared, was the exact reason the Shapers weren't forthcoming.

For three hours, I waited. I'd managed to relax, having freshly fed, and with no small thanks to the nicotine soothing my nerves. I hadn't smoked in at least a decade, and it settled me with surprising ease. I tilted my head back, resting against the wall and staring at the ornate hall clock opposite me. Exquisite in form, but ultimately superfluous to any function beyond its prettiness. Like a newly changed Blood Shade, in that respect.

"Reylan."

I looked up to see Patricia emerge from the room to which they'd admitted Ross. "How is he?"

She plucked the cigarette from my lips and stubbed it out in an ashtray on the hall table that looked like it hadn't been used in years. "I know lung cancer can't kill you, but I'm not so lucky. Do you mind?" She dismissed my annoyance with the graceful flick of an eyebrow. "Isobel is well aware that I allow no smoking in these walls. I'm told Ross will recover by tomorrow evening. His injuries were severe, but Elspeth doubts they were meant to be fatal. The attack seems to have been motivated by panic, not malice."

"I gathered that much." I picked up the pack of cigarettes and drew another.

"Do you know how this happened?" Patricia asked, taking the cigarette from my lips. She flicked it into the ashtray before I'd so much as found the lighter.

"My home was invaded," I replied, with poorly masked discontent.

Patricia remained silent, patiently allowing me to relate events as best I could. I described the boy in the grey hoodie, who'd doubled back on me. Who'd gone back to the house to find Ross.

"I saw the wounds," she said at last. "What do you think did that?"

I hesitated, trying to giving her question every opportunity to be less obvious than it seemed. It didn't help. "Are you trying to insult my intelligence?" I purred, my composure wavering slightly.

"Answer my question. Was it a young man in a hoodie who doubled back on you, or a Flesh Master? I need you to be sure of this, Reylan."

"Whatever it was, it put the fear of God into my cat. Demetrius attacked Ross like he was in some panicked fit. I've never seen him attack anyone."

Patricia sighed, seemingly disappointed. "That would imply a supernatural of some kind. Something other than a Blood Shade."

"You think so? Well, that leaves, let me see, your friend, the Cloak Walker, or a werewolf. Let's see if you can help me narrow that list, Patricia?"

She didn't answer, or even look at me. All I could feel was the temperature of the hall around us lowering a notch. The acrid smell of the cigarette Patricia had extinguished reached my nose. Its bitterness matched her disdain.

"Sarcasm does not become you." Her voice betrayed nothing, not even impatience. "So if Jorgas did this, why did he not take the police files Ross procured for you?"

"Too careless, or in too much of a hurry?"

"Perhaps. Your kitchen was largely undamaged, correct? No sign of a fight?"

"That's right. I doubt Ross even saw him."

"And the woman who lives above you?"

"Dorotha? Not a word. I doubt she heard anything."

"Good. We can leave her be then."

I didn't care to dwell on that implication.

"Do you have some place to go in the meantime?" Patricia asked.

Now it was my turn to raise an eyebrow. In fact, I think I raised two. "Pardon me? Am I being forced out of my home?"

"Young man, you were in perfectly real danger before. I should think that this experience has proven the even greater danger you find yourself in now."

"Young man?" I laughed. "Young lady, I was stalking the evening for companions a century before you were born."

"I address people according to what I see, Reylan. In you, I see a young man and I'm not referring to your appearance."

I didn't ask.

"I will speak to Isobel about finding a safe place for you, temporarily."

"She won't let me stay with her." In fact, Isobel never let anyone stay with her. I'd no idea why not.

"Are you certain? I'm sorry that I can't allow you to stay here. But the Trust's safety is my first priority, you understand."

"And I wouldn't dream of imposing," I muttered. Surely it was better to take my chances with Jorgas than spend a night under the watchful eye of Kelvin. "But Isobel is a very private person, Patricia. So am I."

"Then promise me you will take care of yourself?"

Though her tone remained abrupt and matter-of-fact, I wondered if this was as close to the maternal 'Sister Bakker' as I would get.

"Of course."

"Very well. Did you require anything to assist with your assignment?"

"A .38 with silver bullets will do just fine."

"Must I remind you, that our agreement prescribed no lethal weapons?"

"Sister—"

"If there is nothing else, we will be keeping Ross here until his full recovery. You may leave him. I assure you, he is in the best hands."

"You can't be serious? Lethal weapons or not, I'm going to kill him. Do you understand that, Sister? He forfeited any mercy the moment he touched Ross!"

She stared at me, her expression unsurprised, and unchanged. "Ross will receive the utmost care, but my expectations of you remain as before."

Against all better judgement, I took her at her word.

"Thank you for your cooperation. Good evening."

"I just want to make one thing perfectly clear," I said. "If I humour you and bring this monster in unscathed, and I suspect even a hint of leniency after what he's done to Ross, then it won't be dog I'll be drinking next time I come by. Do we understand each other, Patricia?"

My host didn't flinch, and I wondered if I'd crossed the line. "Don't forget your cigarettes," she looked me over, her eyes inscrutable, "young man."

CHAPTER EIGHT

I couldn't go home. I couldn't go out feeding either. And there was no way I could stay within the Arcadia Trust's walls a moment longer. It was clear I wouldn't see Ross again that night. I'd been forced to settle for the Trust's good word on the matter, whatever that was worth. I'd left the police files there, too. I had nothing to gain by lugging around paperwork. That meant it was just me, alone with my thoughts for the evening.

I wasn't hungry. It was my mind that kept spinning in circles. What did I do for fun when I wasn't interested in feeding? I spent the time with Ross. That was the problem.

I could see Deborah sitting behind the counter of an empty Valia's, leafing the pages of what looked like a thick horror novel, though it was difficult to see from the window. I briefly considered going in for a cup of tea, but it seemed pointless and a little tragic to do so alone. Valia's was our spot, after all. Were we even welcome while Jorgas was still at large? Deborah had made her expectations clear. No trouble in her place. I offered her a tiny smile as she noticed me, but kept walking. The night's solitude would have seemed a lot more worthwhile with a weapon in my hand, preferably a sharp one made of silv—

"Hey."

I turned to see her cheerful smile, beckoning me from the doorway.

"Not coming..." the smile fell away as soon as I stepped into the light. "Oh, honey. You look like shit."

"Thank you." I considered some sly remark about her seeming bouncier than anyone at that hour had any business to be, but decided against it.

"Come on in, I'll make you a tea." She disappeared inside before I could say no.

"I'm really not—"

"I didn't ask."

I squinted as the harsh light crossed my eyes, ultimately sliding behind a small table in a particularly darkened corner.

"Jesus, that bad?" My observant host reached for the dimmer switch. Whether she saw the faint smile I offered her, I couldn't say. "Lousy night. I was just about to close up. Where's Ross?"

"Some business to take care of. I didn't pry." I saw no point in worrying Deborah. She returned with an open beer and placed it in front of me. "When did you get a liquor licence?"

"We're closed," she answered with a smirk.

I took a sip, and there it was, the faintest hint of her blood. "Thanks. You're not partaking?"

"Dry July. God help me." With that remark, Deborah reminded me of why I'd agreed to come inside in the first place. Far from pestering me for what was wrong, she managed to do what only moments before had seemed impossible. She made me laugh.

"So, dare I ask how long you've been getting fairies in here?"

"Ahah!" she snapped her fingers at me, grinning with a look of profound triumph that immediately made me regret the question. "I knew they were out there too!"

"Walked into that, didn't I?"

"You kind of did. So, do you know any?"

"I've... made acquaintances."

"What are they like?"

I shrugged. "You know, delicate, pretty features, wings and such?"

"Yeah?"

"Well, most fairies remove themselves as far from that appearance as possible. Or at least, so I'm told. I'm afraid my experience is rather limited. If you meet one, I expect you'll know."

"Wait. They don't hide, like you?"

"They hide. They hide very well. But you'll know." I tipped my beer at her.

The glint that crossed her eye was instantly familiar. That satisfied gleam that only privileged knowledge could bring. I'd seen it the first night we'd met, when she'd shouted a warning across the street, seconds before some thick-necked thug had tried to clobber me to the ground. I'd carelessly defended myself without heed to the human's presence. But Deborah, in her response to the bloody aftermath, had earned my undying respect and confidence with a single, whispered word... "Awesome."

I'd taken a tremendous risk in leaving her memory of the incident intact. But this charming young woman, the fresh-faced manager of a widely pegged to fail, late-night café on Crown Street, had never once betrayed me to the world. It felt... curious, to count a human among my friends again after all these years. And such a perceptive one. Inquisitive, yes, but also respectful. Had Patricia Bakker once been so perceptive? Had she risen from there to assume her current role in the night's affairs? No. I chose to think better of Deborah. I had to. Who else would sit with such a patient, unwavering smile as I sipped beer and stared at her in silence–which, I suddenly realised, I had been doing for almost a minute.

"Sorry," I mumbled, forcing myself to look down into my drink.

"Don't be."

"You ask me not to bring trouble into your place and here I am, brooding like some—"

"Hey," she put a warm hand over my wrist and squeezed. "You're never any trouble."

That was precisely when trouble decided to walk in the door.

"Can I get your next one?"

I couldn't place the voice until I turned around. My heart jumped, bypassing my throat and firmly wrapping itself somewhere behind my ears. Before Deborah could say a word, I grabbed both her hands and locked her eyes to mine.

"Go," I instructed. "Out the back, and don't come out until we're both gone. Now!"

My host rose from her chair and complied, eyes glazed over in that passive serenity unique to the newly hypnotised. I suppressed a low growl, the violent potential of my hands barely contained as I stared at the bastard. How the hell did he keep finding me?

"Jorgas."

He nodded, surprisingly composed. "You can really do that, huh? Make people obey you, just like that?" His usual sneer was absent. I wasn't sure if that was a good thing.

"Never you mind what I can do." I didn't want to think about it. Erasing their memories was one thing, but I'd seen humans lose all grip on sanity from being compelled once too often. Pulling such a trick on Deborah had been hasty. No doubt, I'd have some explaining to do the next time we met. But damn it! I'd made her a promise and I intended to bloody well keep it, even if it meant shoving her out of harm's way.

"I swear, if you come anywhere near her or this place agai— I didn't tell you to sit!"

He flopped down into the recently vacated chair opposite me. "What do you want me to do? Stand over you, like you owe me money?" Everything about him was different. His clothes were neat, almost passing for sociable. His hair and face were washed up and his usually unkempt grizzle had been tamed to a semi-distinguished stubble. "Cheers." He'd already taken a long pull of my beer before I could answer, and recoiled instantly as he spat it out over the table. "Jesus! What the hell's in that?"

"What do you think?" I asked, opening my lips just wide enough to make a show of my fangs.

He spat out more beer and set the bottle down with a loud thump. "That's disgusting!"

"Not a big fan of your diet either," I pointed out, suddenly losing all taste for the beer. "What do you want?"

He wiped the remaining liquid from his lips and stared at the bottle, conspicuously avoiding my eyes. "Forget it. It's stupid."

I shot out a hand and dug my fingers into his wrist. "In case you've missed it, wolf boy, you are one of my least favourite people right now. So, come on. Out with it."

"Okay, okay! Get off me! Fuck!" He shook me off with a pained wince. "It's just... I heard about your mate. Is he okay?"

I could scarcely believe what I was hearing. "Get out."

"Huh?"

"Get out of my sight! You'll need a damn good head start to keep ahead of what I'm going to do to you."

"Hey, I didn't touch him!"

"Oh, right. That's why you've been following me, isn't it? I'm not buying it, and if we were out of sight right now, I would cut you up where you stand."

Jorgas glared at me with the same eyes I'd come to know and hate in our previous encounters. "Fuck you, bloodsucker. I wanted to find you to apologise."

If nothing else, my enemy had a flair for the unexpected.

"You need help. Where is your head? Besides, why apologise if you're so innocent?"

"I never said that. All I said was I didn't touch your mate and that's the truth."

"Go on." My voice purred in a manner that made verbal threats seem unnecessary. He had me intrigued, and I'd have plenty of opportunity to settle things later.

"Sorry for locking you in that cage. That was shitty of me," he said. "I panicked."

"You're wise in your generation, however inarticulate."

"Look, accept it or not. I don't care."

"Wow, can you feel the repentance on this one?"

"I mean it. I don't know what I'm supposed to do with this thing in me. There's nobody who can explain it or help—"

"What you did to those students?" I hissed, my body shaking as I spat the words.

Breathing steadily, Jorgas looked deep into my eyes, a brave thing to do to a Blood Shade at any time, and damn near suicidal to one so angry. "I don't know what's happening to me, all right? I lose myself, and terrible things happen."

"I'm not your father confessor."

"I want you to kill me."

I felt the same bewildered expression take hold of my face. It had become all too familiar in recent nights. "Great," I said at last. "I don't suppose you've brought something I can use for that?" Caution was one thing. Discarding an opportunity that had fallen into my lap was quite another. I looked down at my adversary. He hadn't flinched. He was serious. "Why don't we take this outside?"

He nodded, and for the first, and I hoped, last time, we

left Valia's together in peace.

*　　*　　*

"I can't live like this. I'm like, an animal or something! I look in the mirror and I just want to throw up. My parents already hate me, Reylan. What are they going to think now? I'm not even human!"

I'd taken Jorgas several long blocks from Valia's, well out of Deborah's sight, to a secluded side street where he could caterwaul out his tragedy in that dead hour of the night.

"Right on all counts," I replied, listening to his epiphany with bemusement. "But why do you want me to kill you?"

"Dude, I killed people. Kids, even!"

"No, no, you're not listening. I know why you want to die. Why do you want me to kill you?"

Jorgas scowled. "Because you can and you want it, don't you? When you grabbed me that night and threw me up against the wall, it was like you were hungry for it, somehow. I could see it in your eyes. You hate me, and you know what? You should!"

"I don't kill people because I want to, Jorgas. What's the real reason?"

"There's nothing else! I just want it to stop! If that's all I've got left, then just do it!" His eyes flared, like they could burn a hole to the back of my skull.

"If you say so."

Jorgas choked down his nerves with an audible swallow.

My eyes narrowed as I leaned against the wall, my arms folded. "Okay. How would you like to go?"

"What? Are you making fun of me?"

"No, not at all," I insisted. "It's a very important question. How would you like to die? I don't suggest drowning. It's slow, painful, and you'll probably panic and get wolfish before we're done. If I'm holding you under, that could cost me an arm and probably more. That simply will not do."

Jorgas shifted uncomfortably between feet. "I don't know. Something quick? I just want this over."

I nearly laughed in his face. Absolution by blood? No, he wasn't getting off that easily. I turned and walked back up the street, leaving the bewildered beast behind me.

"Where are you going?" he snarled.

"Leaving. I want you punished for what you've done, not absolved."

Almost as quick as a Blood Shade, he was in front of me, blocking my exit. "Wait! Where are you going? You said you'd kill me!"

"Oh, I'll kill you." I purred, advancing on him until he was backed against the wall. "But I'll wait until you've started to get comfortable, to feel good about yourself, happy with what you've become. Then I'll come for you."

I hadn't opened the gateway to my inner beast for him, but Jorgas' eyes were still wide as I pushed him back against the brickwork. The boy put on a brave show, all bluster and street smarts, trying to reignite some of the fear he'd inspired the night he'd first attacked me. But it was far too late for that. He'd weakened himself when he'd kissed me, and he was weakening himself now with the whole suicidal charade. The monster—his primary defence—was crumbling around him, and this was my opportunity to finish it off.

"Then, I'll kill you, and it won't be quick. I may not have claws, but I can improvise, Jorgas. Don't ever doubt that. We'll start with a few choice gashes down that furry belly of yours, shall we?" I ran my fingernails down his shirt. "Then, maybe a few deep cuts across your arms and legs? Or shall I just rip those out altogether? That is your preferred method, isn't it? I think the remains of a nice young man near Blaze can attest to that."

Jorgas swallowed, sweat beading on his brow as he licked his lips. He wasn't just crumbling, his nerves were peaking, and I hoped, to whatever god was watching, that he wouldn't change.

I couldn't back down now. "Then, once I've left you a howling, limbless shell of what you once were, I'll take what's left of your vile carcass, sink my teeth into your throat and feed so deeply, that I'll be eating more than enough of your sins." Before his next breath, my hands shot up and grabbed the boy's shoulders. He yelped, wincing under the pain as my fingers drove into his collar like steel rods. "That's what I can do for you, Jorgas. That is the end I'm prepared to offer you."

I felt a wet drop on my hand. He was crying. The bastard was actually crying.

"I don't want to do that stuff again!" he yelled, trying to push me away. "You've got to help me."

His weakened eyes were furred with tears. His whole body trembled like a harmless puppy, until his head fell forward, exhausted. The man I held in my grasp now wasn't Jorgas, but someone I genuinely pitied. A feeble, human response, perhaps. I hated having been human once.

"So you said." What was I supposed to say? What did he want to hear? "Do you really want to die?"

Finally, there came the quiet whisper. "No. But I thought… I don't have a choice, do I?"

An odd, rhythmic sound, a guttural clucking, crept between us as his forehead rested against mine. His breath warmed the cold air around our faces, breaking over my cold lips as I tried to fight the sneer that possessed them. The grip of my fingers softened, the palms of my hands resting on his thin jacket. The awful 'clucking' was me. The laughter built up inside of me as his pathetic confession washed over mental images of Ross' mutilated form. But the image soon faded, along with my laughter, leaving only furious determination as my hands tightened again, my voice rising to an angry crescendo.

"Don't be so melodramatic," I snarled. "You do have a choice, Jorgas. There is always a choice."

"Let me go!" His weakened arms gripped my waist as he tried to force me away.

"Let you go? It's let you go now, is it? What's it to be, Jorgas? Fight for your life, or be done with it? This is your choice, now make it! What do you want from me?"

He stared at me a moment, eyes wide, fringe soaked, beads of cold sweat dripping from it onto my still threatening hands. I don't know why I didn't break the boy's neck when he pushed free of my grasp and kissed me.

Instead, I let my tongue meet his, pulling him deeper into my embrace as his hands held me tight, as though this moment kept him alive. His eyes were closed. How I wanted so much to simply close my own and enjoy the sensation now offered me. I may not be sexual, but to be touched like this? It was the longing touch of affection and desire. And fear, so much fear and anger, from a being beyond human, who knew my true nature. This was a new and wonderful experience.

With a start I broke away, remembering what I held in my arms. A werewolf. A vile monster and killer, in the semblance of a beautiful, if broken, young man. A young man who now leapt on me with such force, I fell to the pavement with his weight on top.

Again, his tongue lapped hungrily at mine. He shook loose his jacket to reveal smooth, muscular arms beneath, which wrapped around to embrace me once the jacket was tossed aside. I tried pushing him away, yet it somehow didn't matter. Part of me wanted this creature, wanted to hold him close and to grant him forgiveness, take him to my bed and feed, gorging myself on his blood, letting it flow like some elixir that would wash away the blood of his victims. But both hunger and compassion would have to wait. In that moment, he was beyond reason, and that was cause enough to know better. I had to know better.

He grabbed my wrist, almost dislocating it as he pressed my hand up against his body. I felt the ripped muscles beneath his shirt. Slowly, he pushed my hand down to his belt and forced my fingers around the buckle, tearing it open.

Puppy boy was hungry, and that put me in real danger.

"Come on, Reylan, I've seen it in your eyes," he snarled. "I've tasted your flesh. I know you want me. You want to know what it means to be alive again."

"I am alive! I don't need you to prove that. You're wasting your time. We're not like that, Jorgas! We don't feel anything!"

"Yeah, I'll bet you don't. Vampire bullshit! I can change that. Horny faggot bloodsucker!"

I cried out as he pinned my arms to the ground, and took the bottom of my shirt in his teeth. He pulled it up, licking at my stomach and chest with broad, slow strokes. I fought his grasp as hard as I could, but he wouldn't move. It was too near dawn. My strength was waning, and Jorgas was feeling just fine.

"Stop!" I screamed.

But the boy didn't stop. Fighting my overwhelmed senses, I tried to think rationally. How long before he bit me? Or worse, changed as a result of his crazed passions? Perhaps he wouldn't change. Perhaps the shell of his human body just wanted mine, to crack me open and gorge itself, feeding his lust with my ageless flesh.

Not bloody likely!

I tilted my head, bared my teeth and drove them into his wrist. An angry spurt of crimson blood erupted from the puncture. He howled, clutching his wounded wrist and staring down at me in horror. My mouth was wet with his blood again as a wicked snarl curled my lips. The 'horny faggot bloodsucker' had prevailed.

Jorgas quickly backed away, taking his weight off me. His hands balled into fists as he brought them up to the sides of his head and screamed behind clenched teeth. "Fuck! Fuck this thing! Fuck all of this!"

"Are you finished?"

"I can't even handle my human side," he mumbled.

"That's your human side? Trying to rape me?"

He fixed me with a mortified glare. "That's not what I—"

"Oh, that's endearing, Jorgas. Absolutely charming. You don't have a human side anymore, understood? As of the first time you changed, that's it. That's what you are. And if you don't learn to manage it, I will make it the personal mission of every Blood Shade in this city to track you down and tear you apart. Is that clear?"

"I thought you were already going to?"

That was all I needed. My resolve, self-weakened in the eyes of my prey. I decided to at least get some answers, in the wake of my collapsed soapbox. "So, what was that little show all about?"

"What show? You asked me what I wanted."

"And you said you wanted to die. Now, you want me?"

"I don't know!" he snarled. "But those guys are going to track me down and kill me anyway, aren't they? If they don't, somebody else will. Jesus! If you aren't going to help me—"

"What guys?" I asked, already knowing the answer.

"At that big house you go to, in Paddington? I checked them out a couple of times. That's how I knew about your mate. I followed you when you left. Those people? They're like us, aren't they?"

"Impressive," I conceded. "You're lucky they didn't find you snooping on them."

"That's how I knew what I was, too. I don't want this thing in me, Reylan."

"Yes, I got that, and no. No, no, absolutely not. We are not going through the whole 'baby supernatural in denial' epic tonight, thank you." I'd heard enough of those—cleaned up after enough baby Blood Shades to know how that song went, and there were few things more boring to me than a whiny, supernatural teenager. "Last time, Jorgas. What do you want from me? Sex? Sympathy? Silver through the spine? Out with it!"

Jorgas shook his head, straightening his clothes as if to reinforce some sense of sexual purity. Too late. "Fine," he mumbled, "I think you're hot. Happy now?"

"You don't say," I sneered. "We're built that way, Jorgas. It's how I attract prey. That's all. If it's sex you want, I can't give you that."

"I know, okay? Vampire thing, right?"

"Blood Shade."

"Oh, whatever!"

I caught myself before the sniping escalated. Ross had almost died. Irrespective of Jorgas' supposed crimes, this was not the time to argue terminology.

"Where are you going now?" I asked.

The boy just looked away, unwilling to meet my eyes.

Again, I saw that same weakened young man in a strong, preternatural body. A bizarre mismatch of gym junkie, street trash and monster of folklore. I couldn't let him go again.

"You're not going home."

"What?"

"Damn it. If you want my help, then fine. But I'm not killing you, we're not having sex and at no point are you to leave my sight. Not for an instant. Is that clear?"

His suspicion tightened into a troubling scowl. "You want me to come back to your place?"

"Would you suggest an alternative?" I didn't have time to take him to the Trust. Not tonight. "Stay close, and don't get behind me. This doesn't make us friends."

Any familiarity with my home would also betray his guilt over the attack on Ross. Had his motive been jealousy? Another man in my house? No. That sort of thinking was foolish and paranoid. And I'd still not the slightest proof.

Not yet.

"Do you know what it is you're doing?" he snarled at me. "Get over yourself, bloodsucker. Bringing someone like me into your house is very, very dangerous. Are you sure you can handle that?"

"Jorgas," I whispered. "Refusing me right now would also be very, very dangerous."

CHAPTER NINE

"Nice place. You live by yourself?"

"Thank you," I said gruffly as Jorgas surveyed my lounge room. I suddenly found myself wondering which of my belongings were too bulky to steal. "I own the building, but I've a tenant upstairs"

"Oh? Who?"

"A retired Polish widow, whose cooking can clog a man's arteries at ten paces. You're not to go up there for any reason. Are we clear?"

"That for her safety or mine?"

"Both."

Jorgas' smirk gave way to an impertinent grin I didn't care for. "Bit risky, isn't it? I thought you'd be more private than that."

Dorotha respected my privacy just fine–though Jorgas was starting to push his luck.

"That's another thing you need to learn," I said. "How to approximate a human lifestyle. Human behaviour."

"I've been doing that for twenty-two years."

"Yes. I suppose you have. But it's easier for Blood Shades. The reason 'vampires' have grabbed human imagination and culture like no other species is that we're not really all that different. We look like them. We hold similar values. They think they understand us, even if they don't believe, and we've encouraged them in that delusion."

Jorgas challenged me with a sarcastic glare. "Except for the whole drinking blood, no sunlight, crosses, garlic, running water, can't enter a home without—"

"Lies. Our lies, in fact, apart from the blood and sunlight."

"Wait, your lies?"

"Try to understand. Humans use myth, storytelling and culture to help them process reality. For us, that presents an opportunity. Over the centuries, there have been inevitable breaches of the cloak protecting Blood Shades from human eyes. So, we propagate myths so preposterous that humans safely dismiss our existence as impossible, to the point they don't even look for rational explanations. Mythology protects us, and others, like yourself. We hide, right in front of their eyes."

"But you feed on them! There's no hiding that."

"Hypnosis," I explained. "If I may demonstrate?"

"You better not!" He backed away with a low growl.

I couldn't resist a smile. The boy still had so much to learn. But it would wait for another night, and for a tutor more patient than I. "Lounge… bathroom… try not to fight the cat for the litter box."

"Yeah, you're not funny."

"Oh, and let me say this once. If you eat Demetrius, I eat you."

Jorgas winced. "You think I'm going to eat your cat?"

"Are you leading me toward a tired joke about eating pussy?" I asked.

"Oh, hah bloody hah. For your information, I like both. Guys and girls."

"How very multicultural for you. I don't care. Though I thought you didn't much like 'fags.'"

"I don't like a lot of people."

"The kitchen," I continued. "I assume you know your way around?"

"What do you mean by that?"

"Just checking."

I bit my tongue. Subtle, Reylan. Subtle. Still, there was every chance that antagonising him could get me answers—or get me killed. I was getting used to the balancing act.

"You still think I did it, don't you? That I cut up your mate?" Jorgas snapped.

"If I thought that, I'd have killed you in the street." I led him to the bedroom.

"Hey, I'm not sleeping with you!" Jorgas protested.

"You've changed your tune in twenty minutes."

"Beer goggles wore off. You're really not all that."

"Cushion my fragile, vain ego."

"Don't you have a spare room or something?"

"After what you've done, whatever that may or may not include, you're not leaving my sight. You want my help? You follow my rules, exactly."

"Dude," Jorgas sighed, "this is all kinds of wrong."

"A bit late for second thoughts, wouldn't you say? Besides, I think you'd look rather sweet curled up at the foot of my bed."

"Stop trying to piss me off. What now?"

"Now, I need sleep." I yawned.

"I don't, and when you do, I'll kill you."

I was thankful in a way. I'd almost lowered my guard. Maybe I was wrong. Maybe he did have a human side. I just had to ignore it, if I wanted to stay alive. "Kill me, or sleep with me? Any chance you'll make your mind up before dawn? Because you're just being tedious now."

Jorgas snorted, ignoring me.

"All right, dog boy, as you wish." I was behind him in an instant, one arm around his throat, the other, pressed firmly into his stomach. He cried out, clutching at my grasp as I squeezed the air out of him. Then, with a small choke, he fell limp in my arms.

Checking he was still alive, I laid his body down on the bed—a heavy bastard, for his size. Was it the preternatural density of the beast he became? I knew so little about the lupines. I carefully removed his socks, shoes and jeans, before easing off his shirt. Just one week prior, I would have laughed at the idea of stripping a werewolf naked in my bedroom but things had changed so much in that week. I'd promised Jorgas to the Arcadia Trust, and I didn't plan on presenting him naked, having ripped off his clothes during an unforeseen change. Still, the job wasn't finished. I opened my closet, and immediately found the ball of silver twine with an orange cat wrapped around it, glaring at me with vicious indignation and a cautionary growl as it guarded its prize.

"Oh shush!" With some effort, I managed to wrench the ball free. Demetrius bounced out of the closet and onto the bed, skidding to a halt as he saw Jorgas' sleeping body. In a movement that defied anything I thought I knew about animal mobility, he sprang high into the air, hissing and spitting at my captive before landing clumsily on the edge of the bed and darting out of the room.

I brought the boy's feet together and wrapped the twine securely around them, once, twice... five times. This made me nervous. Jorgas' feet were remarkably large, though probably not unusual for his kind. I'd never been this close to one before. Not without fear of an imminent, gruesome demise, anyway.

I secured the bind and rolled him over, tying his hands behind his back. The silver thread cut into his skin, but I didn't dare loosen it. A few light burns to his human form didn't concern me. If disaster struck and he changed, the thread would cut right through his flesh and bone, at least in theory. Using this as a failsafe seemed harsh, but I preferred the sight of Jorgas with severed hands and feet, to the sight of my head in his wolfen jaws.

I stepped back to inspect my handiwork, unable to resist a smile. His flesh was warm, his body inviting. Just a taste, I could take some more of his sweet blood before we slept if… no, forget it. I couldn't possibly puncture his skin without waking him. I'd lose whatever trust I'd gained. Worse still, he might shape shift in panic. I knew the bloody consequences of that.

Though it seemed perverse, he did look sweet, curled up, bound and naked, the infernal tattooed tiger fiercely guarding its sleeping master. He reminded me of the rough, beautiful youths I'd taken back in Europe, when I'd first changed. Boys, or girls for that matter, who worked on farms, or hardened trades apprentices. How easy it had been then, to find satisfaction in a companion. They'd carried so much pent-up frustration in those times, desperate for release, the pains of manual work bringing out those delicate individual flavours, particular to the last gasps of the pre-modern age.

None, however, had been so pleasing as Jorgas. They'd been only human, after all.

*   *   *

Blood Shades don't dream. Even in the comfort of sleep, we remain completely focused on the world around us, alerted to even the slightest disturbance to our surroundings, and awakened, should that disturbance mean us harm.

This time, I felt no warning.

I woke slowly, my mind dragging itself from sleep as warm breath teased my skin.

"It's about time."

Jorgas. My head had rested on his chest as I'd slept. I felt strangely... embarrassed.

"Why didn't you wake me if it bothered you?" I eased myself up and looked him over.

"That'd mean dealing with your personality. It's not worth it."

I rolled my eyes and got out of bed as moonlight overtook the room.

Jorgas' bonds were gone.

"How the...?" I hurriedly searched the floor for the silver thread.

"Here." Jorgas lazily pointed to the twine on the bedside table, uncut, and untied.

"What the hell are you?"

"I'm good with my hands," he smirked. "But I don't like being tied up and that shit burns. Don't try it again."

I leaned over him to collect the thread. "You said you'd kill me."

"I thought about it."

I flinched as he ran a hand through my hair.

"Didn't think it was fair. You trust me enough to sleep here. I respect that."

I searched his eyes, determined to find any malice, any sign of deception or cynicism, but there was none. He just looked back at me, open and honest, with at least a hint of the respect he claimed. I shivered as he tenderly stroked my shoulder. His blood radiated warmth against my own bare skin, which looked pale and hungry in the moon's subtle light. I barely felt his hand take hold of mine.

"Do you believe me?" he asked. "That I didn't attack your friend?"

I didn't know what to believe. "Tonight I'm taking you to the Arcadia Trust. They deal with... issues, for people like us."

"That's them, isn't it? That big house in Paddington?"

I nodded. Jorgas could have been innocent. He'd not shown any familiarity with my home. But if the attacker had not been him, then who? Or what?

"And they're going to deal with me, for killing those people?" Jorgas' lip began to shake, the first tears welling in his eyes. Tears he fought back with dogged determination.

"I don't know. They'll want to talk to you. To be honest, I don't think they were expecting me to bring you to them alive." I could scarcely believe my own words. Far from an abomination, all I saw before me now was a frightened young man. His grip tightened around my hand, but it wasn't aggressive. Far from it.

"Then they're going to kill me?"

I wasn't touching that. "Ross is important to them. He's the Blood Shade you... who was hurt."

Anger flashed through Jorgas' eyes, forcing away tears. As a werewolf, everything ran deep and I knew part of him wanted to reach out and take off my head, while another wanted to curl up and cry. I could see every impulse, however briefly it surfaced.

"Is that what you think? About what happened to Ross?"

"Does it matter what I think?"

"To me, yes."

The scent of his blood drove me to distraction as he held onto me with rough, strong hands.

"You're hungry," he observed.

I nodded silently, swallowing to keep my composure. I couldn't lose control, not with Jorgas lying there, vulnerable.

He ran a hand through my hair again, resting it on my back as he craned his neck, exposing the hot, flowing artery beneath. "Go on, take what you need."

"What? No."

"Please. Feed from me." His voice was a whisper. The soft, tender skin of his throat glowed hot as he pulled me closer.

Though my face was frozen in protest, it was a hollow resolve. All I could hear was the beating of Jorgas' heart, its rich red nectar taunting me as his breath grew quick and shallow. My cheek now pressed to his body, I could feel his pulse against my skin. The beating echoed through my head, engulfing my senses with the sound and smell of his blood.

I suckled at his chest, slowly, gently, as though it could coax the blood beneath.

Jorgas moaned, both hands now clutching me tighter into his chest as my tongue caressed his throat. The painted flames on his arm licked the tip of his shoulder, accompanying the beast that guarded his beating heart. They were mocking me, daring me to take what was mine.

Why was I fighting this? I owned this bastard. His body, his blood. I couldn't squander my second chance to claim him. And Jorgas wanted me. I had his blessing.

I bit him.

The scream lasted only a moment before fading into moans of ecstasy. My hunger was quickly satisfied, only to be replaced by a new sensation, raw desire.

Jorgas choked on another scream as I bit deeper into his skin, my arms now wrapped around him. My hands clutched his back, scratching with long, manicured nails. He tried to scratch mine, futile hands grasping at me—the tender nape of my neck, the smooth, muscular curves of my back—anywhere he could reach, as I syphoned the strength from his body.

He forced his head over and kissed me, his punctured artery baptising us both in his sweet juice. But the werewolf didn't care. He just drank more of me in, running a hand down the front of my torso. I flinched as he took hold of my once faithfully apathetic manhood, now animated of its own selfish accord in Jorgas' hand. I let him manipulate me as he pleased.

As I pleased, for my pleasure. Pure, undiluted pleasure, that was all too human. Terribly human. I felt sick.

I tried to climb off of him, only to be stopped by the wolf's rough hands grabbing my waist. I tried to push them away but he was having none of it, sending us both tumbling until he straddled me again.

"Jorgas, this isn't funny." I smarted as he pinned my wrists to the bed.

The boy grinned at me. "Yeah? Tell it to your dick."

"Get off me!" I must have panicked when Jorgas' grip on my wrists tightened. I lurched forward, throwing him off.

"You arrogant—"

His taunts were cut short as my hand balled into a fist and cracked across his jaw. My newly fed strength sent him tumbling off the bed. For a moment, he just lay on the floor and stared at me in disbelief. I didn't blame him. What was I doing? I didn't hit people. The boy's sneer was soon back to remind me, he wasn't 'people'.

"That all you got?" he growled.

I didn't get a chance to respond. He slammed his weight into my body, sending me sprawling backwards. Jorgas leapt to his feet, his nakedness taunting me as he held my head firm against the wall.

"You like the taste of me then, pretty bloodsucker? You want to feed on me?"

I looked down at his twitching, impatient sex. Had my scorn excited him so? Or just the captivating rush of the feed? Probably both. It excited me too. I felt strong, and in my current state of fury, there was no telling what damage I could do to him if I lost control. But I didn't want to. The smell of him was too overwhelming.

"Take it!" he screamed, wrapping his hands around my shoulders.

His blood? His cock? All of him?

His whole body shook in his attempt to dominate me, sending two trickles of blood down his chest, over the hard muscles of his stomach. I licked his abs clean as I slid my way down the wall, not wasting a drop of his sweet, life-giving juice as it mingled with sweat and sprouts of hair. I no longer cared about his attitude, his stupid werewolf arrogance and pride. There was only him—only the beautiful taste of him.

I ran my fingers through the soft brown hairs that blanketed the small of his back, then followed the trail down, caressing the soft fur of his thighs. His body shuddered again as I raked his cock's tender flesh with the tip of my fangs. I could feel the heat of his blood, hear its throbbing rhythm, even over the steady pulse of his lust.

"Oh God…" he panted. "I'm so close."

"No, you don't," I snarled, lifting my hands to tease the furry curve of his behind. He moaned again, swearing as he tried to penetrate my lips.

"I said, no you don't!"

He yelped as I rewarded his impertinence with a hard smack to the backside. "I'll tell you when we're done."

"Fuck you!"

That did it. The rhythmic pulse of his thigh had been calling my name. He howled as I bit into it, his body rigid as the blood surged to meet my kiss. It was more than the boy's lust could stand. He came over my shoulder as I greedily siphoned blood from his leg, then pushed back, forcing my touch inside him.

"Jesus! That hurts, man!" He was whimpering now, like a puppy.

With the speed his fresh blood afforded me, I licked closed the punctures on his thigh and rose to full height. My bloodied lips smeared his face as I whispered to him. "I told you, not yet."

He grabbed my shoulders and shoved me into the wall with painful force. Not so pathetic after all then? Good.

"You can throw me around all you want, Jorgas. Your blood's still mine."

"Vampire fuck!" He delivered a crushing punch to my midsection, doubling me over.

I took a moment to breathe–if only to make sure I still could–but in that moment, Jorgas threw me face down on the bed. He straddled me, crushing an arm into my back.

The sensual warmth of his blood trickled over me from the wound that remained open on his neck. I let out a small moan as I stirred with appreciation. Jorgas was still heavy, but in truth, it felt good–strangely comforting, having his weight pressed against me. But he couldn't win. I wouldn't let him.

I landed a fast elbow to his chest which cracked against his sternum, forcing him to stumble back. I grabbed the scruff of his neck and swapped our positions on the bed.

He snarled as I took hold of his wrists and held them fast behind his back. "If you want to control me, then just do it!"

Arrogant bastard dog! With Blood Shade speed, I was inside him before he could stop me. His threats diminished to puppy-like yelps, his body shuddering to the steady rhythm of mine. He tried to free his arms, only to have them pushed firm against his back. His tortured wincing gave way to a satisfied grin.

"Wait," he panted. "My shoulder..."

"What?"

"Bite me!"

I obliged, unable to resist a grin of my own as he screamed again. His blood washed over my lips, my ravenous appetite reawakened. Don't sass me, wolf man. Not while I can move faster than you can see.

Jorgas pushed me away from the wound, blood spurting as he turned his head and kissed me. His body shuddered in time with my own, his yelps dissolving into moans of pained ecstasy. Our bodies synched as he surrendered to me. The boy finally rose to his haunches, nuzzling me as I clamped my mouth back onto his bloodied shoulder, wrapped my arms tight around him and continued to drink.

My entire body twitched, as though the blood I'd taken from him had swelled to all my muscles at once. No companion had ever done this to me, no one's blood had been so potent. Simon had been close, but Jorgas transcended even that. I drew deep from him once more, hearing his ecstatic cry as he climaxed again. Resealing his wounds with a tender lick, I eased myself back.

"No," he whined, wrapping a hand around us to hold me fast. "Don't move. I want to feel you." His tongue clumsily licked at my face as he tried to kiss me.

It was so tempting to bite him again and finish what I'd begun, but I couldn't. Not now he trusted me. I think I hated that most of all. I'd done this with humans, many times. Gone through the motions and sated a companion's lust before feeding. But this was different. This was desire. Real, physical human desire that I'd not felt since… well, ever, as far as I could recall. And it had been with a werewolf. It had been with a damn werewolf.

What the hell was wrong with me? What did I think I was doing? This wasn't me. I felt sick. I forced Jorgas away, scrambled out of bed and headed for my bathroom.

The bastard followed.

"What is your problem?" I demanded.

"My problem? You don't do this much, do you?"

"All the time," I scoffed, "but I don't feel anything—"

"Yeah? Now who's in denial? That was amazing, and you were loving it. So, spare me this shit about not feeling anything!" Jorgas stared at me, his hair a shaggy mop and his body a mess of smeared blood, offsetting his tattoos. He looked like some naked rock star that had been brought back from an overdose and was now lost in a drug dampened haze.

I shuddered to think what I looked like.

"That was…" I couldn't speak. Christ, I had to speak. "That was wrong. We can't do that again. Not ever, do you understand?"

"Why not? Look at you. You're so turned on, you're still—"

"Don't! Just don't!" I snapped. But he was right, and I couldn't explain it. "I told you, I can't give you sex."

"Then what just happened?"

"I don't know. But never again, you understand? It's not normal!"

"You got that right," he grinned. "That wasn't normal. That was the most awesome fuck I've ever—"

"Look, why are you so fixed on me, if that's all you want?"

He scowled. "I don't know why, but I kind of like you."

"Is that what you like, Jorgas? Somebody punching you? Biting you? You said it hurt? Well, I believe you!"

He shrugged. "But I liked it, feeling wanted, like that."

I shook my head as I began running the shower. I didn't have time for this.

"Don't you ever get tired of it?"

"Tired of what?" I growled.

"Being alone. What are you afraid of?"

"Get out of my bathroom or I'll give you something to be afraid of," I warned, stepping into the water.

Jorgas pushed his way into the shower and kissed me, his tongue breaking through my lips as the storm of water, steam and blood surrounded us. I almost vomited. This was wrong. Far too wrong. He was a killer, an abomination, and I wouldn't have him in my bed or my mouth again.

He cried out with a start as I pushed him out of the shower, stumbling flat on his backside as he tripped out into the hall. Bloodied water ran off his skin, and his eyes returned to me with that same murderous gaze. "You're right then," he growled.

"About what, exactly?" I tried to sound bored and dismissive, keeping my anger controlled. Not like him. I was nothing like him.

"This doesn't make us friends."

Good boy.

"Shower's yours in five minutes. Don't touch anything," I instructed.

Jorgas placed a hand on the bathroom door, and slammed it shut.

CHAPTER TEN

I didn't speak to Jorgas as the car approached the Arcadia Trust. He hadn't fought me. In fact, he'd been strangely compliant. When Patricia had insisted on sending extra muscle to guard him, I'd refused. I didn't know why. 'Trust' seemed too strong a word. Part of me simply knew Jorgas wouldn't fight. He hadn't met my eyes since I'd thrown him out of my bathroom. He'd meekly showered himself clean, pulled on the same jeans, shirt and jacket he'd been wearing the night before and sat silently in the lounge under my meticulous gaze until the car arrived. The driver had brought restraints, just in case, but I'd dismissed them. Jorgas had then spent the entire journey staring vacantly out the window, without a word.

He hated me. Good. That was as it should have been.

The sky was unusually dark. Even the streetlights seemed to break only a few feet before their light was swallowed. It suited my mood. As we arrived at our destination, Jorgas waited for me to open the car door and haul him out. Shaking me off, he walked with surprising dignity toward the Trust's front door, like a condemned man at peace with his crimes. An admirable façade, but I knew better. His fearful, guilt-ridden heart would find no peace here. Perhaps not for a very long time.

The antiquated wooden doors swung open, and only once we'd crossed the threshold, did the car leave. No sooner had the doors shut behind us than I heard a startled cry from Jorgas. His hands had been pinned behind his back. Yet, I saw no assailant. Just a pair of handcuffs, locking his wrists. Silver handcuffs.

"You like them, Reylan? Not exactly Tiffany's, but I've got another pair if you want to try them on."

Kelvin. I was almost impressed by my own restraint. I could smell the faint burning of Jorgas' flesh, though his face would offer Kelvin no satisfaction, nor reaction to the pain. He just gritted his teeth and for the first time since the shower incident, looked straight at me. His eyes were furious, burdened by just a trace of helpless desperation.

I averted my gaze. I didn't need the distraction. "Where's Patricia?" I asked. "I have a fee to collect."

"Jesus, Reylan! Are you stupid?" Kelvin snarled. "I'm amazed this freak hasn't ripped you apart."

I didn't know how big Kelvin was, but he was strong enough to give Jorgas a solid shake. Either that, or Jorgas had given up fighting.

"I've seen those photos, you sick fuck," the Cloak Walker continued, I assumed to Jorgas. "I'm going to watch you burn, wolf boy. Watch you burn real slow and scream like the kids you've killed."

"If you're quite finished?" I said. What did it say about my life that my current allegiance was caught between an accused serial murderer and a sociopathic vigilante? Or that I'd slept with one and been saved–begrudgingly–by the other? First world problems? Not bloody likely!

The slam of a heavy door solved my dilemma. Patricia had arrived.

She didn't speak as she approached, drawing close to Jorgas' face until her nose stopped no more than an inch away.

She looked him up and down, regarding him like a museum piece as she circled him, stepping around Kelvin's unseen form. As she returned to face Jorgas again, her hand shot up and grabbed his chin.

He flinched as her nails took hold, but she held firm. She was staring him directly in the eye. The human eye may have been a window to the soul, but the gaze of a supernatural could all too often open that window to something much darker. When nothing of this nature happened—as best I could tell—I caught myself in a sigh of relief. What? Had I really been concerned for Patricia's safety?

She started sniffing Jorgas around the throat, as if getting the scent of his jacket, then put a hand over his chest, her eyes closing as she focused on his heartbeat. Jorgas seemed as perplexed as I, and a good deal more frustrated.

"I agree with Kelvin," Patricia said. "In so far as he's strong, Reylan. You should have been more careful. We would not have been responsible had—"

"Nothing would have," I interrupted. "I made sure of it."

"How so?"

Only then did I notice Patricia and Jorgas eyeing me, the nun with a resigned dignity and her new acquisition with a cautious glare.

"Pardon?" I asked.

"What precautions did you take?"

Precautions, indeed! "Well, I—"

"What he means to say," Jorgas sneered. "Is that he locked me in a cage in his basement for the night. Real fucking nice, Reylan. How many guys have you—"

"Thank you," Patricia cut him off. "I... understand."

I wasn't sure whether to be embarrassed or relieved, which no doubt was the response Jorgas had been hoping for.

"You want me to bark like a dog?" His sarcastic expression faded as he realised she wasn't biting.

"Curious," she murmured. "Kelvin will accompany you to your room, and I expect best behaviour from both of you."

The werewolf stumbled as he copped a hard shove from behind. His wrists were still burning.

"Come on you," Kelvin's voice snarled.

Before any of us could intervene, Jorgas' hands were free of the cuffs. He swung a solid punch in mid-air, hitting his unseen target with a loud crack, followed immediately by Kelvin's cry of pain. The boy rounded on Patricia, stopped only by the silver blade of a knife she now held at his throat.

"That's quite enough of that, thank you. Don't force us into more cautious measures."

Jorgas nodded as Patricia lowered the knife. Aiming a wry smile at me, he held up the handcuffs. Again, they were intact. Again, his method eluded me. Patricia plucked the cuffs from his grasp and neatly folded them inside her coat.

"You can't be serious!" Kelvin protested, his voice now muted and somewhat nasal. Had Jorgas broken something? Good.

"Kelvin, accompany Jorgas to his suite. Quickly."

There was some incoherent mumbling as Kelvin led a mildly happier looking Jorgas away.

Patricia looked to me and said, "Well, haven't you found a bit of work?"

This seemed a prime candidate for understatement of the century. I knew better than most. "He's a little too much work. What are you going to do with him?"

"Nothing."

"Nothing? Are you mad? Those children... Ross!"

"There was another last night while Jorgas was with you. I'm not saying this proves his innocence, but for the time being, we should avoid making rash assumptions."

She could have staked me then and there. I doubt I would have felt it. Another one, while Jorgas had been with me? In my home. My bed, no less!

"Well…" I managed to get out. "That sends all our theories to hell, doesn't it?"

"Speak for yourself. I'm rather relieved."

"Relieved, why?"

"Your part in this is complete. Thank you for your assistance. Your payment will be arranged shortly. In the meantime, perhaps you'd like to wait in the library where the other part of your remuneration is waiting?"

It took me a moment to find words beyond the obvious 'What?' "Excuse me?" I kept my voice as low and even as I could manage. "I've helped you get this far, and suddenly I'm redundant?"

"Reylan, your involvement in this matter was never intended to be long-lasting. I asked you to find Jorgas for us and you have done so. Congratulations and thank you. We'll take it from here. Goodnight."

"Now just wait a minute," I blocked her path.

My host-come-client fixed me with an annoyed glare. For all Patricia's skill at hiding emotions, she wasn't impenetrable. "I fail to see the problem. You've made your feelings toward us perfectly clear, and I can assure you, they are quite mutual. Now, if you will? The library, please. Third door on the right. I've a great deal to get done this evening."

Ensuring I turned my back first–if only to salvage what shred of pride might remain available to me–I went in search of the room. Patricia was right, of course. So far as I was concerned, this was over but for my reward. But what exactly did that mean? The terms of this arrangement had been unsettlingly vague.

"One more thing, Reylan."

I stopped, but refused to look round, instead offering her a barely interested glance over the shoulder.

"I've spoken with representatives from the House of Magick. They've agreed to your request. One favour. That's one."

I smiled to acknowledge this and continued on my way. One favour from the Shapers was one I would make count.

*   *   *

I soon discovered that the library—if the term could be considered adequate—kept by the Arcadia Trust was the kind of room that not only had its own personality, but also seemed to impress that personality the moment one breached its threshold. A little dust fell from the doorway as it creaked open, which seemed out of place in a room that, like the rest of the house, was otherwise spotlessly clean. There were dull overhead lights and even dimmer lamps sporadically placed around the room, but none of them seemed to pierce more than a few feet into the darkness. The shelves creaked with each step I took and the books I passed seemed to sigh for their rejection. Endless rows of brown and grey leather.

Old, old books, and I was sure more than one of them had been bound in human flesh. Such things are no confections of imagination. Superstition is a beastly master.

Books, the likes of which I'd not seen since leaving Europe. Books I never thought I'd see in the New World. On some, the lettering glinted in the light, gold against the ancient leather. But more often, the print had faded to nothing, leaving an empty spine that begged rediscovery, to be cracked open and skimmed through once more. How tempting it was to answer that cry for attention. Countless volumes on Blood Shades, werewolves, witchcraft, theology, alchemy,

Egyptology, Greco-Roman and Celtic lore. Ancient belief systems long lost to the world. But where to begin?

"One week."

"What?" I started, looking around for the voice that had broken the musty silence.

"You may borrow any text you choose for up to one week, though only to you at Patricia's request. We don't normally offer our collection to outsiders. You're not to pass them on. Do you understand?"

I turned around to find the source of the gruff little voice that had instructed me so boldly. A child. I was being chastised by a child, in the Arcadia Trust. "Oh, yes that's fine... I suppose." I almost laughed.

The boy would have been ten at most, his mousy brown hair cut into a neat little fringe over his spotty features, which scowled up at me like some angry garden gnome who'd stumbled across a burglary. "And don't be all night about making your selection either."

A tuft of white fuzz shifted its weight in his tiny pale hands, which I'd only just realised were petting a large white rabbit. The creature had already shed stray fur across the child's navy-blue sweater.

"What are you staring at?" he demanded.

"Sorry. I just... that is, I wasn't expecting Patricia to have children here."

The boy suddenly lifted the rabbit to his mouth and bit into its neck as though it were the most natural action in the world. The animal screamed as thick blood ran down its white fur as well as smearing the boy's lips. Its head thrashed as it fitted out its death spasm, white paws thumping against the child's face and neck as he drank, deep and steady as one who'd been feeding for years.

It made more sense now. Soon, the rabbit's frame went limp as the juvenile Blood Shade withdrew his teeth and mopped his mouth clean with a handkerchief. I brought my own hand up to my mouth to try and hide my disgust, but it was plain to see. Animals… and common rabbits at that!

"Giorgios!" a voice rang out behind the boy.

He wiped the congealed blood from his lips and glanced at the girl who'd snapped his name.

"How many times have I told you not to feed among the collections?"

Another child. A little taller than the boy, but not much older to look at, maybe twelve or thirteen. Her straight, red hair hung down past the frilly shoulders of her delicate white blouse, which offset a black skirt, stockings and sensible shoes. Perhaps most notably, in the centre of her face, were a set of piercing, bright pink eyes. Although myths existed to the contrary, pink eyes were incredibly rare among Blood Shades, and the individuals born with them couldn't help but grab attention, particularly the children–or Prematures, as they were usually known–Blood Shades who changed before adolescence.

As a species, we aren't known for elephantine memories, but we all remember our change to a lifestyle of shadow. The confusion of our sudden hunger for blood, our bodies' rejection of mortal food, and the pain of tearing blood vessels as they rewired themselves to our digestive systems. Then, the agonising task of keeping our 'difference' a secret. Most Prematures didn't survive the transformation. Furthermore, back when I'd first turned, it had been the House's standard policy to hunt down and kill those who did, for their own sakes. 'Purging' it had been called. A cruel idea, perhaps, but a being dependent on blood, trapped in a child's body, never to age or grow up, was difficult to hide. A lone child, wandering the night, searching for blood was far too conspicuous, a potential danger to all of us and to itself. Hiding them away as glorified librarians seemed a wonderful idea, in comparison.

The girl turned her attention back to Giorgios and his rabbit. I shuddered as I looked at it. The creature's hapless shrieks still reverberated in my mind.

"Take it away then, silly. Can't you see you revolt Patricia's guest?"

"No, that's all right," I lied.

The boy retreated to the shadows with his drained carcass. Only when he was gone did the girl turn to acknowledge me.

"Patricia must think highly of you." She inspected me up and down, like I was a prospective nanny. No Mary Poppins, judging by the look I was getting.

"I doubt that," I muttered. "We agreed on terms, that's all."

"Very well." The girl walked ahead of me, a slight, youthful spring in her step. "You can choose anything you like from the Trust's collection. The shelves are roughly catalogued by publication date. Not a precise system, you understand, but it should serve your purpose as it does ours."

"The Trust's collection?"

"Any volume in this room. And also, this." With neither grace nor ceremony, the girl thrust a small leather-bound book into my hand.

Even with my Blood Shade vision, I strained to read the text in the dim light. Precious little of it was in English, or Danish, my mother tongue—which I'd not used in decades—or indeed, any of the seven other modern languages I could read. There was one chapter in centuries old Germanic, another in what looked like Estonian or Finnish. I couldn't be sure. A patchwork of languages and cultures—mostly European, but not all—wrapped in well-worn, mahogany leather binding, with only a trace of gilt paint left to suggest the book's contents. On the back, however, was embossed an eight-pointed star, each point shaped to a perfect forty-five-degree angle. It vaguely resembled the Rub el Hizb of Islam, except each crossing line that framed the centre of it had been bent inward.

I ran my fingers over the embossing, certain that I didn't recognise the symbol from my own collection. Two points were directly vertical, two others, horizontal with the remaining four set between. A perfect hollow axis menaced only by the bent inner lines. The emptiness between them felt wrong, though I couldn't think why. I turned the book over and thumbed through it once more. To my frustration, there was no reoccurrence of the symbol.

"Very nice," I murmured, "and this would be?"

"Yours to keep, I understand, from the Shapers. A 'thank you' for dealing with some werewolf problem I'm sure you all find fascinating. Though, frankly, it's taken up enough of my time."

Marvellous. Now I was being admonished for interrupting the academic schedule of a twelve-year-old. At least, in so far as her appearance.

"Well... that's very kind of them."

"What kindness? The House of Magick owed you a favour, did they not?"

My mouth fell open. This had to be a joke—a sickeningly unfunny one. Goddamn it! Not tonight. I was not in the mood.

The girl just stared at me blankly. She was serious.

"This is... ridiculous!" More than ridiculous, it was insulting.

"Then clearly, you should discuss it with them. Now, if you'll excuse me?"

"Wait, did they at least—"

"Four drops. No more, no less. Page two-forty-four. They said you'd figure the rest out. They've more faith in your intuition than I." The corners of the girl's mouth snapped upward into a false smile as she departed.

"Four drops of what?" I demanded.

"Of blood, silly. Goodnight."

She skipped off through the shelves, leaving me with an ancient book I couldn't read, an uncomfortably cryptic recipe involving blood–presumably mine–and an inability to form coherent words.

Page two-forty-four, for its part, was in Cyrillic, which made it all but useless to me. I'd not been to Russia since the revolution and my memory of the language was shaky at best. With a little concentration, I managed to translate the title, The Wolves of Varna, but soon gave up on the rest.

I skimmed through the rest of the book, this time, spotting a chapter in archaic Latin that I vaguely understood.

Cruento immortalis, cruento vernificus... The blood of the immortal, the first Blood Shade, and the blood of the sorcerer, the first Shaper. Our very own creation myth. Though I'd only ever heard it in Danish, its familiarity transcended the barriers of language or culture.

My late mother knew quite well the secret that flowed within the veins of her family line. And while most mothers enthral their children with tales of Mother Goose, mine thought it best to fill my imagination with the story of these two men–or women, nobody remembers which–whose blood was spilled in a great and terrible battle. Their mingled blood soon seeped into the rivers until it had tainted all the waters of the world, and as humankind began to drink, a number of its children began to change. Some grew fangs, their insides tearing themselves apart as their hunger roared its wicked new appetite for blood. Others grew fur and claws, as the wolf's daemon spirit opened their souls to Cerberus' call, consuming them with the fury of the beast. Some embraced unspeakable blasphemies, wielding tricks of reality in mocking imitation of the gods' own power. While many others just disappeared, never to be seen or heard from again, often despite their best efforts.

Traverse several thousand years and here we are, spread across the globe. The 'hidden people', as Mother used to call us. My father often had grave concerns about his son.

Encouraged by this successful, if modest, translation, I began wandering the stacks of the library. The scent of books blended with a peculiar sweetness I couldn't place. I allowed my lungs to fill with several deeply satisfying, even invigorating breaths. The scent was stronger now. Almost on top of me.

"You're blocking the light," said a familiar voice.

I rounded the end of the shelf and met Ross, who stood dressed in a simple polo shirt and fawn pants, reading a text that claimed to be the memoirs of Elizabeth Bathory. To my undisguised delight, he was up and about, and perfectly whole. Better than whole. His face seemed unusually healthy and ruddy, framing a cheeky smile. That was the Ross I remembered. The newly changed Blood Shade boy I'd so eagerly taken under my wing all those years ago. Unspeakably beautiful, effortlessly charming and just slightly clueless.

"What are you doing in here?" I asked.

"Reading."

"Yes, alright smart mouth. What are you reading?"

"You saw the cover. You've heard of her of course?"

"Of course. Bathed in the blood of virgins to stop ageing. Sounds lovely."

Ross nodded at the book. "She wasn't crazy either. It apparently works."

"What the...? Let me see that."

Ross shook his head, snapping the book shut and putting it away. "Not that I don't trust you, old man, but it creeps me out just reading about it. And considering the availability of blood in your lifestyle—"

"Virgins? On Oxford Street?"

"Fair point. Anyway, it's not that simple. The book claims she also mixed in a pint of Blood Shade. That shit's not cool."

"Right." I shivered. I didn't buy the theory, but it still wasn't something I cared to think about. Especially not now. A pint of Blood Shade? I wished Ross would choose his words with greater care...

Then it hit me.

Had the sweet scent on the air been him? I'd tasted him, hadn't I? Savoured drops of his blood before I'd known what it was, then stupidly tried to lick closed his wounds, no doubt imbibing more? There was no mistake. I could still smell it. For one brief, horrible moment, I was tempted to take Ross in my arms, pierce his sweet flesh and drink. Anything to taste it again, to feel its burn on the back of my tongue.

"I'll assume that's not how you patched up so well?" I was suddenly scared to breathe. Scared to inhale the scent.

He turned to me with a smile. "Shapers make pretty awesome medics."

More words I didn't care to hear. Though I had to admit, Ross probably owed the witches his life.

"I was worried about you," I said, more to keep my mind off the scent of his blood. It seemed to be working. The aroma didn't seem as strong now. I even managed to offer my friend a faint smile. This was silly. I'd allowed the stress of recent nights to get to me. At four times Ross' age, what kind of example was I setting if I succumbed to something so primal and reprehensible as supernatural blood addiction?

"Not easy keeping me down," he beamed. "You know that."

I wanted to hug him, but thought better of it. At least until the last pangs of temptation went away. "I guess not. I don't suppose you got a look at him? The thing that attacked you?"

"Well, he was big, about eight feet tall, bent over a bit in your kitchen, obviously, with these massive claws that ripped into my gut. No Reylan, I didn't get a proper look at him, or see his human form. First thing I knew, he had his claws in me. After that, I could barely hear myself think over the screaming–my own, by the way."

"Of course. I'm sorry." I don't know why my heart sank at that point. Perhaps I'd been hoping for some proof that Ross' attacker had been something else. Anything else but Jorgas. I forced the thought away. Why was I rationalising to defend that bastard? Still, if Patricia was right, there could have been another werewolf out there. But not another one that knew where I lived, surely?

"So, you like the library?" Ross asked, snapping me out of my pondering.

I regarded the collections with a shrug. "I haven't really had the chance to look. The curators are... interesting."

"Yeah," Ross laughed. "Well, don't be late with your returns. That's when Sophia gets really interesting. What happened to me last night has got nothing on what she considers an acceptable late fee."

"Sophia?" The Premature Blood Shade girl, I presumed.

"How old is she?"

"A little more than you, I think, but not quite two hundred."

"But that would mean she survived the Purges?"

"I know. She's a smart little thing. Picked up a fascination with Blood Shade history and now here she is. Patricia's happy to have them here as long as they want. Got to keep them off the streets, right?" Ross grinned.

I nodded. While I couldn't quite shake the prejudices of my generation, I could appreciate the logic. If the Prematures were to live out their immortal lives, better it was done in a protected setting, serving a purpose. Patricia Bakker earned yet more points for practicality. I ran a finger over the inviting spines that lined the shelf. There wasn't a speck of dust on them. Somehow, that didn't surprise me.

"So, what are you taking?" Ross asked.

I considered showing him Sophia's 'gift' but decided against it. After what he'd endured, the last thing Ross needed to hear about was another book that called for blood sacrifice, however small. "Maybe a couple of volumes on Blood Shade lore. I'm not sure."

Or a twelve-step program for supernatural blood addiction? I bit my tongue. That wasn't funny.

Ross picked up a book bound in dark purple velvet and handed it to me. "See what you think. Not exactly scientific method but, if you get time..."

I opened the bare front cover and felt my eyes widen as the author's name leapt out.

"Vlad Tepes? *Conditions of the Damned?* I thought his connections to... us, were a myth."

"They are, in so far as his being a Blood Shade. A lot of nonsense made up by enemies over the years, descendants of the regions he conquered. But this is where it comes from. He studied us, like a macabre hobby. The church in his time made something of a vendetta out of it, which didn't help his reputation."

"Or maybe it did," I smirked.

"Tepes of course, had no clue what he was studying, so I wouldn't put much stock in it. But it's an interesting read. Only three copies are known to exist."

"And the other two?" I asked, flipping through the barren pages.

"Probably the centrepiece of some collector's shelf. It's woefully inaccurate, so the Trust never followed it up."

"I'll take a look. Any others?"

Ross glanced over the books before taking out a small black leatherback and passing it to me. "I haven't read it. Nobody in the Trust has. It was written in the sixties by some radical occultist-slash-feminist-slash-pacifist in San Francisco, so you can imagine the credibility that earned it in academic circles. The House of Magick kept track of her for a while, but her research was so far off the mark they decided to leave her be."

"Esme Moonflower," I read aloud, opening the front cover. "*Nightly Bites: The Secret Covenant of the Vampire*? Oh please."

"Give it a try... just to spite Patricia. She prides herself on reading all the texts before anyone else does and if you got to it first—"

"I'll take it." I conceded, placing it atop the Tepes volume.

"You don't change much do you, old man?"

"Leopards and I have been known to share that trait." I scanned the rest of the books. Hmm, *Composite Thoughts and Ethics*. That sounded like a riveting night in... yawn.

"Oh, and I saw this one." Ross added another book to the pile. "You might find it a bit more useful."

No Man's Friend: A History of European Lycanthrope Myth promised the cover. Of course, because Jorgas was all about old world European class!

"Why should I be interested in werewolves?" I asked. "Patricia wants to take over from here, and for me to keep my distance. So, that's what I'm doing. She's welcome to him."

Ross nodded. "Well, good, but did she tell you?"

"About the murder last night? Yes."

"Still no pardon for Jorgas as far as I'm concerned."

"What do you mean?"

"Besides what happened to me? There's still that guy he killed right in front of you. That guy from the club."

"Rory."

"You remember their names? I'm impressed."

"I remember him lying there after Jorgas cut him up. He was begging me."

"So… Jorgas didn't kill him outright?"

"Does it matter? He would never have survived those wounds."

"So? What did you do?"

I stared blankly at Ross. Surely, I didn't have to answer. Ross was smarter than that. Still, his jaw dropped. "You didn't hear him whimpering, pleading for help," I pointed out.

"So you killed him? You're a big help, Reylan. Great work."

"I did the quickest, easiest thing I could to end his pain and keep the whole thing quiet. I broke his neck. He didn't suffer, I promise you."

Ross shook his head. "That's the real curse, isn't it?"

"Sorry?" If he was going to get existential, I was leaving.

"Being immortal. Being part of the House. You hear people go on about the so-called 'vampiric curse'. It's that responsibility. Keeping everything hidden from humans. Living forever's the easy part."

"I can understand that, coming from you. Most of your close friends are Blood Shades. You'll never have to watch them grow old and die."

"Did you?"

I was sure the temperature in the room had dropped several degrees. Whether it had been gradual or sudden, I couldn't say. Ross had chosen a lousy time to probe me with deeply personal questions. "No."

"Not at all?"

"I said no, Ross."

White lie. I had, in fact, briefly looked in on my mother, only once, on her sixtieth birthday. Her once lustrous dark hair had turned mottled white, dirty with streaks of dark grey and insipid blonde. Her face, once the smiling, ruddy countenance of a prosperous peasant accustomed to the rewards of sacrifice, had thinned with the exhaustion of a life well lived. A life I'd been absent from for almost twenty years. One irreparably ruptured by the passing of my father. In that moment, I'd resolved never again to witness time's assault on a mortal I loved. This was not a story I cared to share, even with Ross.

"Is that why you never get close to anyone?"

"You and Isobel are all the family I need."

Ross prudently dropped the subject. "So, what happens to Jorgas now?"

"That's Patricia's choice, not mine. I don't care."

"I'm all for dismemberment, if you want."

"Give it a rest, will you?"

"No, I will not!"

The outburst astonished me. I'd rarely seen Ross angry.

"We don't know he's the one who attacked you."

"Who else knows where you live, Reylan?"

"Well Jorgas shouldn't have, for a start. Look, I appreciate you've been through a terrible ordeal, but try to relax. There's still something out there killing these people. Shouldn't you be doing something about that? I mean, once you've fully recovered and—"

"Ssshhh!"

We looked up at Sophia, who sat at her desk hissing through her tiny fangs. Silence in the library, indeed.

"Oh, we will be." Ross' tone was now so clandestine it was almost threatening. "Maybe you're right. Maybe Jorgas has a wolfie girlfriend somewhere, who tracked you down and took a piece out of me. But you go back to your clubs, Reylan. We'll take it from here."

The bastard was mocking me.

"All right, that's it. I'm glad you're fine and all, but I've had it with your attitude!"

"Reylan?"

I turned to face Isobel, whose gentle intrusion had probably spared Ross a backhanding.

"Is everything all right?" She regarded me with the kind of quizzically playful expression one gives a cat chasing light from a laser pen, as though my frustrations were some experiment to satisfy her curiosity. I could have done without the implication.

"We're good," Ross said, pushing past us. "Excuse me."

Even ignoring his quarrelsome tone, I was relieved to have him gone from the room. His beauty, the scent of his blood... how much longer would it torment me?

"Shhhh!" The sound of Sophia's hushing filled the library, as though a battalion of enraged snakes had been loosed into the darkness.

"Is he all right?" Isobel asked.

"Still tender, I think."

I could tell she wasn't listening, her attention firmly fixed on the book in my hand—at the bottom of the pile. The book from Sophia. From the House of Magick.

"A little present," I explained, "from the Shapers."

"May I?"

I saw no harm. Isobel was far more likely than I to have some insight into the text, and hopefully, she'd share. Hopefully.

"Jorgas seems okay," she mumbled as she flipped through.

"You've spoken?"

She nodded, not taking her eyes off the book. "He's frightened, of course. He feels lost. Angry. But he's not a bad kid."

"Then he's all yours," I mumbled, shoving hands deep into my pockets.

"You're not planning on seeing him again?"

"What's that supposed to mean?"

Isobel was barely listening. I couldn't make out the page she had open, but she seemed fixated.

"Did the Shapers tell you anything else? How old it is?

Anything at all?"

I shrugged, making mention of the chapter detailing the creation myth and explaining the vague, second-hand, 'four drop' instruction Sophia had given me. When I mentioned The Wolves of Varna, Isobel looked up, a glint in her dark eyes.

"I noticed that story, among others," she explained. "Each page is a different myth. Another chapter in supernatural lore."

"So, it's a history book?" I asked. No doubt, one of many in the stacks of this room. Oh, generous favour, indeed!

Isobel turned the book over and frowned at the embossed star on its back. "Let's find out."

CHAPTER ELEVEN

"Isobel, what is this? Where are we going?"

"Testing a theory. We need open air. Come on!"

I shivered, pulling my jacket tighter as I tried to protect my clothes in the now drizzling rain. I'd nothing but respect for Isobel's curiosity, but tonight, I was hungry, cold, wet, and sorely missing the glorious sensation of curling up in my own warm bed, alone. She'd picked a lousy night to go scrambling through the trees in Moore Park.

"Have you got the book? Don't let it get wet."

"What's it going to do? Multiply?"

"Just find page two-forty-four. Trust me."

Trust was one commodity I did not have in abundance.

"I'm hardly in the mood for Bulgarian folklore, Isobel."

"Do you have a knife?"

"Have you ever known me to carry a knife?"

Before I could stop her, she took firm hold of my wrist, held it over the page, and bit hard into the skin.

"Ow! What do you think you're playing at?"

"Shhh!"

I felt the throb of fresh blood seep from the punctures as Isobel squeezed my arm. A drop spilt across the Cyrillic text on the page, then another, then two more.

Isobel quickly re-sealed my flesh with a lick. "Four drops, correct?"

"Are you insane?"

A stain of dark blood spread across the pages.

"We'll see." She'd quickly begun to withdraw, her eyes never leaving me. Never leaving the book.

"What're you doing?"

"Getting out of the way."

"Isobel? Come back here, damn you!"

"Whatever you do, don't drop it."

"What?"

But my friend had already disappeared. So had the rain, Moore Park, and any other trace of the city that not a moment ago, had surrounded me.

*　　*　　*

It was the woman's piercing scream I noticed first. Shrill with agony, a scream borne only of two things. The first pangs of life, or death's final throes.

The night seemed so much darker than it had in the spotlit serenity of the park. I quickly realised why. The only light emanated from small campfires spread around what was neither a village, nor an encampment, but something in between. A colony or settlement, but one well accustomed to sudden relocation. Its shelters were hastily assembled huts of fresh cut wood, with blankets for shelter. And there was something else. My clothing and hair were now perfectly dry. Nonetheless, I was cold. Freezing, actually. A chilly wind swept across the fires. Too cold for Sydney, even in winter. I tucked the book away tight inside my jacket.

Kansas, be damned. Where had Isobel sent me?

"Sir? Sir!" The old woman's gnarled hands were upon me before I could object. "Please, you must come. You must help. Fetch blankets. Quickly, please!"

These words were not in English, nor any language I spoke at all. And though I understood them—I thought it best not to reason how—they dashed any last hope that I was still in Australia. Assuming, of course, that the scene before me was in fact real and I wasn't just losing my mind. What had I just put away in my pocket? Just what kind of hell ride had I agreed to take, by shedding four drops my blood?

"Please. Hurry!"

Certain I'd get no further explanation, and growing tired of the claws the woman had dug into my skin, I went in search of the requested blankets. I quickly scanned the camp, moving from shelter to shelter until I'd collected several from its nervous, but oddly obliging inhabitants, most of whom were much younger than the one who'd grabbed me—around my age, in fact—and all of whom spoke the same language, some out-dated Balkan or Romani tongue, by the sound of it. Most of them were young couples, unusually healthy looking, for the setting, their mouths, full of flawless pearl teeth. A number of the women were heavy with child, which I thought odd, given that throughout the settlement, I'd seen no children at all. Not one. Had I stumbled upon the first generation of this strange community of nomads? Or had my mind created them? I'd not yet ruled out the idea that I was tripping.

"In here!" the old woman barked again. Like the strength of her hands, her tone was unimpaired by the frailty of years. Hers was not the voice of some old crone, but a powerful and resourceful leader, loved and trusted by her people.

Another roar from the shelter that needed my help. Literally a roar this time, both hollow and inhuman. I handed the blankets to a pale young woman I took to be the midwife. Her face looked gaunt. Hungry, in fact.

I saw little of the mother to be, covered as she was in layers of blankets, but she was not a small woman. Her shoulders were every inch as broad as her husband's. The man, his skin as pale as the midwife's, clutched his wife's hand so tightly, I feared he'd draw blood.

Another low growl came from under the blankets.

The old woman pushed me out of the way. "Give us room, please," she barked, taking out a string of charms from the folds of her clothing.

Thinking it unwise to argue from my current position of total ignorance, I complied. The old woman, who I now took to be some kind of lawgiver in this community, began to mutter some incantation, too low for me to hear over the woman in labour. This continued without interruption–save the mother's birth screams–for at least twenty minutes. It was twenty minutes I simply did not have.

Damn Isobel! If she found all of this so fascinating, she could make the journey herself. I was going home. With a polite nod to the pale soon-to-be father, who had been eyeing me with disquieting suspicion, I excused myself from the shelter and flipped through the book that, at least in mind, had landed me here.

Two-thirds of its pages were now blank, including what should have been page two-forty-four.

This was impossible. I flipped more of the pages. Was I imagining it? Had I gotten the page number wrong? No, that was equally impossible. Isobel had made such a point of the story, The Wolves of Varna, or whatever it had been.

I carefully punctured my wrist with my teeth and allowed four drops to seep into the page. They vanished into the paper, leaving neither trace nor stain.

Shit!

"Sir?"

I rounded angrily on the voice, calming myself only when I saw the speaker was no more than a child. A boy of thirteen or fourteen perhaps, but still the closest thing to a child I'd seen since my arrival. His complexion was even paler than that of the husband or midwife. He was skinny too, his black fringe flopped over his forehead, his cheeks sunken and his eyes wide, to what seemed almost the point of madness.

"Hello." Having found my only apparent means of escape null and void, I was more than open to any hint the locals could give me, including this boy. And for that, I needed his trust. "Are you all right?"

He shivered, shaking his head with a nervous swallow. "Hungry."

"And why is that? Do your people not have enough food?" Unlikely, given the robust condition most of them were in.

"They... won't let me feed."

"Won't let you?"

No answer. The boy just regarded me with a sullen glare.

"What's your name?" I asked.

"They call me Jal."

"Is that your real name?"

His narrow shoulders lifted in a shrug.

"Why won't they let you eat, Jal?"

"I'm a curse. The daemon... he claimed me before I was to be his."

I moved closer, examining his sunken eyes, his firm jaw and pasty skin—a handsome, if criminally undernourished boy.

I suddenly felt like the stupidest man on earth.

"Jal," I resisted the urge to place a patronising hand on the Premature's shoulder. "Would you like to come feeding with me?" I shuddered to think how he was surviving. Rats? Livestock? The occasional missing child from a nearby village? Brutal, I grant you, but this had been the point of the Purges.

"I..." he stammered. "I don't..."

"Do you even know how to feed?"

He suddenly began to shake his head rapidly from side to side, clutching his stomach as he backed away from me. "You shouldn't be here. You need to leave!"

"What? Jal, what's wrong?"

"I am wrong!" He surged forward, fangs bared, eyes glowing, hissing as he tore away the thin layer of humanity that protected the outside world from his natural blood lust, driven to desperate starvation by his peers. "I am death! I am the bringer of their end!"

We both looked up as another scream erupted from the shelter, then a series of shouts and roars. The sounds of crashing, and, loathe as I was to recognise it, tearing flesh.

"Wait here," I commanded Jal, running toward the noise as though someone's life depended on my haste.

I smelt blood. Gallons of it.

It soon became clear that my perception of this place was not bound to the constraints of linear time or logic. Whatever commotion had wrought such terror within the shelter had long passed. The midwife and the old woman were nowhere to be seen, but the walls were thick with blood, the mother's once strong, healthy body now torn open and ragged. The father lay not far beyond in another great pool of blood, his throat opened, skin shrunken to his bones like parchment and his fangs bared, sharp, futile reminders of the Blood Shade he'd been, the man incapable of protecting his mate from whatever had—

His mate? Who'd died in childbirth?

More shrill screams.

I rushed outside, my once rational mind now freshly awakened to that which in my world, time and place could be firmly dismissed as impossibility. Yet with the wind's icy sting on my lips, the marshy ground squelching beneath my shoes and the decaying, acrid smells of an age long before my birth, heavy on the air, it had become impossible to dismiss this world as any less real than my own. Without a comforting shred of doubt. I was living it.

The question was, for how much longer.

The gory scene that had greeted me in the couple's shelter seemed barely a hint of the strife that now surrounded me throughout the settlement. Men and women emerged from their homes, screaming and bloodied, wielding primitive weapons including their own claws and fangs. Their human veils now shed, Blood Shades and werewolves—yes, that explained the larger ones, the muscular, ruddy looking ones I'd seen with such slim, ghostly companions. Some of them had changed, wielding their wolf forms with a lethal grace that seemed far beyond the brutish instincts of someone like Jorgas.

I should have run. Should have clutched the book tight to my chest and bolted for the edge of the camp, never to look back. But I couldn't move. It scarcely occurred to me that I'd come to a standstill, barely remembering to breathe as I watched their majestic movements with the grim awe of a man watching a suicide bombing he's powerless to prevent.

It was only when I recognised the pale, screaming, Blood Shade midwife, splattering me with blood from the stump of her arm, her eyes now crushed, empty sockets marking the middle of her face that I fully realised the danger I was in.

But this was a curious carnage. Neither Blood Shade nor werewolf had raised tooth, claw or weapon against the other. The reason for this became clear when I was set upon by their true enemy, who tore at my flesh with tiny, razor-like talons.

I screeched as the creature knocked me to the ground. No bigger than a puppy, yet bearing the weight of a being five times its size, its skin was pale and wet with a gelatinous film that defied description. Its eyes were wide and black as Hell's gullet, tiny batlike ears seemingly tearing back its cruel face. A snout, perhaps two inches long, eagerly snapped at me with a jagged curtain of cruel incisors. I grimaced as the claws dug deeper into my skin, the delicate smell of my own twenty-first century blood rising to mingle with the putrid carnage that saturated the air.

Another scream, one of defiance, anger and determination, this time. I caught the flash of what looked like a sickle in the light of the fires, the sound of metal slicing through flesh and bone. A great gush of dark red blood poured over me as the monster was lopped in two, its halves falling to either side of the foetal ball into which I'd shaped myself.

"Come!" yelled Jal, lifting me effortlessly to my feet. "You must go, now!"

"What the bloody hell was that?" I shuddered in horror as I saw a werewolf lift one of the creatures high, breaking its back in mid-air.

Everywhere I heard the awful squeals. How many there were, I couldn't tell. But they were dying. The settlers had won this battle, but at a heavy price. The air was thick with the stench of death, Blood Shade, werewolf and abomination alike.

"Please!"

The echo of Jal's scream evaporated on the air. Only the cracking embers of the fires around us remained. The surviving Blood Shades and werewolves stood, battered and bloodied in their silence.

They were staring at us.

I glanced at Jal. The boy's knees were shaking, the first drops of crimson tears forming in his eyes as the old woman—the shaman, priestess, whatever she was to this place—stepped forward.

"*Ryebyenok dyemona,*" she muttered, not as an accusation, but as a solemn statement of fact. It was directed at Jal.

"Harbinger!" one of the werewolf men screamed, his blood-drenched face wild with fury as he stared at us.

The priestess sternly silenced him with a raised hand and repeated the words. "*Ryebyenok dyemona.*"

I felt as though my heart were plummeting through my insides, dragging the temperature of my blood with it as it fell. Daemon child. Not Jal, but the newborns. Created by union of Blood Shade to werewolf.

For all my ignorance of where I was or how I'd arrived, I knew the nature of scapegoating. Jal wasn't responsible for this horror, yet I knew what difference that would make to his anguished community. Not a damn bit.

The boy didn't move.

"Leave him!" The Blood Shade midwife barged her way through the crowd with her still attached arm, the slowly regrowing stump of the other a ghoulish reminder of our species' gifts. One of her eyes, now regenerated, glared over the crowd, before settling on the fuming werewolf priestess.

The old woman muttered what sounded like another incantation, too low for me to hear, until she was abruptly cut off.

Literally.

I hadn't seen the midwife draw the blade, but its once stainless surface was now thick with blood in the moonlight.

The crowd stared in disbelief. Then came the murmuring, and the shouts, too fast and angry for me to make out with any clarity. But I got the gist. In this camp, surrounded by their beloved dead, Blood Shade had raised sword against werewolf in defence of a scarcely tolerated daemon child. And with it, the first blame had been laid.

All this could not have transpired in mere minutes, so I knew my perception had surged forward again. For that, I was thankful. If neither of the two species had raised weapon, or tooth, or claw against the other while facing their mutual enemy, they certainly did now. I didn't need the gory details.

"P-please?" a frail voice stammered.

Jal.

The boy's neck had been chopped almost through. The cut bled down his chest into the ragged mess of his clothes. His mouth was full of blood, his face covered in red tears. I heard a roar behind me and spun around, bracing myself for the heavy swipe of werewolf claws. Instead, a sword went straight through my body, just below the heart.

And with that, as suddenly as it had first appeared, the world of the colony vanished.

*　　*　　*

Only when I found myself returned to Moore Park, face down in the grass with the pelting rain driving against my frozen back, did I realise, I'd coughed up blood. Lots of it.

"Reylan?" Isobel was shaking me as though I'd overdosed on some hallucinogen—not an unfair assessment, all things considered. "Reylan? Say something! What did you see?"

"What the bloody hell did you do?" I screamed over the rain, spitting blood as I lurched to my feet and rounded on her. "I mean it, Isobel! What the hell did you just put me through?"

"I'm sorry." She took out a delicate handkerchief and wiped the last of the blood from my lips, kissing me as she dabbed it away. "Are you all right?"

In truth, I'd not the slightest idea. At least the bleeding had stopped. Some part of me knew it had all been an illusion. A singularly realistic and humourless one. But my body was still shaking. I still felt the sting of the monster's claws. I still saw Jal's body and heard his whimpering.

"I... I bled on the book," I said, piecing the experience together, more for my own sake than Isobel's. "Four drops—"

"A temporal echo," Isobel explained. It was the kind of cryptic explanation that was anything but. "It's a fairly simple spell. The record of an event, imbued with the essence of a witness. Cast properly, it reacts with the senses of the user to recreate that event within the mind's eye. I've seen it referenced in a number of texts, but to actually find one... Reylan, what did you see?" she asked again. "I have to know."

"See? I was almost killed!"

"It's not real. You can't be harmed."

"And you know this, how? I assure you, it feels very real!"

She still looked at me with expectation, so I described what I'd seen, hoping Isobel could make sense of it.

She did, lapping up my words with hungry fascination. "Would you like me to hold on to it? See what I can find? It would save you having to ask the Shapers why they felt you should have it."

I couldn't refute this point, and Isobel had both a knack and patience for scholarly research that I sorely lacked. "Knock yourself out," I said, handing her the book. "I'm going home."

CHAPTER TWELVE

The rain had returned as I stretched out on my lounge and tried to relax. The stack of books from The Arcadia Trust sat beside me. I'd skimmed the text on werewolves, but had soon lost all motivation. Compared to the Shapers' little gift, the other books seemed... quaintly human.

Part of me could care less if Isobel kept the thing.

I was exhausted. The sound system had gotten stuck on single disc and the 1970 Broadway cast recording of Company–not a word–had quietly looped a third time in the background.

After three hours 'relaxing', my nerves were still rattled.

This was insane. What did I care what happened next in this ghastly saga? Everything was back to normal. The Arcadia Trust was out of my life, save a few books I had to return and the clothes Patricia had borrowed. Jorgas was gone and the nights were free for hunting. I could even bring Deborah the good news next time I dropped by Valia's. All in all, my place in the world wasn't a bad one right now.

So why could I not relax?

Ryebyenok dyemona. The words bounced around my head. Daemon child. Unholy offspring of Blood Shade joined to werewolf. What had the Shapers been thinking? Why single out that page—that story—and show it to me? I doubted either Jorgas or I would be spawning daemon children any time soon.

I heard a faint tapping on the front door and hauled myself off the couch to greet my visitor, and the orange bundle of cat she cradled in her arms.

"I know you busy, Mister Raymond, but I find him outside."

Demetrius was shivering, only becoming more violent as Dorotha passed him to me. His white paws beat against my chest as he twisted his body to escape.

"Hey," I whispered. "What's wrong? What's the matter with—Ow!" I pulled my hand back with a start, inspecting the bleeding scratch with disbelief. My cat never scratched me! He twisted out of my arms and fell to the floor, retreating to the kitchen. At least this time, I had the cat flap locked.

"Oh, dear!" Dorotha mothered. "I know just the thing. I come right back."

"It's okay. Happens all the time," I lied, still partly mesmerised by the wound. "I keep a good antiseptic." My saliva. You couldn't buy better.

"If you say so. Poor thing. I find him on my stairs. He shake like crazy. At first, I think he cold, so I take him inside, give him warm milk and herring. But he not eat! He just shake, like you see."

"Well, it's cold, and he hasn't been well." I had one hand on the door, ready to bid her goodnight.

"Don't be foolish, Mister Raymond." She'd taken on that admonitory tone I didn't like.

I rather enjoyed having Dorotha upstairs. For all her petty irritations, she was not a meddler—at least, not outside of her attempts to marry me off to Ross. She hadn't interfered when he'd been attacked. She hadn't made herself known when I'd brought Jorgas back... I had a bad feeling that lapse in judgement was going to haunt me.

"Something scare Pooska. Scare him, to an inch of his little life!"

"Why should he be afraid?" I smiled, hoping she'd relax.

She didn't. "That man. The one you bring to your house last night, after Mister Ross leave."

My shoulders tensed. Had she seen Ross' wounds? The Shapers?

"You go out to club, and you bring that strange young man home with you. I hear you from upstairs."

No, she hadn't. Thank Christ.

"At first, I think he just like all the others, but he—"

"His name's Billy. He's just some punk kid. Cute, but dim, and kind of hot headed. I won't be seeing him again."

Dorotha shook her head at me like I'd just tried to defend Jeffrey Dahmer. "He have a bad face, Mister Raymond. Bad face, in one so young? Bad heart. Even Pooska see it. Why not you?"

"As I just said," I snapped, "I won't be seeing him again. What else do you want me to do? Leave the kid alone. He's... got problems. That's all."

"All right, then. You know best." She gently wrapped a cold, wrinkled hand over mine, just below the scratch. "You always know best."

I politely but firmly shut the door behind her and returned to the kitchen to find Demetrius. The cat glowered at me from under the kitchen cupboards, hissing as I approached. Afraid, indeed!

Demetrius may have been off food, but I wasn't. I'd surely earned a 'no strings' treat, after the hellish history lesson Isobel had put me through! I retreated to the study, and turned on my computer, taking a seat in the plush leather chair. I relaxed in the dim light of the monitor as it whirred to life. Hungry as I was, I didn't have the energy to go out.

It wasn't my preferred form of feeding, but there were times when one just had to order in.

I can remember when the Internet first became available for public use. I'd purchased my first computer in the early nineties, and after a fortnight's perseverance with the beast, had come to the conclusion that those religious fanatics in the newspapers were right. This new invention was in fact, the Devil, come to condemn the mental states of mortals and immortals alike to Hell. Five years later, I'd summoned the courage to try again, discovering that I'd evidently not been the only one to find the information superhighway—nineties slang for it, as I understand—to be a Mensa puzzle in a box. The whole system was now far easier to grasp.

Of course, something about it seemed cheap and definitely tawdry. Having been alive for the birth of the electric light, the telephone, the radio, film and television, air travel—still tricky, for the sun-sensitive among us—and countless other revelations, I'd like to think myself an expert on the impact of technology upon human society. Then along came the Internet, all knowing, and all serving for anyone who called its name. No longer a Mensa puzzle in a box, but simply a lazy way to accomplish one's tasks.

What do I care? I can't get fat.

I half-heartedly opened the relevant site and scanned the list of names. Identities of lonely mortals reduced to the crudity of a double entendre laden moniker. Nonetheless, this was the digital buffet, and I wasn't feeling fussy.

It would be a few moments before any of the prospective prey said hello. I didn't bother sorting through the names myself anymore. Not to sound narcissistic, but for all appearances, I'm twenty-three, independently wealthy and aggressively dominant, all wrapped up the irresistible allure of a Blood Shade façade. Why should I make the effort when I can filter offers?

I used the time to start a search for werewolf material online, in the unlikely hope of finding something useful, perhaps even, against hope, some reference to the 'Wolves of Varna'. It had been months since I'd used such a search. The last time had been an elusive companion who ran a prestige car dealership in Alexandria. A waste of two hours memorising the extravagances of overpriced German cars, only to get through a boring hour's conversation and a less than satisfying feed. Allure or no allure, I can't always get a hit.

One more thing annoyed me about the Internet. I couldn't use my gifts, so cheating by eye contact was out of the question. That said, I've never put Blood Shade hypnosis to the test over a webcam. Perhaps one night, I shall.

4,128,102 search items found. This did not bode well for holding my interest. I scanned the results with dismay. Old myths, silver weapons, Lon Chaney pictures, a pretentious role-playing game… yawn.

AlteredSpace: "Hey, what's up?"

I opened his user page. No face photograph, but the boy was twenty, a student, and liked it rough. Lunch was served.

Reyth1856: "Hello. Not much, you?"

I went back to perusing the nonsense turned up by my search. Nothing about the colony–no surprise–but something about the idea of werewolf 'packs' was familiar.

AlteredSpace: "Rey? It is you, isn't it?"

My eyes widened a little as I rechecked *AlteredSpace*'s profile. I don't like being remembered.

Reyth1856: "Who is this, please?"

I continued reading as I waited for a response. The article was from the Ludwig Maximillian University of Munich. That at least gave it a little credibility:

It has been theorised over decades and suggested by folklore that lycanthropy breeds a canine instinct towards pack mentality, or—

AlteredSpace: "It's Simon, remember?"

With a grimace, I did remember, and apparently so did he, strong-willed little bastard. But that was impossible, wasn't it? He'd met my eyes before leaving. I'd made sure of it. That should have erased his memory of the night. Damn it to hell!

AlteredSpace: "Thanks for the other night. Was so hot. Want to hook up again?"

Hmmm... Good. Humans who remembered being bitten didn't usually ask for seconds.

Reyth1856: "I'd like that, but to be honest I'm more a one-shot type of guy."

AlteredSpace: "One-shot?"

I ignored him for a moment, continuing to read.

—some kind of familial society within its species. Newer studies have brought this into question, particularly in the light of folklore. These claims—

AlteredSpace: "What? You mean you won't play with the same guy twice?"

Reyth1856: "That's right."

—are given credibility by such familiar tales as Red Riding Hood. What we must remember is the study of these creatures is hardly a new science.

AlteredSpace: "Tart."

Reyth1856: "Manners."

AlteredSpace: "Why not?"

Reyth1856: "It's just safer that way."

AlteredSpace: "Seems old school to me.

I chose not to take this personally and kept reading.

Both older and more contemporary opinions offer valuable insight into the lycanthrope social structure. A theory commonly attributed to Dr Karl Heimdahl's research suggests that the behaviour and tendencies of 'werewolves' while in the wolf state reflect the circumstances of their human lives. While it is likely that any control over their actions in such a state may take several years to refine, they are likely to be influenced at a subconscious level by their long-held human values. In essence, lycanthropes who lead solitary lives prior to their first change are likely to remain solitary predators. The consequences of having such a creature forced into close proximity with another of its kind are open to speculation. Though it has been suggested—

AlteredSpace: "I can be discrete. My parents think I'm dating this girl from church anyway."

Church? I finished reading the sentence.

—in the late 1920s by Professor Frank Bakker of University of The Hague that a lycanthrope with antisocial tendencies would struggle to cope with better adjusted rivals of its own kind, most likely with violent results.

Bakker? I reread the passage. It had to be a coincidence. And if the man was linked to Patricia in some way, didn't that just better qualify her to deal with Jorgas? I closed down the article, which had more or less ruled out Ross' 'wolfie girlfriend' idea.

AlteredSpace: "You there?"

It was time to do a little first-hand research into Jorgas' pack habits. How fortuitous, to now have one of his peers on chat. Hell, life owed me some good fortune at this point.

Reyth1856: "Well, maybe I can make an exception, for you. Nobody else."

AlteredSpace: "Hah! Knew you liked me."

The tip of my tongue tapped against the point of my left fang as I wracked my brain for words, only to delete them. What kind of head swelling flattery would persuade a twenty-year-old trust fund brat to cooperate?

"You're very swee—" Ugh. Delete.

"I don't meet many as cute as—" Okay, I may vomit.

"You're a smart guy. I respect tha—" Right, because we'd spent the night discussing Keats between rounds of Scrabble. Delete.

"Mmm, loved the feel of your smooth, tight—" Oh, Jesus! Decorum, man! Decorum!

Reyth1856: "Yeah. Yeah, I do like you."

Okay, so Keats, I'm not.

AlteredSpace: "Haven't shown you half of what I can do yet."

This wasn't the 'cooperation' I'd had in mind, and I was running out of patience.

Reyth1856: "Question, your family goes to Saint Barnie's, right?"

AlteredSpace: "Yeah. Hey, don't even think about telling anyone at church!"

Reyth1856: "Relax. I was just wondering if you knew somebody. Billy Myers?"

Thirty seconds passed, then a minute.

Reyth1856: "Simon?"

AlteredSpace: "What do you want to know about Billy?"

Reyth1856: "What do you want to tell me?"

AlteredSpace: "He's not my type. Next question?"

Reyth1856: "I heard some of your friends don't care much for him either."

AlteredSpace: "Well, no offence, but you don't know anything about my friends."

Reyth1856: "No, I don't. Care to enlighten me?"

AlteredSpace: "About my friends, or Myers?"

Reyth1856: "Both."

AlteredSpace: "What do you care?"

Again, my tongue rested at the tip of my fangs. Honesty was out of the question.

Reyth1856: "I know Billy. He's in a bit of trouble. I'm just trying to help him out."

AlteredSpace: "Look Rey, I don't know how long you've known him, but you don't want to get involved there. Trust me, he's bad news."

Bad face? Bad heart? Bad news? I'd surrounded myself with alarmists.

Reyth1856: "I think that's my choice, don't you?"

Another pause. The quiet hum of my computer's cooling fan was suddenly deafening.

AlteredSpace: "I have to go. Heading out tonight."

I closed down another chat window that had popped up from some random pleasure seeker. A hookup site really wasn't the venue for this discussion.

Reyth1856: "I need to speak with you. Where will you be?"

AlteredSpace: "No way, man! Not about this!!!"

Reyth1856: "Simon, it's important."

One… two…

AlteredSpace: "Look, I can't tell you much. I really don't know the guy. And I'm not talking with you about this in front of my friends."

Reyth1856: "Then make a suggestion."

Another pause. I held back a low growl.

AlteredSpace: "Meet me at the church in thirty."

Reyth1856: "At Saint Barnabas? Is that a joke?"

AlteredSpace: "No, man. It's private. I can tell you what I know, okay? Then maybe ask Father Isaac. Billy talks to him, sometimes."

I had an imperious nun summoning me to emo clubs, and a closeted North Shore guppie in training summoning me to church. When did my life get so complicated?

Reyth1856: "Talks to him sometimes? Can you be a bit more specific?"

AlteredSpace: "That's my suggestion. Take it or leave it. I'm doing you a favour."

I could almost hear my teeth grinding. The boy had better lose the attitude or I'd repay his 'favour' in his own soft, white flesh.

Reyth1856: "Fine. See you there."

AlteredSpace: "Good, because I'm leaving now."
Reyth1856: "Okay."
User '*AlteredSpace*' has logged out. Your message "Okay." was not delivered.

Someone was in a hurry. I shut down the computer. Just to be sure, I returned to the book I'd left beside the lounge, flipping to the page I'd been at when I'd put it down, concerning pack habits. Sure enough, it agreed with Frank Bakker. Werewolves, like us, were not necessarily pack hunters. And Jorgas sure as hell didn't fit into the 'pack' that was the Saint Barnie's brats. That confirmed exactly what had been nagging me since I'd arrived home.

CHAPTER THIRTEEN

Saint Barnabas was one of the last bastions of Gothic architecture left in a city increasingly determined to leave the trappings of European tradition behind. The church's mission long predated my own arrival, having begun as a token philanthropic gesture from the upper middle class, in service to the Irish migrant community of Surry Hills. In recent decades, spiralling rents had forced blue-collar residents to move on, enticing the Catholic rich to reclaim Saint Barnabas as their own. Its current board of trustees ensured that all who passed by knew this was now a church for the well to do. While I didn't care for the excesses of faith-inspired design, it was hard even for me to ignore the detail of the crown balustrades lining the top of the building, almost fractal-like in their perfection. No human would have noticed the narrow gaps where intricately carved gargoyles sat by day. But I noticed. Three, perhaps four of the irritable little beasts had no doubt abandoned their posts soon after dark to go feeding.

The rain had stopped, and the steps leading to the building's main arch were slippery under my feet. Cold, polished marble, replaced every five years or so. No crack had ever gone more than a week before repair. The original sandstone columns that rose from the top of the stairs had been replaced some decades prior with steel pillars, wrapped in a sandstone façade. The gargantuan wooden doors were wide open, which seemed odd for night-time hours, but with that said, I'd never seen them closed. They too, had enjoyed the same level of care as the steps. Polish, repair, replace, repeat.

Yet atop this mighty doorway, was a simple wooden cross. Unlike the rest of the structure, the cross had been allowed to weather and to my memory had never been replaced. A symbol of Christ's humility, or so one of the faithful had told me some years ago.

Any trace of humility however, was erased the moment I breached the mighty doorway. Even with dim street lighting, the stained-glass window sent the darkened hall into an explosion of colour. And although the illuminated windows of several offices offered glimpses of modernity, no electric light pierced the church's darkness. Instead, scores of candles lined the pews and altar, their light dancing across the ornately carved columns that supported this astonishing monument to God—or his donors.

"Reylan!"

My eyes flicked around the hall, trying to find the whisperer. The twitching candlelight was giving me a migraine.

"Reylan, I've been waiting! Over here."

"Twenty minutes," I pointed out. "Aren't we at least going to have an intimate heart to heart in the confessional? I feel ripped off." I sauntered over to where Simon had sunk into one of the pews.

He smirked at me. "We can if you want. Wouldn't be the first—"

"Simon," I interrupted. "Out here's fine."

"Fine," he said with a dismissive snort. "If you're gonna be boring, I've got some friends waiting, so let's make it quick. What do you want to know?"

"I want to know about Myers. I want to know about the family, what you know of Billy's history, and just what your problem is with him."

"Listen, I don't have much time."

"Good, because neither do I," I growled.

"His family… they're okay, I guess. No brothers or sisters—"

"That, I know."

"Well, what do you want me to tell you? His dad's a defence lawyer, mostly. Specialises in hard cases, ugly stuff nobody wants to take on."

"You mean sex crimes? Murder?"

Simon shook his head, beckoning me to keep my voice down, though we were barely whispering. "No, no. Stuff that nobody thinks they can win. Fraud, dodgy CEOs—"

"So, Billy's dad has a reputation?"

"Well yeah. But he donates enough to the church to buy a few friends."

I rolled my eyes. "And He cast out the money changers from the temples, saying unto them—"

"Spare me," Simon groaned.

"You're not telling me what I need to know. What's Billy like?"

"I thought you said you knew him?"

"Not well."

Simon stopped, eyeing me with suspicious reluctance, now utterly focused on our conversation. "How do you know Billy? Tell me."

"He…" I fished for some excuse–any excuse. I hadn't come prepared for this. "We've… met a few times. That's all. Kind of gotten to know each other."

Simon's eyes widened. "You two have fucked?"

The word bounced around the hall. A silent penitent looked up from the front pews and glared at us. Simon covered his mouth and shrank down in his seat. Innocence? He wasn't fooling anybody.

"We've… been intimate, a few times. That's all." Saint Barnabas already had its share of lies. What was one more?

"So, you'll fuck him more than once but not me?"

"That's none of your concern, and will you give it a rest?"

Simon shrugged, his flirtation finally defeated—either by my refusal or by revulsion at the idea of sharing a bed partner with Jorgas. Probably both. "I thought Billy was straight."

"So are you, according to your parents."

"Hah. Yeah, that would explain a lot."

"What would it explain?"

"Tell me what kind of trouble he's in and I'll tell you." Simon smirked.

"Tell me more about him and I won't tell Father Isaac you're a whoring sodomite," I growled.

"Oh, geez man, he knows. Okay, my parents don't, but he does. He knows about everyone."

"Does he, now?" My curiosity about Father Isaac was growing by the minute. "Do you think he knows about Billy?"

"Doubt it. Billy doesn't talk to anyone."

"I thought you said he talked to the Father?"

Simon shrugged. "I guess. Father's probably worked it out. He works everyone out. Not sure how. Like I said, you should talk to him."

"Is he here?" I asked. The opportunity was worth exploring.

"I saw him head out the back to his office just before you arrived. You can probably catch him."

The silent penitent drifted past us and shot a quick glance in Simon's direction. The boy hastily tried to hide his face, before watching the woman leave.

"You're in a hurry?" I muttered.

"I told you I was."

"Are you sure there's nothing else you want to tell me?"

Simon looked up and stared into my eyes, as if to prove his sincerity. "Look, Billy's got a temper and worse. He doesn't deal well with people. He…" The boy seemed to forget about his pressing appointment as he fumbled for words. "I heard he hurt Sarah."

"Friend of yours?" I asked.

Simon shrugged. "I don't like her much better than Billy. She's a total... I mean she just sleeps around a lot, so I hear."

"Pot paging kettle?"

"Oh, give it a rest! Plus, she's kind of dumb and snooty. She's all about looks and how much money you make and what places you can get her into. Real plastic, you know? But Billy's so… when he loses it, I mean really loses it... I don't know."

"Don't know what?" I could believe it. Jorgas liked to play, and I knew first hand, he liked to play rough. "Do you think he hurt this girl?"

"Yeah, I think he could."

"I did not ask if you think he's capable. Do you think he harmed her or not?"

The boy stared at me, shifting uncomfortably at the question.

"You're making a pretty serious accusation there, Simon. I need you to be sure."

"I've heard all that before," he snarled, before straightening his shirt, trying to regain composure. Too late.

"I'll bet you have. Did you give the police a statement?"

"Look, what do you want, man? With me? With Billy? What does it matter to you? I don't know if he touched Sarah or what, but his dad got him off. So, what does it matter?"

"Matters quite a bit to Sarah, I should think."

Simon shook his head. "I've got to go."

"Nothing else you can think of?"

"Look, yeah, there is. But it's complicated. The point is that Billy and I aren't ever going to be close. That's how I like it. I don't hate him. I barely know him. But we're not friends. Billy doesn't do friends."

I sat there in silence until I was sure he'd finished. None of this helped me find the other werewolf, but it did explain some of the previous night. "Thank you, Simon." I sensed a little of the boy's defensiveness falling away.

"You care about him, don't you?" he asked.

"No." My sharp response echoed around the empty church. But there was nobody left to turn and stare. Besides, the echo inside my head was even louder. Did I care about Jorgas? Was that even possible?

"I'm sorry, I didn't mean to—"

"It's all right." I said, putting a hand on Simon's. He didn't fight me. "Billy's just an interesting guy. That's all." I gave the hand a comforting squeeze as I let it go.

"Hope he appreciates you, looking out for him."

"I'm quite sure he doesn't. But thank you."

"Honestly?" Simon offered me a nervous smile. "I'd be a better boyfriend, if that's what you're after."

I couldn't tell if he was joking or not, but in one sentence, the boy had made me feel as disconnected from humanity as I'd felt in years. What did humans seek in a partner these nights? But Simon now looked me right in the eye. His expression wasn't desperate or needy, simply open and honest—and very charming.

"Then you should find somebody who deserves one," I said.

He stared at me a moment longer, then put an arm around my neck and kissed me. It was a fast, even careless kiss, which left me a little stunned as I watched him scurry out of the vast hall. I eased back into my seat, admiring the grandeur of the building once more. I must have closed my eyes. It's the only explanation I have for not noticing the priest come up behind me, until a gentle hand tapped my shoulder and I spun to face him with a start.

"I'm sorry. I wasn't sure if you were awake." The man almost beamed, making his apology. "I know it's late, but we don't allow sleeping in the parish."

"No," I sat up and straightened my shirt, allowing the priest to sit beside me. "I just have a lot on my mind at the moment."

The priest smiled at me. Did he expect more? I couldn't help but smile back. Perhaps it was my host's plump, ruddy cheeks or the wispy, dark grey hair desperately coiffed to slow increasingly apparent baldness.

"You look suitably fatherly." I offered, almost biting my tongue as the words emerged. Was I mocking him? If I was, the priest didn't seem to care. Good. Neither did I.

"Thank you. But I'm a little surprised to see you here."

Curious phrase to hear, from a stranger.

"It's been… a while, I suppose." I murmured.

"I know."

I tensed, only a little, but I was sure the priest noticed.

"That is to say, I guessed. You must be rather special though."

"Special?"

"You're the first boyfriend Simon has brought here."

Boyfriend? Boyfriend? Then, I remembered Simon's kiss.

"Oh, no. He's just a friend. I was actually hoping to speak to somebody named Isaac. I understand he's one of the Fathers here?"

The priest emitted a deep chuckle that made me feel foolish. I wasn't accustomed to humans making me feel foolish. Especially not the clergy.

"Well, that would be me. Father Isaac O'Baer. But please, just Father or Isaac will do."

"Reylan." I extended a hand, which was warmly accepted.

"And Simon suggested you come here?"

"He insisted on meeting me here. I guess he doesn't want to be seen with me in front of friends."

Father O'Baer looked down at his hands, as though perplexed by the shape of their chubby digits. "Well, knowing his friends, I can't say I'm surprised. May I ask the nature of your meeting?"

"Father," I cautioned.

O'Baer raised both hands apologetically. "Please, I didn't mean to intrude. Tell me to mind my own business if you like. On the other hand, we are alone, and I can promise you discretion. It was merely an offer."

"I'm not confessing to you."

"Well, thank Christ for that. I don't have all night."

"I'll try not to take that personally."

"Oh, no insult was intended. But you do carry yourself as a man of some gravitas. Emotional weight, perhaps?"

My glare narrowed somewhat. "You could put it that way. Honestly? It's not my confession that I wish to make."

I was expecting some rhetoric about the personal nature of one's relationship with 'God,' but none came.

"Guidance for a friend?" O'Baer asked.

"An acquaintance."

The priest nodded.

"Do you think," I continued, "someone with an… affliction—something monstrous, that they don't understand and can't control—can benefit by embracing it?"

The priest shifted his weight in the pew, regarding me in silence. I'd been as literal as I dared already. If O'Baer wanted more, there was no comforting lie I could retreat to.

"Am I to suppose, that we're talking about a member of my congregation?" O'Baer asked.

"I didn't say that."

"No, but why else would you come looking for me? You're a stranger to God, Reylan. I can tell. The only answers you could hope to find at Saint Barnabas concern those within the church family and yet, you are here. So, I must assume—"

"I doubt this acquaintance has attended here in some time." I smiled a moment before looking into the man's eyes, expecting the false warmth of religious compassion. But there was none. Father Isaac's eyes were curious, even fascinated, and a little apprehensive. They also bore more than a hint of recognition. The smile fell from my lips as he stared back at me.

"Who are you?" the priest asked.

"That's a very complicated question."

A mortal never would have seen the changing glint in the priest's eye. But I did.

"You have something in common with the boy, don't you?"

"Simon?"

"The Myers boy, Billy."

Cluey priest.

"I don't wish to offend, Father, but that's really none of your—"

"Be quiet."

I straightened my back. The audacity of the command had left me rather stunned.

"Billy has parents who love him, Reylan."

"Do they, really?"

"Yes. For all their faults—and they have many, I know—they do. But they will never be able to love *him*."

I didn't like the sound of that. Did the priest know Jorgas was wolf? He was so close to an admission of knowledge that I was tempted to break his neck right there. But I couldn't take a man's life so casually, not on such a flimsy, cryptic statement.

Still, what if I was wrong? What if he did know? If I left the man alive, Jorgas could be in serious danger. I'd seen more than my share of loony 'demon' hunting priests over the years. They weren't inclined to wait around for proof, so why was I? And Christ, just how many humans in this city had dared to pull back the proverbial veil? Whatever happened to the Sydney I loved—the city of cynics who believed in nothing beyond a quick buck, a stiff drink and their next lay?

"You're talking about Billy's 'affliction', I presume?"

"You know I am. I've served Saint Barnabas for fifteen years. I've watched Billy grow up. He needs family, Reylan. A family that can love him in his entirety."

My breath grew shallow as the priest's words turned over in my mind. "What if family can't? What if it's just one—" I caught myself before saying 'man' "—person?"

O'Baer offered me a sympathetic smile, which, though it was gone in an instant, let me know my correction had been redundant. "It would take a very particular man to do that. One who's seen great evils, and has a unique understanding of the world, and of people."

I'd certainly seen great evils, though I was starting to doubt my ability to understand people. "I know there was an incident—"

"I'm not talking about what happened to Sarah, and you know it."

That was all I needed. I shot out a hand towards the preacher's throat, but before my fingertips grasped him, a flashing blade was whipped from his cassock and driven through my hand, pinning it to the pew between us. I screamed as blood dripped from the wound, rich, red blood that I couldn't afford to lose. I hadn't fed yet, but if I managed to free my hand—oh, it had been months since I'd last had a little priest!

"You wish to protect your new companion. That is admirable, nothing to be ashamed of. But if you raise hand against me again, sir, I'll cut you down without hesitation."

"What are you?" I grimaced as my hand smarted. "You will tell me!"

O'Baer eased himself out of his seat matter-of-factly. His manner, so threatening only a moment prior, had returned to the fatherly bearing of his introduction. "I'm very busy," he said. "Now, if you'll excuse me, I have an important meeting. And I did promise the other party that we would meet alone."

I screamed again as the priest yanked the knife from my hand. He cleaned it on a handkerchief and replaced it within his robes. I stared at the wound where my palm had been so neatly impaled.

"You may lick it closed. You've nothing to hide from me, Blood Shade."

I growled at him before relenting, my saliva instantly numbing the pain as the fibres of my skin fused back into place, until it was just as smooth, tender and flawless as it had ever been. "I think an explanation is in order before you go anywhere, O'Baer. Because I am not leaving without one."

"It will suffice to say that I have known Billy Myers for the duration of my tenure here, and I have known of his 'affliction'—and yours—since long before he was born. In that time, I have studied and observed, bringing no grief to any of your kind."

"I could bring you plenty of grief, O'Baer. You have no right, do you hear me? No business—"

The priest cut me off. "Your secrets are safe, I assure you. Now, if you'll excuse me. I cannot help you."

I clenched and released my fists angrily. How tempting it was to seize hold of the man and drain him dry, but I resisted. Right now, I was too impulsive. Too angry. "Can't or won't?"

The priest regarded me with soft, patronising eyes, as though I were some small boy, crying over a lost puppy. "I have agreed not to. Good night, Reylan."

I checked my hand for scarring once the priest was out of sight. The man would keep.

The closing of the front doors echoed through the hall. Composing myself, I withdrew to the shadows of the nearest wall, keeping a pillar between myself and the new arrival. O'Baer's appointment, I assumed. My eyes closed for only an instant as I heard the priest's feet scamper down the aisle to greet his guest. O'Baer seemed in an unusual hurry to get their meeting underway—or over and done with. When I saw the other party, I realised why.

Patricia Bakker did get about of an evening.

This explained a lot. Unable to retreat, I drew closer to the column behind which I'd taken refuge.

"Father O'Baer, thank you for seeing me. I trust the hour is not too late for you?"

"Not at all."

"Of course, you already know Isobel?"

What?

"Father." Sure enough, the voice was Isobel's.

"We've met, briefly. Don't think me rude, Sister, but I was not informed that she would be joining us."

Nice to know I wasn't the only Blood Shade on O'Baer's prickly side.

"I wasn't aware that was required."

"Please, is it possible for us to speak alone? I mean no disrespect to your colleague," the man protested.

"Anything you have to say to me can be said in front of Isobel, I assure you."

True to form, my old friend was the voice of diplomacy. "Patricia, it's all right. I'm happy to honour the Father's wishes. I won't be far if you need me."

The few seconds that followed were eerily silent. Not even the creaking of furniture or the hum of a car outside. Nothing but the icy moment of Patricia's pondering.

"Very well. I'm rather pressed for time, Father. Please don't waste it. Your office?"

"Follow me, please."

I didn't dare poke my head around to see where they'd gone. But three sets of footsteps could be heard through the hall. Two going down the aisle toward the altar, and one heading straight for me. Damn it! Wasn't she supposed to be curled up reading, somewhere?

"Reylan, what are you doing here?" Isobel hissed, making sure the other two were out of sight.

"Me? What about you? Don't try telling me you've suddenly found religion."

Isobel relaxed a little, with Bakker and the priest out of sight. "Of course not. Patricia asked me along. She knows O'Baer, just."

"Just?" I snapped. "And tell me, do you 'just' know him too? Because the good Father seems to know a lot more about me than he should."

"Calm down." She put a hand on my arm. "Nobody's told O'Baer about you. At least, nobody from the Trust. But Patricia's been studying and interacting with supernaturals for over thirty years. You didn't seriously think she'd be the only one? Lots of humans believe in us, Reylan. Of course they're going to find each other and compare notes."

"I don't much care for the fact that she's even involved with us and now you're telling me she convenes the local research group? Just who the hell is O'Baer and why hasn't he been dealt with?"

Isobel crossed her arms, grimacing. "Before you decide to go all old school Inquisitor on his hide—"

"Oh, that's flattering! Thank you, so much!"

Blood Inquisitions–supposedly to protect our secrets. Another ugly chapter in the House of Blood's history. For all the things I could have done to O'Baer, nailing his eviscerated organs to door frames up and down the streets of his village seemed a slight overreaction.

"Look, O'Baer has Patricia's protection, and that means he has the Trust's. Put it out of your mind."

Joy. A week ago, I'd never heard of the Arcadia Trust, and now, it seemed they were everywhere. "I don't suppose I'm going to be told what he's done to warrant that?" I eased my clenched teeth as they started to hurt.

"What do you want me to say? I've only met him once. Patricia has known him for years. Forget about him. He's not a problem."

"The man put a knife through my hand, Isobel. I consider that sort of behaviour problematic!"

"Did you provoke him?"

I didn't answer until Isobel smiled. "I'm sorry, something amuses you?"

"Not at all. Are you okay?"

"No thanks to the good Father, but yes."

"Well then, did it occur to you that he just wanted to be sure you're a Blood Shade? He's not like Patricia. He doesn't seek us out. I'd imagine it was quite a thrill for him to meet you in his church."

A thrill? My eyes widened. "He wasn't sure? What if I'd been human?"

"Well, I suppose that would have been… awkward."

I opened my mouth but no words came.

"You still haven't answered me, by the way."

"Answered?"

"What are you doing here?"

"You're surprised to see me?"

"You entered a church. You, Reylan. I'm surprised not to see you in flames."

"Don't be snide. I'm just seeing what I can find on... actually, never mind."

"I wish you'd just asked me. I could have told you, you won't find out anything new about Jorgas here."

My dear friend, as astute as ever.

"Besides, we know he's not responsible for the killings. Patricia told you that. She's taking care of it."

Patricia seemed to take care of a lot, and it didn't satisfy my curiosity. Whoever or whatever the real killer may have been, they still needed to be dealt with.

"Reylan, I know she's only human, but she's very smart. She can do this, I promise."

An eerie silence crept between us. I was seldom one to question Isobel's judgment, but just letting Patricia Bakker handle this after what I'd gone through—with Ross, and with Jorgas—felt wrong. Far, far too wrong.

"Fantasy," Isobel murmured.

"What?"

"The last murder. They found the guy's body near Fantasy. A few people at the club had seen him around. Twinky, circuit boy. Look, if you really need to do this, I'll meet you there once Patricia's done."

"No," I growled. "I'm sorry, no. I want to do it alone." Isobel cradled my chin in her hand and tilted it so our faces met. "No, you don't."

"Isobel—"

"You don't want to be alone at all."

I opened my mouth to object, but she hushed it closed with a finger.

"Behind the Trust, through a trapdoor in the courtyard, there's a wine cellar. He's in there." She gently kissed me, her lips surprisingly warm against the church's cold draft. Then, she shivered, as though trying to force down some unwelcome sensation.

"What's wrong?" I asked.

"Did you feed on him?"

I stared at her, wondering how to answer that, or if I cared to at all. This dubious practice of kissing to determine the identities of my recent meals had to stop. "Yes, I did." I couldn't lie. Not to Isobel.

"In his human form, I assume?"

"Yes, what of it?"

Isobel shrugged. "It's probably nothing. I need to run a few more tests."

I didn't like the sound of that. "Did you take a sample from him?"

"Do you have any idea how rare it is, to have access to a live and cooperative werewolf? I'm not going to waste this opportunity. Initially, I wanted to study his blood toxicity, but unless I can get close when he's in beast form, that's not going to happen. Still, I did find—"

"Have you gone completely barking mad? You can't just—"

"No, listen to me. I found abnormally high concentrations of zinc and yohimbine in the blood composition of his human form."

I shook my head, my patience fraying. "Meaning what, exactly?"

"His hormonal levels. Sexual impulses. They may be slightly… unbalanced. And if you drank from him… just be careful, Reylan."

Careful? It was a bit late for careful. I'd lost all control of my senses. Been overcome by petty, human lust and gorged myself on the boy's flesh, all because I'd tasted his blood. Had it just been sex? Or had his wolfen blood forged something deeper between us? If so, was it mystical or chemical? Did it occur naturally, or was it a curse upon the bloodline?

"The book," I murmured. What I'd witnessed–what I'd been through at the settlement now made a lot more sense. "The colony I saw? That spell—"

"Blood Shades bound to werewolves," Isobel said with a nod. "Method to my madness, you see? I'm still working on it."

My Blood Shade hearing picked up the faint sound of O'Baer's office door opening.

Isobel heard it too. "I'll try to hold them here a while. You need to go, quickly."

Keeping to the shadows, I swiftly took my leave, shivering as I took one final look at the great hall of Saint Barnabas and rejoined the frigid night.

CHAPTER FOURTEEN

It was nearly midnight as I made my way through Surry Hills, back toward the clubs. The streets were already teeming with every walk of life in a thousand different pedigrees of blood, though most of them were the clubbing crowd. I soon regretted my decision not to feed, and considered the risks of a return to Saint Barnabas. How satisfying would it have been, to take O'Baer by surprise? But it was too late now. If I wanted blood, I'd have to take a companion off the street like a common thug. I hated that.

I finally reached the lights of the café strip on Crown Street, letting the faces fade to a white blur under the lights of closing restaurants. The rain had begun to trickle down, but it was still early, so I managed to hail a cab with little effort. Well, little effort for me in any case, as the driver of the occupied cab pulled over, ordered his patrons to vacate and let me in. I don't encourage the hypnosis of any target behind the wheel of a moving vehicle, but needs must when the Devil drives—or needs a driver.

My plan was simple enough. Get in, get Jorgas, then get out and find a killer. A better knowledge of the building would have helped, but I didn't have that luxury, only Isobel's hint about the wine cellar.

The cab pulled over two blocks from the Arcadia Trust, just as I'd requested. Paying the driver a heavy tip for his discretion, I rounded the block and was pleased to find the Trust backed onto a small laneway, protected only by a locked gate, barely six feet tall. I pulled myself up and over with ease, dropping gracefully to the ground. The movement startled a scrawny, orange cat from its waste bin home.

I winced as the loud bang of unbuckling sheet metal echoed off the walls of the house. I stood still a moment to let the night settle around me. I had no way to tell what variety of Shapers Patricia kept on site. There were the medics, certainly. But there were also Shapers who dealt in the laws of serendipity and paradox, those advanced in the supernatural detection of other beings, or the natural born trouble-makers who could cast the light of day from their very hands. So many different fields of study—wherever their schooling in the faux-magicks had led them. For all I knew, Patricia Bakker had an entire range, ready and waiting on a nightly basis, particularly in her absence. But surely Isobel would have warned me, if that were the case?

Then it hit me. Kelvin, perhaps others like him. I could run straight into them and never know. I stuck close to the fence and hoped my dark clothes would protect me, trying to keep my pale face down. I licked my lips, turning the mundane possibilities over in my mind. Motion sensors, dogs... God, how poorly had I thought this through? But I was here now, committed, and nervous. I took a few deep breaths and darted forward, flattening myself against the wall of the building and out of sight. No lights, no barking.

For all their bluster and posturing, the Arcadia Trust were not big on security—not of the mundane sort that humans favoured, anyway.

I still couldn't shake my nerves as I sniffed the air. No Kelvin. No Shapers—at least, not yet. I scanned the courtyard that sprawled out behind the house, trying to keep my fog-laden breath to a minimum in the cold air. I could see the trapdoor to the wine cellar, a clear twenty feet away from my hiding spot, in open, moonlit view. I threw myself forward, scrambling for it. My fingers wrapped around the ancient iron handle and pulled, freeing the heavy cellar door from the ground and letting the light spill out into the night above. I jumped down, pulling the door shut quietly, still unseen, as far as I could tell.

Though its door was antique, the cellar itself was a modern, temperature-controlled chamber housing a wide variety of reds, all lit with god-awful institutional fluorescents.

"Oh, it's you. What do you want?" a familiar voice growled.

I peered into the dark corner from which the voice had emerged, finally making out the speaker. Sure enough, Jorgas sat on an uncomfortable looking bed without sheets. He was wearing the same jeans and shirt he'd been in when Patricia had taken him for 'debriefing'. But something was wrong. He looked wrong, somehow. He looked sick, like it was an effort to even sit up. His eyes were lazy with dark shadows beneath them, and his jaw hung lax on his face.

"I need your help." I said, still unable to get over his exhausted appearance.

"Hahaha! Do you, now? Piss off, Reylan!"

"What on Earth did she do to you?"

She? Patricia? Isobel... I forced the thought away.

Jorgas grimaced. "Nothing, just... nothing. It's a sedative, that's all. It's supposed to stop me changing."

"You look like hell."

"I'm fine! Now, get out. I don't want to see you again. Not ever."

"Sorry, this isn't a debate. You're coming with me." I walked over to the bed and took his arm, easing him up. To my surprise, he didn't fight me.

"Why?" he asked.

My stomach almost turned at the sight of him. Whatever the Trust had put him through, the drug had taken its toll.

"Because I believe you," I explained. "And we have to prove you didn't kill those kids."

He shook his head, throwing my arm away with a strength that belied his weak appearance. "You don't know that. Hell, I can't even remember what I do when I change. How can you—"

"There's been another murder," I said, cutting him off.

"Last night, while you were with me."

Jorgas eyed me with a suspicion I didn't like. "Another one?"

"Yes. Couldn't have been you, could it?"

"I could have put someone up to it. Got somebody else, like me to—"

"You would have had to have done that in human form. Diplomacy? When your beast is out? Don't be ridiculous. And having been in human form, you'd remember the conversation, which you clearly don't." I knew Jorgas could see the truth in my words, but accepting that truth meant leaving behind so much fear, so much hatred. "Can you stand?"

He flashed me a familiar scowl, and for a moment, looked himself again. "What do you think? They're not transferring me to the zoo." He got up off the bed without my help and straightened his clothes.

"Fine. But if you start dragging your knuckles, I'm getting you a 'don't feed me' sign."

"So where are we going?" he muttered, ignoring me.

"Dressed like that? You're going nowhere. Don't you have anything else? Anything at all? Didn't they give you—"

"Listen, bloodsucker, I'll do your whole covert ops thing but I'm not playing fashion parade."

It was going to be a fun night, I could tell.

"Fine," I said. "Here's hoping the bouncers don't notice a two-day old outfit and growth. We need to get that cellar door open again. Better kill the lights in here so we're not seen. Where's the switch?"

"Oh sure, I know where the switch is. I've just been lying here trying to sleep with the lights shining for the fun of it."

Without another word, I grabbed him and shoved him against one of the racks of wine. The bottles rattled as one came loose and smashed against the ground, spilling its deep Cabernet across the floor like blood.

"Jesus! Will you chill out?"

"You do not want to push my buttons tonight, wolf man. I am in absolutely no mood for it. Are we clear?"

Jorgas sighed, his bravado giving way to a faint trace of humility. "Sorry, I'm being a prick. It's this drug, okay? I don't know what's in it. I feel bloody awful."

I hadn't realised how heavily I was panting. But Jorgas had.

"You're not so great yourself," he offered. "You're hungry again, I can see it. Go on, take it."

I shook him violently against the wine once more.

"Hey!" he barked. "I'm just trying to—"

"We don't have time! Every second we waste here is one less second to find the monster you nearly just took the fall for, understand? I'll be fine."

He nodded, putting a hand on my shoulder, which I guessed was some form of apology. My eyes lowered uneasily as his lips curled into a smile. He looked almost sweet, and I didn't trust it. Then, he seemed to glance past me.

"Hey," he observed. "Light switch."

I turned around and there it was, right under the steps into the cellar. I flicked off the light and waited for my eyes to adjust, then gingerly pushed open the cellar door. We eased ourselves up onto the courtyard above. This time, with no tell-tale light to betray our movements.

Too late.

"Nice night for a stroll, ladies?"

Kelvin.

"Move!" I commanded Jorgas, bolting for the gate I'd vaulted to gain entry to the grounds.

But there was no second warning. Two shots rang out through the night, and I heard Jorgas cry out with a yelp as at least one tore through his flesh. I looked back to see him limping, holding his side as blood trickled from the wound. He stumbled to the ground.

"Don't worry about him," Kelvin scoffed.

Jorgas convulsed with pain as he was sharply kicked by the attacker's unseen foot.

"I've got Shapers standing by. They'll patch him up," the Cloak Walker said, making no effort to hide the arrogant sneer behind his words.

Ever since I'd met him, I'd longed for an excuse. Any reason at all. With every ounce of strength I had left, I lurched forward, my arms spread wide, my face the Devil's own avatar, determined to take Kelvin in my grasp one way or another. It worked. The Cloak Walker shrieked as my ghastly form wrestled him to the ground. Sure enough, he had strength, but it was no match for my unbridled rage. Once I had him, there was nothing he could do but scratch at me with his useless nails. I heard the bastard's cries as I brought down one punch after another, until his screams became wet gurgles and then silence. I felt for the gun he'd kept hidden with the rest of him, and ripped it from his fingers. It shimmered back into view as it left Kelvin's hand. I tucked it into my belt before turning back to Jorgas. The shot's intent had not been fatal. Kelvin feared Patricia far too much for that. But the pain that twisted Jorgas' face sent an icy shiver through my whole body.

I took the boy in my arms and gently shook him. "Jorgas… Jorgas, come on. Stay with me. Don't sleep. You've been shot. I need you to stay awake."

"Rey… Reylan… he shot me. The bullets… they're silver, aren't they? I'm going to die."

"No, no, you're not going to die. And the bullets are not silver, you drama queen!" I gave his cheek a slap, mostly to keep him conscious. I hoped I was right. Surely Kelvin wasn't that crazy.

Then again…

I held Jorgas tightly, trying to stem the flow of blood. "But we need to get you patched." Had I gone quite mad? I had no idea where to start 'patching' a werewolf.

He smiled at me half-heartedly. "Well before you do… have a drink. You look terrible. Shame to waste—"

I silenced him with another slap to the face, harder this time. "That's not funny."

This was hopeless. He was losing consciousness and I'd no way to stop it. Except for one, and that was out of the question, wasn't it? Ethically dubious at best, and certainly dangerous. A potential living nightmare that could plague us for the rest of our natural lives, which could have been a very, very long time.

Jorgas' head fell against my arm. He'd passed out. I shook him again, but there was no response. I found a pulse, but now I had no choice. An unethical, dangerous living nightmare it would have to be.

I gingerly bared my fangs and slit open my wrist, just a couple of inches, allowing the arterial blood to spurt across the ground. Jorgas stirred as a few drops fell on his face. I'd forgotten how potent this could be. Taking a deep breath, I pressed my wrist against his lips and braced myself for the inevitable pain.

It was immediate, as though my blood had awoken some fierce primal instinct within the wolf that needed to devour my essence. He took long, slow, painful gulps at my wrist.

I tried to contain my scream as the preternatural blood left my body on its mission of mercy to heal his. A few seconds was all it took. But the agony, as if the very life were being drained from me. For all real intent, it was.

Our bodies shuddered as I tried to pull my wrist away, but Jorgas clasped it and held it firm. This time, I couldn't help it. I screamed as I brought a fist down across his face, forcing my arm free. He yelped with pain and fell to the ground, groaning and panting as life returned. The animal my blood had awakened, banished deep within its human host once more.

I felt dizzy. The next thing I knew, my body had collapsed under its own weight. The temptation to puncture Jorgas' flesh again, to take back what I'd given him and satisfy my own thirst, was stronger than I wanted to admit.

Jorgas lifted his shirt to reveal flawlessly smooth skin, healed as though nothing had happened. Only the tell-tale tear in his clothes showed where the bullet had entered, along with the faint smell of blood that lingered on the air. He stared at me in amazement.

I was too tired to react. I wanted to vomit, and would have let myself, had I fed. I hoped I hadn't made a mistake. I'd been low on blood already. I couldn't afford to share.

"What was that?" Jorgas asked.

"My blood," I panted. "It'll accelerate the healing process of anyone who drinks it. Gives you just a little of a Blood Shade's power."

Jorgas stared at me, suddenly alarmed. "Why?"

"Because we don't have time to wait for the Shapers, and frankly, I'd rather they didn't know I was here. I need you with me and I need you now. Come on!" I rose to my full height, but quickly had to steady my hands on my knees as the night spun around me.

"Wait," Jorgas said, helping me stand. "Last night, you drank from me, I just drank from you. Do I become a vampire now? Christ, I'm already a werew—"

"No, you don't!" I barked, before remembering to keep my voice down. "Why do people always assume we're out to recruit? You're either born one of us, or you're not. End of discussion. Now, come on!"

It was the truth, for the most part. But to drink of a Blood Shade was to take of its essence—to have some of it inside you, which put you just a little further under its power. For humans, this manifested as a hopeless and relentless need to accompany and serve. I'd never tried it on a supernatural. I assumed, perhaps optimistically, that against a werewolf's much stronger constitution, the effect wouldn't be so powerful. Jorgas' feelings about me were confused enough as it was. I didn't need him in my thrall.

Damn it.

CHAPTER FIFTEEN

From Taylor Square, the Oxford Street clubs spread out before us like a thick forest of lights, into which fate had hopefully spilled crumbs that would lead to our killer. Or at least, lead me to some breakfast, if the opportunity presented.

Fantasy was our best chance, either way.

"So, you think there's another one like me who's doing this?" Jorgas asked.

"That's what we need to find, yes. Somewhere."

"Somewhere? Reylan, there are over ten thousand people in those clubs. Can you be just a bit more specific?"

I nodded, swallowing my annoyance. "Fantasy."

"What?"

"Isobel said the victim last night was some twink boy they found near Fantasy. That's where we're starting."

"Reylan, that's one of the biggest clubs in the city."

"That's right. It's also fruit fly night, so the place should be packed."

"Fruit fly night?"

"Straight girls get in free if they're with a gay guy."

"Do me a favour, okay? Do not explain how they police that."

I remembered the date well. It was the one night every month that Ross' chaps came out of the closet. He never missed it. I just hoped that this month, his injuries had left him in no shape to go. As much as I loved Ross, I didn't need the complication of being spotted by any of Patricia's friends.

"I don't believe this," Jorgas moaned. "I thought you had a real lead."

"Well, we're going to have to do this the hard way, aren't we?" I snarled. "Besides, can't you… I don't know…"

"What?"

"Sniff them out or something? I mean, can't you tell your own kind, like we can?"

Jorgas looked out into the sea of partiers and pointed to a woman in a faded red sweater, who was stepping out of an all-night convenience store with a bag of potato chips. "Her! She's one."

"Really?" I asked, moving to get a better view.

"I don't know!" Jorgas recanted, holding me back as the woman was enveloped by the swarming crowd. "God, do you think if I knew someone else like me, I'd be coming to you for help?"

Immediately, I could see in Jorgas' face that he'd said more than intended. I didn't call him on it. I needed his trust.

"Going to be a long night," I muttered.

"You don't say."

None of the crowd around us seemed in any way remarkable, at least, not in the non-human sense. We pushed our way through them and walked the two blocks to Fantasy. The queue ran halfway down the street and around the corner.

"God, anywhere else?" Jorgas moaned.

"Pedestrian thinking," I scolded him. "I know this is a strain for you, but try to think fabulous once in a while."

"Reylan," he growled. "You will not say 'fabulous' when I'm around. Not ever."

"Awww… is puppy embarrassed?" I smiled.

We briskly strolled up past the crowd of boys and their eager heterosexual sisters in crime—not to mention a healthy sprinkling of lesbians and straight couples. How different, to the Oxford Street of thirty years ago, when the gays had been more counterculture than tourist attraction, determined to stay hidden and not at all keen on sharing their sanctuaries with the mainstream.

Having lived in Paris, Berlin and Copenhagen—albeit, all before the second great war that had sent so many of us scurrying to America—this behaviour had seemed paranoid to me at first, though I'd come to understand it after one particularly unpleasant individual took exception to my kissing a male companion in public, and had forced me to be somewhat… firm, in standing up for my rights. It had been my first and last confrontation with the New South Wales police.

I approached the bouncer, smiling broadly and ignoring the crowd. We mostly went unnoticed. Mostly.

"Reylan! Seriously? What are you doing here? What else do you want from me?"

Of course, of all the dozens of clubs Simon's little posse could have chosen, it had to be this one.

"You didn't mention you'd be here tonight," I said through gritted teeth.

"I told you I was going out. I'm late, by the way, so thanks."

"Are we done here, Reylan?" Jorgas snarled.

I latched a cautionary hand onto the werewolf's wrist. He took the hint and fell silent. I was in no mood to deal with a Saint Barnie's brat fight this evening. Besides, doing so could have meant another conversation with Isaac O'Baer. I wasn't going there.

Simon looked at Jorgas with a hint of trepidation.

"Simon, we're not here to see you, okay?" My hand still gripped Jorgas, imploring him to stay quiet.

"Fine." Simon relaxed a little. "Billy, how's it going?" he asked.

I almost laughed. Surely it was a little late for playing cool acquaintances?

"I'm… doing okay, I guess." Jorgas managed a smile. I couldn't believe it.

"Have fun tonight, okay?" I let go of Jorgas' hand. One crisis averted. My night was improving.

Simon nodded, finally offering a smile. My fingers playfully danced over the boy's chest as we passed. Jorgas glanced at him, and I heard a low growl as Simon looked away.

"There, I can play nice. Hope you're happy."

"Cool it," I cautioned.

"You know that guy?" Jorgas spat the question out with disdain. "You know, he—"

"I don't want to know, Jorgas. You and the Barnie's brats don't have the best history, I get it. But do not assume that I'm curious about the details. Not for a minute. Do you understand?"

"What do you know about that?"

"More than I care to." I stepped up to the head of the queue.

"Sorry boys, no jumpers. Back of the line, thanks."

I smiled. The lazy refusal had come from Angus, one of my favourite bouncers on the strip and certainly my favourite at Fantasy. He hadn't even bothered to look at us. Indeed, he sounded irredeemably bored.

I pouted like a schoolgirl. "What do you mean I can't have a pony, daddy?"

"Reylan, what are you doing?" Jorgas demanded.

Angus looked up and met my eyes, as he had done so often in the past. Surely, he knew me by now, though I still wasn't sure if he liked me or not. I'd pulled his emotions to and fro so many times that I'd lost track of what was real and what was induced. The manipulative quicksand of emotional hypnosis. How I loved it.

"Now, look, I said…" he began, but it was too late as he recognised my persuasive gaze. "Ah, sorry…"

I winked at Angus and ran a finger over his shoulder, down his unnervingly enormous chest. The man was half Samoan and built like a panzer tank, with more than a few scars around the face. I guessed that his threatening appearance hadn't gone untested over the years. A few blows to the head would have explained a lot about Angus.

"Geez, sorry, I've forgotten your—"

"Reylan. You remember, don't you?"

"Of course. Sorry, Reylan. Busy night. Lots of faces through. Go right in, mate."

I pushed past the annoyed crowd. I suspect even Simon grimaced in disbelief, but I couldn't be sure. If it kept him out of our hair a little longer, that was a plus. Jorgas shuffled along after me, but the gargantuan breadth of Angus stepped in his way.

"Sorry dude, it's fruit fly night and if you're his, then you're the ugliest damn fly I've ever—"

I doubled back, pushing Angus out of the way—no easy feat, even for me. I grabbed Jorgas and pushed my lips hard against his. Jorgas quickly got the idea and put his arms around me, his fingers running through my hair as our breath warmed the air around us and his tongue broke through, lapping hungrily at mine. I'm sure I heard one of the girls mutter something about her birthday as we parted.

"Sorry boys." Angus nodded. "I didn't realise. Have a good night, eh?"

"Thank you." I had to smile. To be fair, it was possibly the first time I'd arrived at Fantasy with a 'friend' on my arm, though I usually managed to leave with one.

I quickly shuffled the cover charges to the attendant. I could have gotten us in for free, but while money was no object, I'd no reason to push our luck. I urged Jorgas inside before Angus could get wise.

"What are you, the Queen?" Jorgas sneered.

"Depends who you ask. Remind me to give you a crash course in improvisation. Most of the bouncers are easy to get past if you work them properly. Just try not to be recognised by anyone who saw us, and stay away from your church friends."

"Right."

Jorgas muttered something else as we went inside, but was drowned out by the thick, pulsating beats of the club.

The crowd was fairly typical fruit fly night fare, almost impenetrable, filled to its thousand head capacity. Gleaming, shirtless bartenders dripped sweat from overwork, and whatever passed for dancing that week was already out on the floor. The music was clumsily mashed top forty and the faint, acrid smell of stale sweat pervaded the room—not to mention the myriad cheap scents that tried to cover it.

I pulled Jorgas close to me again and shouted in his ear.

"We should split up. Meet me back here in ten minutes."

"Got it."

"One more thing. Where are the brats?"

"The what?"

"The brats. Simon's friends."

Jorgas scanned the crowd with an angry glare before settling on a half dozen kids dancing in a loose circle on the central floor, most of them conspicuously straight—two of the four boys were barely moving. I half smiled. I should have picked them for the Barnie's brats myself.

"Good, we can rule them out."

"Yeah? Well I'd like to—"

"Leave them alone, Jorgas. I mean it."

"Whatever."

"And let me know if you pick up—"

"Yeah, yeah, wolfie vibes. I told you I can't, but I'll try." He pushed me away.

I breathed steadily as two younger guys drifted past us into the sea of the crowd. Definitely not supernaturals. That was two, plus the Barnie's brats down, only nine hundred and ninety-two to go.

Jorgas was already gone. He pushed through the crowd with an arrogant confidence I envied, and a frank, hostile scowl that unnerved anyone he passed. So much for being inconspicuous.

I spotted a few of my past companions as I surveyed the crowd from the relative safety of the entrance. They could be ruled out right away. Taking one last breath, I descended into the mire of sweat laced bodies and smoke. My eyes darted from face to face, as I came just close enough to each individual to pick up anything unusual or just plain wrong.

Some preternatural speed would have been useful, but with the crowd so dense, any use of it would surely have ended in injury and possible death for some unfortunate mortal. I didn't need the complication.

My paranoid nerves sprang to attention as a low howl erupted through the club. I spun around in panic, my fangs flashing before I could stop them. I put them away, though my eyes still burned, begging to release the monster within. What met me however, was not a werewolf.

It was the Fantasy stage, with a drag queen in cheap Victorian men's regalia that suggested a dollar store take on Jack the Ripper. She held up a cheesy cane prop that I couldn't properly see and howled to some god of obscene vice as the club's latest show began. I tried to relax. The crowd returned the drag queen's howls as three young male dancers in black mesh shirts joined her onstage. At least this would keep them all still enough for me to work. I circled the room slowly. Nobody at the back of the club was interested in the show— the regulars, who'd seen it all before. The werewolf could have been among them, but I doubted it. The deaths were too recent, and most of the regulars had been clubbing on the strip for years. That meant descending into the crowd.

I recognised the first few notes of the drag queen's set, an old Annie Lennox number. I did a quick double take on the act and felt my jaw almost drop out of its joint. Her lips were wet with stage blood.

She was playing a Blood Shade. She dared to play the role of a Blood Shade as she mimicked feeding on the boys around her, sloppily dribbling stage blood over them while they clutched their necks and pretended to choke in mock horror. Every movement was exaggerated, like some tawdry school play. Is that how she thought we looked? How she thought we conducted ourselves? She wasn't even doing Ms Lennox the decency of getting the lip synch right!

I pushed through the crowd, taking just enough care not to injure the hapless humans enjoying the show. But I never took my eyes off the creature disgracing my kind.

Until a rough hand grabbed my shoulder.

"What?" I demanded with a start, rounding fiercely on the hand's owner… Jorgas.

"You're a real fucking ray of sunshine, you know that?"

"The kind that chases ants through a magnifying glass, I'm sure. Now, what is it?"

"Out back, the beer garden, found our guy."

"What? Already? Are you sure?"

"Wet dog."

"Huh?"

"Sensitive sniffer." He tapped his nose. "Come on. I didn't actually see him, but it smells like he was there just a moment ago. I'm sure of it."

"Wait. This won't take a moment." I turned my attention back to the show.

"Huh? Oh, Jesus! Will you get over it? It's just a drag queen!" He shoved me hard in the back.

I nearly snapped again, but he was right. I was being stupid, my judgment clouded by outrage. I liked drag queens as a rule. I liked polished, glamorous drag queens, scrappy, resourceful drag queens, witty queens, creepy and quirky queens…

What I could not abide was a queen who mocked my very nature, then had the nerve to phone it in.

It's very difficult to make eye contact with an entire crowd in the darkness of a club. The first step was to capture the attention of a small group with your irresistible beauty and charisma, which in this case, meant distracting them from the despicable circus currently playing out on stage.

Then, you have to extend the tentacles of your overwhelming personality to their friends, then friends of friends, until you've enveloped the entire crowd into believing not just your every word, but your every thought. It's difficult, but I've done it before. I could do it again. And I had just the group in mind to distract.

"Hey Simon!" I called.

Simon had yet to materialise on the Fantasy dance floor, but the sound of a stranger calling his name was enough to grab the attention of one of the Saint Barnie's brats, a waif-like brunette eager to greet their tardy friend. I wasted no time in locking her eyes to mine, as she smiled sweetly, tugging on her boyfriend's shirt and pointing me out. He too, cocked an arrogant half-smile as I exerted my magnetism further, spreading its influence to their friends, then to the crowd beyond. No small effort, but over and done in less than a minute.

Jorgas, meanwhile, had stayed out of their sight, but shot me such a filthy, furious look that I felt almost guilty.

Almost.

I'd told him to leave the Saint Barnie's brats alone. I'd never promised to do the same. I gave the first girl a final wink as Jorgas bounded through the bodies to the stairs at the back of the room. The energy afforded him by my blood made him damn near untouchable. But I managed to keep up, staying just long enough to hear the shouts begin.

"Get off the stage!"

"You're fuckin' awful!"

"Leech! Leech! Leech!"

What pretty music the mob made as it spoke the truth! Within a minute, the club had descended into chaos. I slipped through the back exit and stepped outside. The beer garden was similarly packed with regulars looking to escape fruit fly night. As with those inside, I doubted any of them could have been Jorgas' 'wet dog.' And now, Jorgas was out of sight. Damn it!

I pushed through the beer garden and noticed the back gate to the club open. That was odd. Fantasy's manager was a tyrannical forty-eight-year-old lesbian who never, ever let a soul in without paying their cover. There was no way that gate should have been unlocked, much less open.

*　　*　　*

Nobody saw me as I stepped out into the quiet back streets. The crowd were all too interested in the riot brewing inside. The music and hum of the beer garden kept up a dull roar behind me, but the surrounding walls proved a surprisingly effective buffer against the sound.

Peering into the gloom, I saw only alleyways, the back of shops and nightclubs, long fallen to neglect, their brickwork cold and filthy. I stepped out further. Wet dog? I smelt nothing, unless you counted the bitter ammonia of urine and slowly decaying garbage. That said, I wasn't a werewolf.

As I rounded the corner, I saw a familiar face.

"Seventy-five a piece? For E? Jesus, man, that's the third time this year."

"Best I can do, Brett. And it's better than E, okay? Don't insult me. Good tabs. Next level, I promise you."

Brett. The same, tall, handsome young man who'd been sporting the 'Karloff by way of Madame Lash' get-up at The Black Soul. I felt strangely... disappointed. He reluctantly took out his wallet—his new wallet, I noticed—and accepted the pills, stuffing three hundred into the sneering dealer's pudgy hand. The dealer was short by comparison, no more than five nine, and by the look of things, younger than Brett. Maybe twenty-two. No threat, so long as he was human. But tonight, I wasn't prepared to risk that assumption. I raised my senses, determined to find something amiss. It was just the three of us in the alley. Wherever Jorgas had gone, he'd meant one of these guys. I could feel it already, and it wasn't the dealer.

It made perfect sense. Brett's cold demeanour, his frequenting Fantasy for drugs. Plus, he had my scent. Had he waited for me outside The Black Soul? Had he followed me home, where Ross...?

The little blood I had left boiled within me as I stepped closer. "I can still get you better for forty," I snarled.

The two men looked up in shock. Brett's jaw instantly fell as he recognised me.

"Hey, I'm going to say this once," the dealer growled. "You leave now, and nobody gets hurt. Unless you're here to shop too?"

"I've much bigger concerns here than your precious pick-me-ups," I replied. "That's your cue to leave, son."

The dealer flicked out a knife and brandished it in my face. Christ, were all the post-teen delinquents packing blades these nights? It surprised me even more when Brett joined him, and I found myself staring down at a pair of sharp street knives.

"Right back at you, arsehole," the dealer seethed.

Fine. Fools irritate me, they really do.

I grabbed the dealer's wrist and snapped it back against itself, forcing the knife to drop. The man screamed as he dropped to his knees to tend the break. It flopped loose with the crunch of bone as he tried to nurse it.

Brett stared in horror until... I'm not sure if it was courage, anger or just mad panic that made him lunge forward and cut me across the throat. I winced as the searing pain took hold for its brief second and then vanished. A hot trickle of blood seeped down my neck. But with so little left, a Blood Shade body my age has the wondrous ability to ration it just so, when injured. Brett backed off immediately, his knife-wielding hand still quivering, stained with my blood.

"Brett, that was extremely impolite and I am most unhappy. What do you think would be... an appropriate response, on my part?" I advanced on him, stepping over the still wailing dealer.

"What the hell are you, man?" Brett whimpered.

It didn't make sense. Why would a werewolf use a knife in the first place? Brett's eyes went even wider. The knife dropped as he stumbled backwards, tripping over his feet as he scrambled away. He began clawing at the frozen brick wall he'd backed against, as though the bricks could crack open and swallow him into their safe haven.

I soon realised I wasn't the reason for his retreat.

The seven-foot beast behind me howled as it bounded up the alley. I'd wondered where Jorgas had gone. I kept an eye on Brett as the werewolf surged toward us. But it reached the dealer first. The man screamed, trying to stand up on the slippery bitumen as the creature sniffed him over. He finally got to his feet and threw himself forward, but it was too late. The claws swooped down and grabbed his midsection, splitting him across the ribs and spilling a bloody mess of pink intestine across the ground with a faint, putrid steam. Then, the broad, hairy snout dove in to maul the man's side.

The dealer screamed again as his flesh was shredded by the werewolf's teeth. Brutalised strips of skin and muscle hung from the creature's jaws as it tried to shake them free.

"Jorgas! What the hell?"

So much for Patricia's drug! I'd been an idiot to think he could control his beast out here, under stress.

Then I saw Jorgas, in human form, panting as he rounded the corner up the street.

"Reylan!" he called.

The werewolf dropped its prey and turned on him.

"Never mind." Jorgas rushed to strip off his clothes.

"What are you do–?"

He threw them at the other werewolf's snout. With a frustrated roar, it clumsily clawed the clothes away, giving Jorgas just enough time to overcome the drug. I watched, frozen as his arms slowly, painfully extended. I heard the cracks of his spinal column as it changed shape, the splitting of his jaw as it elongated into a vicious snout. It was all over in seconds as a coat of thick brown hair shrouded his flesh. His snarls fought to contain a howl as the rapid metamorphosis took over. At last, we had an even match. I looked around nervously. If any human saw this, for even a moment, we'd have a serious problem.

Then, I remembered—too late.

I glanced back at Brett, but he was already tucked into a foetal ball, crying. I could wipe his memory of all this later. So long as he didn't move—just stayed in the dark, out of the way, he'd be all right.

Then, there were the dealer's remains. The man was spread across the street and… ugh. I hated it when they were still alive. But if he was, that meant…

There's a time to swallow one's pride. I was still hungry, damn it. I grabbed the dealer's stubby neck and sunk my teeth in, drawing what was left of his hot, greasy blood. I fought the urge to gag, but it would have to do for now.

The two werewolves slashed at each other with such ferocity, I expected a huge severed paw or head to land at my feet. But their wounds healed almost instantly, as they carved into each other's flesh, only to see it reseal. If I didn't do something, this could go on all night. And not to be speciesist, but I hadn't met many werewolves. They both looked the same to me! Which one was Jorgas?

I threw away the dealer's remains, blood spurting across the street. He wouldn't live long now, and he wouldn't talk.

I was covered in gore, painted like some ancient cultist, fresh from ritual sacrifice. But the wolves could smell it. Both their heads faced me, eyes and teeth glistening in the cool neon that licked the end of the street.

Shit.

As one of them bounded towards me, I ripped Kelvin's gun from my belt and opened fire. The harmless clicks of an empty magazine replied. Throwing the useless weapon at the monster, I turned tail and fled up the street, seeking anywhere, anywhere to hide. A dumpster would have done at this point. I somehow found the courage to look back, to see Jorgas on the beast's tail. But Jorgas was lost to the change himself. I had to wonder, if he managed to get the brute off my track, would I be any safer? Then, from the dark, a tall shape rose and darted away from the two monsters that bore down on me.

Brett. Stupid, terrified Brett.

The first werewolf lunged forward and swatted the man against the wall. Brett fell facedown to the street and was still again as the wolf turned its attention back to me. But in a second, Jorgas was on its back and going for its throat. Their howls erupted through the air, reverberating off the walls and darkened windows of the surrounding buildings

I didn't think. I couldn't have thought. It was madness, I know. But I jumped on the monster's thrashing form, sank my teeth in and let blood pour from the wound. The creature howled again, but this time, I barely heard it as the toxic red bile ran over my jaws. I coughed violently as the buildings spun around me. My fingers ached, clawing in the fur until I was thrown off. I cried out as my head spun with sudden whiplash. The numbing thud of a brick wall clattered against my back and I fell to the street beside Brett. The shape of dim buildings still spun around me and the dance of lights that invaded my mind's eye stung painfully with each flash. I couldn't get up. I could barely move. I vaguely heard Jorgas' nearby scream—a depressingly human sound. Whether the drug had kicked in again, or just his own inexperience, he'd lost the form of the beast. I barely heard the last howl, before the air fell silent, and I lost the battle to stay conscious.

CHAPTER SIXTEEN

I finally opened my eyes, only to slam them shut as the blinding, thick blood of that night's feed curtained down. I wiped the mess away and forced them open again, this time settling for a faint red haze. I'd hit my head harder than I'd thought.

I couldn't have been out long. Five, maybe ten minutes at most. The werewolf was gone, and I still had all my limbs. I considered myself lucky. Luckier than Brett's dealer, anyway.

"Dude… dude, are you okay?"

I knew the voice. Brett put a hand on my shoulder.

"You mean besides feeling like I've been trampled by a stampede? I'll live." I eased back against the wall, and stared at my human Samaritan.

Brett backed off as soon as I looked at him.

"What?" I asked.

"No-nothing," he stammered. "Listen, I'm sorry about before, okay? We've gotta get out of here before those… those things come back."

Come back? Surely Jorgas hadn't run after the other werewolf alone?

I coughed a glut of blood out onto the pavement. Brett backed off even quicker this time. But he couldn't get far. I could see the broken bone that had pierced through the muscles of his leg. It glinted with blood in the dim light. I couldn't let him see that. I didn't need to deal with some hysterical human in shock over his shattered insides. If he was too numb with pain to feel it, all to the good. I just had to keep him distracted.

"What things?" I struggled to my feet, staring him down.

"I… I umm…" He took out his knife and looked down at it with guilt.

"Oh, that's right. I'd almost forgotten." I advanced on him, tilting my head to show my now perfectly healed throat.

Brett tried to shuffle away, his bottom lip quivering as he stared at my neck's resealed flesh. Cheap shot though it may be, I find raw terror to be a marvellous distraction.

Another familiar voice came from a pile of rubbish in the dark. "Reylan, will you just kill him already and get me out of here?" Jorgas emerged from the pile of waste bags he'd been thrown into.

"Oh, that's attractive," I muttered.

"Shut up, Reylan! Where is it? Did it get far?" He was naked of course, his clothes this time strewn across the street where he'd shed them for his transformation. Except now, he reeked with garbage. He shot Brett a nasty scowl.

The man jumped with a start, wincing as his leg smarted. Looking down, the first thing he saw was the shattered bone. "Oh… oh shit!?" he screamed. "That's my leg, dude. That's my fucking leg!"

"Brett, don't look at it. Focus on my voice. Can you hear me? Talk to me."

"So, what's the problem? He's seen too much, deal with it. I've seen you do it before," Jorgas snarled.

Before I could stop him, Jorgas kicked Brett in the chest, sending him sprawling across the bitumen. The human screamed as the leg crunched under his weight. I pushed

Jorgas aside and went to Brett's aid. The man was struggling for breath now.

"Don't you touch him," I barked, taking Brett in my arms. I could feel the damp, warm blood that had seeped through his shirt. Brett's blood, which now covered my hands. Jorgas was right. We had to deal with this now.

"He tried to kill you," Jorgas growled.

"So did you!" I snapped. Then I realised, my teeth had flashed. I hadn't even thought about hiding them.

"Let me go! What the hell are you?" Brett struggled against me.

"We can't leave him," I said. "Not with that leg, and he's bleeding badly. He'll die."

"So? Finish the rest of him and let's get going."

"No!" Brett screamed, his words wheezed out between great, panicked sobs. "I won't tell anyone. Oh, God! I'm sorry! Don't kill me. Pleeeease!"

"Shhhh..." I ran a cool hand over his forehead until he'd stopped squirming. He just stared at me, eyes full of fear and wonder. Though he had tried to kill me in the heat of the moment, he'd also risked his own life, to stay with me until the danger had passed. I gently brushed the blood-spattered hair off his face and lifted my wrist to my mouth.

Jorgas shot out a hand and grabbed it. "Oh, you're not."

"I did it for you," I reminded him.

"Yeah, there's me, and there's a plain vanilla human. I got to read up on some of this stuff at the Trust and there's a huge difference in effect. You're not making him your blood puppet."

My mouth flattened into a steely grimace as I met Jorgas' eyes. "You should have read then, that it's not your decision. I'm aware of the differences, and I don't know why, but I like this boy. Now, find out where that animal's gone and put some pants on for Christ's sake!"

Jorgas was not a patient man, so I'd learned in my short time knowing him. But with an angry harrumph, he did as he was told. Pulling on his pants, he sniffed the air, trying to find any trace of where the other wolf had gone.

I held Brett's head firm, and gently raised my wounded wrist to his mouth. "Drink this."

"No!" He was spluttering, trying to keep the blood out of his mouth as it spilled over his face. "You're not making me one of you! I know how this works. You can't make me!"

God, how I hate Hollywood.

I jammed my wrist into his jaws. As the first drops of sweet blood hit his tongue, Brett's screams of protest became long gulps of ecstasy, holding my wrist to his hungry maw. He would have sucked me clean and dry, had I let him.

As I said, drinking my blood will always leave a being somewhat in my thrall. But a true mannequin can only be borne of a human, an agonising process, to say the least. A little of the human inside the recipient dies to make way for its new life, both inherently painful processes in nature's canon. Once the change is complete, the Blood Shade effectively owns them. It was something I didn't do lightly. Brett was only my second. My first, Yvette, was lost to the Great War. I was very fond of Yvette, but I'm not one to bore with details.

Brett's body thrashed about as if seized by some daemonic entity, writhing and spitting blood out onto the street. How the man screamed, his form fitting in pain and terror as his fragile life force was replaced by my own. His leg was healing, the bones fusing themselves back together as my blood swelled to their aid. His pupils dilated. His muscles tore themselves apart, only to rebuild as preternatural strength filled them, drawn both from my blood, and his own will. I could barely stand to watch. Had I any reason to fear God, I might have prayed that I'd made the right decision.

Jorgas soon rejoined us. "It's okay. I think it's heading away from the main street. Will you hurry this up?"

Brett's eyes rolled back in his head. He was still spitting blood. A gurgled, piercing shriek escaped him as he suddenly sat upright.

Jorgas jumped back in fright, narrowly avoiding a shower of blood. "Reylan, are you crazy? It's not working! He's dying! Just cut his throat or something!"

"No, he's not." I folded my arms as Brett's fitting slowed.

When Brett's body finally stopped convulsing, I squatted down to face him, gently wiping the blood from his mouth like some nurse cleaning up after a child.

"What was that?" he stammered. "I feel… I feel great!"

"I know. I'm sorry, Brett."

"What for?"

I balled my hand into a fist and slogged him across the jaw, knocking him out cold to the pavement. "For that." I shuffled his unconscious body aside into the dark.

Jorgas stared at me, utterly bewildered.

"We're in a hurry, aren't we? I'll pick him up later."

"What if he wakes up first?"

"Then he'll find me," I said, briskly heading in the direction Jorgas claimed the monster had gone.

"You have problems, Reylan. Seriously."

"I know."

*　　*　　*

Jorgas picked up the wolf's scent again soon enough. The creature was moving slower now, and it wasn't far away. No reason for us to slow down or be complacent, but it helped.

The beast had avoided the garish lights of the open street— and I hoped, any human sight—as it headed deeper into the Surry Hills warehouse district. That meant a fine line. Half the old warehouses had been converted into apartment blocks, and I couldn't bear the thought of another human dying that night because of us. Since there were no humans in sight, I picked up the pace. Then, a little more, until I'd reached a speed only a Blood Shade could manage. Jorgas cried out to me as I rushed past, but I didn't need his tracking skills on the scent anymore. I'd seen the bastard. Just a flicker in shadow as he rounded a corner, or dove over a barricade blocking the street. I couldn't tell if he was still a full-blown wolf or if he'd reverted. But he was there, in my sight, meaning I couldn't wait for my accomplice to catch up. As we mapped the dim back streets, vaulting old wooden fences, clumsily piled boxes and garbage bags with ease, I could make out his shape so plainly, a small, pitiful, human shape. A werewolf in human form. Oh, so tasty.

The sight spurred me on. I could feel my legs straining, burning blood too quickly. I'd taken so little from the dealer. Not enough, but it didn't matter. This would all be over soon, as I set my sights back on…

He was gone.

I couldn't help it. I screamed and slammed a fist into a nearby drainpipe, crushing it against the wall and ripping my hand away in pain. Stupid, Reylan! You arrogant fool!

Now, I'd lost Jorgas, and this thing, in pathetic human flesh had escaped me. I rested my hands on my knees and struggled not to collapse to the pavement. That's when I saw blood on the ground.

I slowly forced my legs to move. There was a dried drop here, a fresher drop further up the way, glimmering in the dull lights of back entrances to stores and wholesalers. High above were the apartments of mortals I hoped were safely in bed or out, off their faces. The trail turned, leading under one of the closed doors. I carefully grasped the handle, determined not to shake it. If this guy was as wild and poorly disciplined as

Jorgas in his changes, or perhaps worse, then he could have changed back into wolf form already. If he had, I'd be dead before I got six feet inside the door. But what else could I do? Leave him? Knock?

I forced the door open in one hard and fast movement, threw myself behind it and slammed it shut. I instantly ducked out of the way of whatever claws might come swiping toward me. But there were none. He was in here somewhere, in the dark, almost certainly in human form—and I'd no clue where.

I sniffed the air gingerly, trying to get the scent of blood again. But however severe my prey's cut had been, it was now healed. The scent of rats and fresh fruit wafted through the air, the latter ready for the city's weekend markets and the former hoping to get the best deals ahead of time. Nowhere could I smell a bleeding werewolf. But my search didn't last long.

"Whoever's there, leave me alone!"

I glanced over at some boxes in the opposite corner of the room.

"I mean it! Just go away and you won't get hurt, okay?"

There was a curious hint of sobbing in that threat that belied its credibility. The voice was familiar too.

I paused in front of the boxes that hid the creature. "Stand up," I instructed quietly.

"Go away!"

I carefully rounded the boxes and stared down at the frightened, naked young man behind them. I had to look twice, and then again. Once I was certain, there was nothing I could say.

Simon.

Not the same cocky, carefree boy I'd seen trawling the clubs for one-off partners, or the one who'd so happily given his downright opinion of Jorgas, but a hollowed shell, fighting to keep a monster tucked away inside. Simon the lycanthrope.

Simon, the cashed-up Saint Barnie's brat, who now seemed so pitiful, I felt revolted just laying eyes on him as he shivered, trying to avoid or repel my gaze. His own eyes glowered from beneath his long black fringe, soaked with sweat and fear.

"Listen," I forced out.

He shivered again, drawing closer into the wall.

"Come with us. We'll take you to people who can explain what's happening to you. What you need to—"

"No!" he growled. For a second, I jumped. Even his tinny, human voice carried the jagged edge of a werewolf's snarl.

I tensed, expecting a sudden change. But the boy remained human.

"You don't get a choice." My voice had all the sternness I could muster, which by this point wasn't much, but I'd make do. "You've done some terrible things."

It made perfect sense. How good he'd tasted the night he'd spent with me, the latest murder, right near Fantasy... All circumstantial, perhaps. But what we'd just seen in the alley left little doubt.

"No, I haven't! I haven't done anything wrong. Just get this thing out of me!"

"I know you can't remember. That's normal. But you need help, or it'll keep happening. You understand that, don't you?"

Simon wiped away icy tears, swallowing another sob.

"I guess you didn't meet up with your friends tonight after all?" I tried not to make it sound like a joke.

The boy violently shook his head. "They wouldn't understand any of this. How do I explain it? I can't!"

"Don't worry about that. Nobody is going to tell them." It sounded more like an imperative than reassurance. It probably was.

"I... I don't have... I..." Simon's words choked as tears overcame him.

I almost took him in my arms, but thought better of it. I knew how to talk a young Blood Shade down off the roof. A young werewolf was a different story. If physical contact made him feel threatened or patronised, he could be the last thing I ever touched. As for Jorgas… well, I'd been lucky there. I didn't trust that luck to hold out twice. I heard the clattering of the iron door as Jorgas bumbled his way inside.

"Reylan! Stop, don't kill him!" He skidded to a halt as he looked down at Simon's shaking form. "I take it back," he growled. "Kill him."

I regarded the two of them side by side. Both supernaturals, yet they'd turned out so very different in human form. Simon, the clean-cut North Shore boy from a family with too much cash to flash, and Jorgas, from a family so similar, yet he'd turned out a shadow of what that young life could have been. Lost, angry and violent, even before his dual nature got in the way. Ultimately, their backgrounds didn't matter. This had to end now.

"Nobody's killing anybody." I looked Simon in the eye.

He met my gaze, but I was weak from blood loss. I couldn't hold him with my stare, either to inspire terror or love. The only hope I had was that he would see reason and come without a fight.

"Reylan…"

"Shut up, Jorgas." I never took my eyes off Simon.

"Jorgas?" the boy asked.

I didn't wait for the third-party explanation. "Think of it as an alias. You'll need one too. You've got a lot to learn."

Simon began to shake, trembling as he slowly stood up and faced me, never taking his eyes off mine. I nodded, trying to look reassuring as he carefully took a step toward me.

I caught him as he suddenly fell forward into my arms, a great flood of tears bursting all over his trembling face.

"Reylan," he sobbed. "Help me, please? I don't understand this. I don't get any of it."

I tenderly kissed his forehead as I stroked his naked back, my fingers running through his sweat-soaked hair as warm tears trickled down my shoulder. They belied the ice cold of his skin, frozen in the night air.

I heard a growl.

Jorgas was staring at me, perhaps waiting for Simon to pull himself together. But I suspected more. It was hard to say what, especially in my current state of distraction. The smell of Simon's blood washed over me and I couldn't help but inhale the delectable scent. I remembered the night he'd been my companion, how rich that blood had been, how vibrantly textured. The blood of a werewolf in human form.

"We'll get you some help. Just trust us," I whispered, trying to take my mind off the aromatic bouquet.

"What did I do?" he sobbed.

I wasn't sure I should answer, but Jorgas was happy to fill in the details. That, I did not need.

"You killed some people. A boy, two girls, and another guy last night."

Simon's head sprang up from my shoulder. He glared at me through tear-stained eyes. "Last night? No, that's not possible! How can you—"

"It's true," I answered calmly. "We've seen the photos. That's why you need to come with us."

"No, I didn't! I haven't done anything. I just want to be normal!"

He tried to break from my hold, but I was ready for that and held him firm. Jorgas started toward us but I held up a hand, signalling him back. If I was going to do this, I was going to have to do it with trust.

"Simon, don't fight me. You've screwed up, didn't know what you were doing and now you have to fix it. It's all right. Nobody's going to hurt you."

"Liar!"

I felt the searing pain of claws in my back. My eyes clamped shut as I tried to not to scream. I didn't see the hair that had sprung from Simon's chest, nor the teeth that had begun to form in his rapidly extending jaw.

The creature was coming home.

I don't know if it was his anger, or what remained of his human side trying to get me out of harm's way, but Simon shoved me violently into the darkness. I hit one of the market carts with an impact that would have broken a rib in any human—such force in fact, I was actually winded. I wanted to cry out, but the sound choked in my throat. Before I could stop him, Jorgas darted forward and pinned Simon against the wall. The attack seemed to halt his change, though I'd be damned if I knew how. Sudden shock, perhaps?

"Oh no you don't!" Jorgas barked as Simon tried to push him away.

The world swayed around me as I tried to cry out again. My efforts produced only a faint trickle of blood from my lips. I felt ill, as though one of my ribs really had been broken.

"Billy? What are you doing? Put me down!" Simon whined.

"Who's the scum now, arsehole? Who's the trash now?" Jorgas violently shook Simon against the wall. I heard the crack of bone.

"Jorgas… put him…" I choked out the almost muted words.

"It wasn't me, all right? I'm sorry!" Simon pleaded.

"Oh, Christ." I was too weak for either of them to hear as I watched the old wounds of the Saint Barnie's brats reopen in front of me. I coughed once more, sending a spurt of blood over Jorgas.

"Watch where you're spitting, Reylan."

"Jorgas… let him go," I begged, my throat now clearer.

"Stay out of this. I mean it!"

I didn't have much choice. Had I been at full strength, I could easily have broken the two apart. But just then, if either of them changed, I'd surely be killed if I interfered.

"Thought I was going to take the fall for you again, you bastard?" Jorgas continued.

"What are you talking about? The fall for what? Put me down!"

Wherever Jorgas had hit him, Simon was bleeding. I could smell it.

"Why don't you tell him, Reylan? You read the police file, right? That's what the nun said," Jorgas taunted.

"Jorgas, I am not going to warn you again. Put him down!" I could feel my strength returning, however slowly, as the blood's aroma grew stronger.

"Oh yeah," he ignored me. "I've got a real nice record there, Sarah Bateman, right? Sarah Bateman, who I've never even said two words to? That didn't stop me grabbing her while she was wasted and trying to jam my dick in her, did it? Some nice big bruises, a couple of broken fingers—oh wait, that wasn't me. It just sounds better, doesn't it, huh? Couldn't have been someone else, could it? Not some little closet cocksucker with something to prove! You lying piece… of… shit!" The last three words echoed around the room in time with the sickening crack of Simon's body being shoved against the wall, accompanied only by the boy's cries of pain.

"Okay, okay! Stop!" Simon whimpered, choking on the words. "I didn't want to, all right? I swear! The other guys… I tried to ignore their bullshit, but Ritchie, he wouldn't let it go. He was gonna tell Mum, Dad... everyone, if I didn't... So, they got her smashed. I was scared! They made me—"

"They made you?" Jorgas yelled, bashing him against the wall once more.

Simon screamed again, but this time, the scream mutated to something otherworldly and terrifying. A howl of fury and pain, as the boy's neck bulged, breaking Jorgas' grip. His lips pushed out into a snout, and his spine cracked as it expanded to its monstrous form.

I couldn't wait. I leapt forward and forced Jorgas away. He was too surprised to fight me. I bared my own teeth and sank them into Simon, his still half human scream echoing through the dark room as blood spurted from his throat and cascaded down my own, delicious as it had been that first night, the poison of the change not yet taken hold. I felt the impact of Jorgas' fist through the changing werewolf's body, and Simon fell to the ground. His wolf hair and claws receded, leaving the harmless form of a young man lying on the ground in front of me, still as death.

I glared at Jorgas. "What did you do?"

"Hit a pressure point on his spine. He'll be fine. I did that for you."

"What's that supposed to mean?"

"You want him alive, don't you? Whatever. But only for you. I'd much rather see the son of a bitch burn."

"Yes, I got that. For God's sake, Jorgas! What is your damage?" I licked closed the punctures I'd made on Simon's throat, then checked his pulse to make sure he was indeed still alive. I was impressed. For all his other failings, Jorgas could land a precision blow. "How did you know where to hit him?"

"I read a lot, okay? What? You surprised?"

I shrugged. I was, a little.

"Anyway, that charge on my file?" Jorgas looked down at Simon with a derisive snort.

"Oh, no. No. I am not buying this. Simon's gay, Jorgas. You expect me to believe he—"

"You heard him yourself. He went along with it. Had to prove he was a man. When she came to, he gave her my name, told her it was 'Billy' who ripped into her. She was too wasted to remember any better, and all his mates backed him up. They're gutless bastards, Reylan! I'm not taking the fall for him again."

"So, who's this guy, Ritchie?"

"What does it fucking matter?" Jorgas shouted, his temper erupting. "They're all the same. They stick together like a pack of—"

"Shut up, Jorgas!" I snarled.

The room went silent.

"I don't know why, but part of me wanted to believe you were worth my doing this. That you were worth standing up for. Worth finding the real killer for. But I have had enough of your attitude. I have had enough of your little vendetta and your criminal past. I have had enough of your little North Shore cliques and the small-time chaos that lies in their wake. I am here to do one thing only, and that is to bring that boy into the Arcadia Trust. Where they feel Simon should go from there, be it the police, his family or the bloody dog pound, I'll leave to them. I am done with both of you! Do we understand each other? Because if we don't, I have no problem, not one, draining you both dry and letting the Shapers try and fix you. So, either help me, or stay out of my way!"

"And those dead kids?" he growled.

"Tragic. But if we're being perfectly frank? They're not my problem. I don't care."

More silence as I rolled Simon face up and put a hand underneath his head. He was still unconscious.

"If we take him back to that nun, she might kill him," Jorgas muttered.

I nodded. "She might. You'd like that, wouldn't you?"

"Wouldn't you?"

"I beg your pardon? Are you trying to aggravate me? Because that would be a very unwise thing to do just now."

"You really don't care about those kids? Or about Sarah?"

"Not personally, no."

"And what about Ross?"

I stared at him, fury burning behind my eyes. Very good werewolf, now twist the knife counter-clockwise with a little salt…

But Jorgas just stared back. It was an honest stare, a questioning, earnest stare. A stare that made me think very carefully before I spoke again.

"I want you to answer me this, right now. Did you come to my house early last night? Did you attack Ross?"

Jorgas didn't answer right away. He didn't break eye contact either.

"Did you?" I barked.

"No. Reylan, I didn't even know where you lived until you brought me there."

I glanced over at Simon again. "He did." The words were little more than a murmur.

"What?"

"He was my companion, a few nights ago. He knew where I lived." I flinched as Jorgas grabbed my shoulder.

"And you still accused me—"

"Get your paw off me or I'll remove it from both of us."

"Reylan," Simon's voice forced out.

I looked down at the boy in my arms, leaning close to hear his words.

"I didn't kill anybody, I swear."

"You wouldn't remember," I interrupted.

"I do. I remember everything and I—"

"Shut up," Jorgas snarled. "Or we'll kill you right here and now!" He went instantly quiet as my eyes levelled on him.

I turned my attention back to Simon. "What do you remember?"

"I remember you taking me back to your house. How rough you were, how beautiful it felt. I thought I was just drunk. But you bit me. I know you bit me. It was… incredible."

I thought about lying, protesting that it was all in his head. But it seemed foolish. "How do you remember that?"

He didn't answer. I looked at Jorgas, who just shrugged at me. Perhaps it was in the lycanthrope's nature. A mental fortitude rendering them immune to our gifts. I doubted I'd ever get the chance to test that theory.

"I thought maybe… just maybe you could help me with the changes."

"Help you?"

"I wasn't sure. I didn't know anywhere else I could go, so I came back to your house. There were people out front… a cab. So, I came around the back and waited."

I froze, looking at Jorgas again. This time, he wouldn't meet my eyes. I didn't like where this was going.

"First your cat freaked out on me, and then I felt it coming. I tried to run, tried to get away from you. But then it stopped, so I came back. I thought it was safe, and I had to talk to you—"

"Shut up!" Jorgas barked again.

"Then I saw that guy at your place, and something in me freaked out and… Oh, God! I'm sorry!"

I slapped him silent, not wanting to hear any more. I don't remember what I was thinking or feeling, if anything.

My entire body–and curiously, my mind–was numb, as though every nerve right up to my brain had shut down somehow and all I could feel was the gentle tattoo of my quickening pulse. I eased Simon to his feet, and sent Jorgas off to get a set of roughly fitting clothes for him. It took a few guesses to find the right market stall zipped up in its weather coat, but he soon returned with a suitably plain pair of jeans and a white t-shirt with some tourist promotion on it. I barely noticed the detail. The stolen clothes would do.

Simon could walk, barely. Jorgas' blow to his back had been blunt and powerful. But that wasn't what bothered me. Jorgas kept looking at me with slight, apologetic glances, like a child afraid of a parent's disapproval.

The half-changed blood I'd drunk a moment earlier bubbled up through my gut, its ascent delayed by Simon's unfinished transformation. But it was still so potent. So... oh, God!

I had to let go of Simon as I dropped to my knees and coughed some of the toxic red bile up onto the street. The boy ran off. Jorgas ran after him, but he was far too slow. Simon was terrified, and I was the only one who could stop him.

Running ahead of Jorgas, I leapt forward and grabbed Simon's shoulders, forcing him to the ground. I heard a sickening crunch, perhaps one of his ankles as he screamed. I threw a hand over his mouth. My free arm wrapped tight around him, its weakened, blood-starved grip trying to pin him against me.

The scent of Simon's blood was unbearable. Its lycanthropic sweetness heightened by anger and terror as I pulled the boy even tighter. His head twisted, staring at me. His eyes were wide, his gaping mouth muffled by my hand. Frozen tears were still fresh on his cheeks, melted by new ones from the pain of his ankle. My arms were thrown from around him when Jorgas' weight slammed into us.

Another thin strain of poisonous, congealed blood hung from my lips as I tried to spit it to the street. With some effort, I looked over to see Jorgas trying to grapple Simon and force him to the ground. Trying, but not succeeding. Despite his broken bones, Simon pushed hard against Jorgas' assault.

My swaying, blurred vision could barely make out the thick brown hairs that had begun forming on Simon's arms, then Jorgas'. Simon let out a brutal, animal snarl. He had Jorgas pinned. I caught a look at Jorgas' eyes. They were yellow—wolf's eyes—and they wanted Simon's blood. I laboured to my feet. This had to stop. Another transformation from either of them could mean exposure, or worse.

"Jorgas!" I called.

But I got the wrong wolf's attention. Simon's head spun, piercing me with the same hateful yellow eyes I'd seen in Jorgas only a second ago. Eyes that named me prey—named me meat. But Jorgas wasn't done yet.

Simon howled as Jorgas' claws lashed out. They drew long, deep gashes into the boy's face before Simon grabbed the offending paw and bit it, tearing away the now hairy flesh of Jorgas' wrist and spitting it out in a callous show of victory. Jorgas howled, a low, hollow sound that was only choked off when Simon seized hold of his thickening throat.

I hauled Simon off Jorgas and pinned him to my body once more. The boy thrashed against me. The smell of blood—his own and Jorgas'—raked across his face and in his mouth. My tongue flicked out to sample a drop before I could stop it, but I soon slammed my mouth shut, gritting my teeth to stop the scream as Simon's claws buried themselves in my side.

I was more than injured. I was injured and starved. My only chance was to weaken Simon. I sank my teeth in again, drawing more blood as he withdrew his claws and clung to my back, now lost in the ecstasy of my kiss. It was foul at first. Toxic werewolf blood. But I forced it down, until I felt the boy's body shrink in my arms. The sweet, exquisite blood of his human form soon followed. Jorgas called my name twice as I drank, but all that mattered now was the man clinging to me, holding my mouth fast to his throat, as the blood rushed to greet my hunger. He whimpered, moaned in pain and joy as I drank, but I didn't stop. I felt his heart slow and I didn't stop. I couldn't do this. I hadn't in decades. It was terrible, evil and depraved. But why should I not? This creature had attacked Ross. He'd attacked Jorgas. And in doing so, he'd attacked me.

These thoughts came and passed before Simon's last scream became a high-pitched whine. He clawed my neck, pushing me deeper into his own. Then, I felt his heart slow to a full stop, the last of the blood bubbling over my tongue. As I broke from the hold, I stared down into his lifeless eyes, brushing the bloodied hair from his now re-sealed forehead. For the first time in I knew not how many years, I'd killed a man while feeding from him. A werewolf. A beast, perhaps, but still a man. My mouth, the front of my clothes—all bloody testament to that decision. I looked up at Jorgas, who'd safely returned to human form, his wrist now healed. In the short time I'd known him, I'd never seen him look so utterly white.

"Reylan—"

"Don't," I cut him off. "We need to get him back to Patricia. Are you coming?"

Jorgas nodded. Taking one end of Simon's dead body, he helped me move him out of sight.

CHAPTER SEVENTEEN

Patricia Bakker declined to meet us at the door. Instead, the two Shapers who'd attended Ross' wounds greeted us. The woman scowled at me as they gently took the weight of Simon's body from our shoulders–without touching it–and floated him through the narrow hall, out of sight. The still, dead body glided effortlessly through the air, its eyes shut, its limbs and fingers frozen in death. It was the single most eerie sight I'd seen in years. They'd been expecting us.

Jorgas shrugged as we were left alone, though his eyes never left me. Indeed, his stare almost itched. Then came faint agitation of a different sort. A sweetness on the air, rich and appetising.

"Reylan! My God! Are you all right, old man?"

I turned to face Ross and froze, recognising the scent that had aroused me. My friend's blood. "I'm fine," I got out. But I wasn't. I could feel Jorgas' eyes burrowing into my back.

For a moment, I almost wished his gaze could melt me into the floor, or bash me unconscious against the wave of guilt I felt over the night's events, guilt compounded by a sudden desire for Ross' blood. I forced myself to breathe. Blood lust was a childish impulse, one I had to control.

"I saw Kelvin and—"

"Is he alive?"

"Yes. But he's got daggers for you," Ross said, pointedly ignoring Jorgas. "I wouldn't be visiting our infirmary anytime soon."

I finally managed a half smile. One less life on my conscience, as much I despised its owner. I stopped Ross as he moved to hug me and I suddenly remembered the taste of him. Damn it! How long would this last? Surely these feelings couldn't haunt our relationship forever?

"Are you sure you're all right?"

"Ross... later, please?"

He stared at me, all trace of our earlier quarrel gone from his gentle eyes. "Is there anything I can do? I mean, at all?"

He still refused to look at Jorgas, and I knew that this apology, this restoration of all that was good and lasting in our friendship, was for me alone.

"Yes," I said. "You can tell Patricia I'll be waiting in the library."

He planted a tender kiss on my cheek. "You know how much I care about you, right?"

For the first time that evening, I felt a very fortunate man.

* * *

The room was as dark as I remembered. Even on my first visit, the light had been too dim for a human to read by—which perhaps was no problem in this place.

"I returned your boy's wallet."

The voice had emerged from the room's far wall. I stepped forward, peering deeper into the inky void. As the corner of the room became lighter, I could just make out the shape of a young woman, her feet tucked up in a big armchair, a familiar volume on her lap.

Isobel.

"You're referring to Brett, I assume?" I tried to find the light source. But there was no lamp, not even a candle. It was Isobel herself. I stared for a moment, bewildered. Was I seeing things? She never looked up, her eyes darting critically over the page. Could I be imagining this luminescence from her? She had never... no. This was Isobel, who I'd known for almost a century. I had to be imagining it.

"He turned up here, all pale and trembling, looking for you. I sent him to your house."

"Thanks." I peered forward at the page Isobel was reading. I didn't even recognise the alphabet, much less the language. "Is that what I think it is?"

She primly snapped my book shut and smiled. Her eyes were still that deepest shade of mahogany. Her black hair flowed freely down her shoulders, a supple cascade offsetting her alabaster skin. It betrayed her Iberian roots. How human men who'd seen us together had envied me–though not so much the type of men whose company I'd kept in recent years. "Doubtful, considering it's not even what I thought it was."

Why did I get the impression a headache was suddenly imminent?

"It's a religious text," she explained. "It contains temporal echoes, all right. But I wouldn't take them any more literally than the six-day creation story or the parables of Christ."

"Parables?" I murmured. "So, what I saw, the whole incident, the colony, Jal, could be a myth?"

"Not entirely. The echo needs to be imbued with the blood of a witness. Something had to have happened. I think the caster saw something that grew out of unions between Blood Shades and werewolves. Not children, I wouldn't think. Otherwise, why would someone think it's relevant to you and Jorgas? But something else, that needed a warning so horrifying, it would never happen again."

Scare tactics. Laughable in the modern world. But sewn deep within centuries old supernatural religion? It was as good a reason as any for the House of Blood to look upon werewolves with such disdain. Why relationships, even friendships between our two species were almost unheard of. Yet for all its harshness, this 'warning' wasn't what disturbed me.

"What someone?"

"Pardon?"

"You asked why someone would think it was relevant to me."

"I don't—"

"How did they know?" I snapped under my breath. "How did anyone know?"

She shrugged. "The simplest way would have been a fate scrying. Look into the past, possibly the future, depending on when it was done—"

"When would a witch have been close enough to me to do that?"

"Who said it was done to you?"

Jorgas. Newly changed and ignorant of the supernatural world now open to him. Someone had gotten to Jorgas. O'Baer? I'd no way to know. I felt a twinge of anger, as if the thought had awakened some deep, protective instinct.

"And Patricia?"

"Doesn't know. Neither of you would be allowed back here if she did. Interesting, though, that whoever it was chose to give you the book outright. Something so powerful and valuable? They must think quite highly of you."

"Or they're bribing me to stay away."

Isobel stood up, passing the book to me as she took both my hands in hers. "Please, just promise me you'll be careful?"

"I will," I smiled, kissing her forehead. Was I lying? Could I even make that promise anymore?

"Reylan."

I really disliked hearing my name used in that tone of voice.

Patricia leaned against the doorframe, her arms folded, a piercing glare levelled on me as she approached. "Isobel, please leave us."

No stretch of imagination could adequately describe the presence of Patricia Bakker in that room. The woman I'd met previously couldn't compare to the one I saw now. She was dressed in the same trim, well cut cream suit with sharp trousers she'd worn for her meeting with O'Baer. Her face wore an even sharper expression that betrayed no clue to the fact that it was past 3am, or that Bakker was a mere mortal struggling against fatigue's insidious clutch. For all I knew, this was the height of her business day. Striding toward us, dignified and cold as one could ask, was an individual who transcended judge, mother, or headmistress. I felt almost as if I were in the presence of God.

And she was pissed.

Isobel raised a 'good luck' eyebrow to me as she departed, leaving me holding the book like a baby–an unfortunate metaphor, in this instance.

"Your favour from the Shapers?" Bakker nodded at the book.

"That's right. Quite lovely, isn't it?" I said, not caring if she thought I was mocking her. The fact was, I didn't want Patricia to know what I'd been through, or to deduce that I'd slept with Jorgas. Her curiosity had caused me enough stress already. In any case, I had other concerns. Just seeing Patricia's face had unlocked a flood of realisations about the night's events, none of them good. "Tell me," I murmured, my rage simmering beneath a thin veneer of civility. "Are all the Saint Barnie's brats werewolves, or just the two?"

"Just Simon and William. To my knowledge, no one else in either family has changed."

That bitch. She'd known too. She'd known Simon was wolf and said nothing.

"Why didn't you tell me of your prior connection to the boy?" she asked.

"You're in no position to chastise me for withholding information right now, Sister. You, or O'Baer!"

"Isaac O'Baer, whose acquaintance it seems you've also made behind my back, knew both boys better than I. He'd noticed Jorgas becoming more distant and antisocial. Until tonight, Simon had shown no sign of instability or violence."

"You think so, do you?"

"I thought we had an understanding," she sighed. "Your task was to bring Jorgas to us so he could be suitably educated in the ways of his kind, which you did. Then, when Isobel brought last night's murder to our attention, it changed everything."

"Isobel? Isobel reported the last murder to you?"

"Yes. Her contacts within the police were kind enough to leak the preliminary report."

I closed my eyes, driving my fingertips against my temples as my mind made connections I wished I could drive away. I felt foolish. No, I felt positively idiotic.

"O'Baer had to be told. Simon trusted him. Just as, when it became clear you wouldn't be dissuaded, I trusted you to bring Simon back to us." Despite her words, there was no anger anymore. Her face was suddenly empty. Dull and lifeless, as though she'd paused for breath and 3am had caught up in a sudden rush. She stretched out a hand. "May I?"

Against all better sense, I handed over the book, turning my attention to the darkened stacks as she satiated her curiosity. Part of me hoped it would spontaneously combust, taking her along with it.

"Patricia," I lowered my voice, trying not to sound accusing, now that she'd apparently stood down her defences. "What do you hope to accomplish?"

"Pardon?"

"All of... this. The Arcadia Trust. Why would you create such a thing?"

"The Trust is my family, Reylan. My calling."

"Calling? From God, no doubt?" I scoffed, without looking at her.

"Or the Devil. I cannot deny I'm unsure which."

"You'd answer a calling from the Devil?"

"Been there," she said. "Done that, wouldn't you say?"

Ouch. Nerve.

My smirk was gone as soon as I turned around. There, thumbing through the pages of the book, was not Patricia, but a young man. His blond hair, like hers, was combed straight back. His features were fine and delicate. Even his clothing was of similar style. But he was very much a man.

"It's now perfectly clear to me that you've no desire to understand our work," he said, his voice still unmistakeably Patricia's. "Nor respect for our methods."

"What... what are..." I stepped closer, sure that the light had fooled me. It hadn't. Even the hands were male.

The figure looked up at me, his eyes gentle, kinder than Patricia's. Finally, he smiled, handing back the book. "*Ryebyenok dyemona,*" he purred. His breath was brisk and frigid, his voice, teetering on some strange nether-ground between male, female and not entirely human.

I snatched the book from his grasp and averted my eyes. When I looked back, I saw only Patricia, showing no sign that she'd ever been anyone else, and looking just a little outraged at my sudden, rude retrieval of the book. Any trace of 3am was now gone as her steely determination returned, business as usual. Too much business.

"What in the hell—" I stammered.

"I've shown you who we are. What we can do. You can be with us or against us, Reylan, or ignore us completely if you so choose. But until you do decide to be with us, you're not welcome at the Trust, is that clear? I will tolerate no upset to all we've accomplished here."

I took this statement as my cue to leave. There'd be no further answers for me here–or perhaps I was just too confused to argue. Unwilling to give Patricia the satisfaction, I turned on heel and headed for the exit. "I wouldn't dream of it, my dear. I wouldn't dream."

CHAPTER EIGHTEEN

"But why can't I have some more now?" Brett twitched with anticipation and a thirst I couldn't satisfy—at least, not yet. His leg had fully healed, but its recovery had left him hungry, his eyes wide, imploring me. I'd tried explaining his new dilemma, and the opportunities it presented him. But training a new, ill-disciplined member of the household took time, and my patience was waning.

"You have to understand. My blood is highly reactive to your body chemistry. To give you more now would probably kill you. More to the point, it would definitely kill me."

Oh yes, my patience had waned.

"Umm… I'm not going to start eating bugs or anything, am I? I'm really not cool with that."

"Brett, I want you to go home and take out every… vampire novel, movie or television program you own and donate them to some charity shop. Preferably one that's not Catholic. Can you do that for me?"

"Is that such a good idea? I mean, shouldn't I try to learn everything I can?"

I raised a knowing smile, one that took him into my confidence and welcomed him behind the veil. It was time to abandon vain tales of fantasy and embrace the hidden realities of the night. Time to grow up, my sweet, young friend.

"I'll teach you. Now, go home, get some rest, and stay safe."

Brett took a few slow steps toward my front door before turning back. "Can't I... can't I just stay? Be with you and do things for you? You know, be close?"

"Brett, this is a lot for you to take in. I think you should do it on your own terms. Take a long walk. Go see a cheesy movie. Nothing with vampires in it."

He whined like a petulant child. "But I want to stay with you. Not in a queer way. I'll sleep on the couch. Even on the floor, or maybe... maybe I can sit in your room and watch over you while you sleep? I want to be with you."

"Brett. Vampires are real. Or Blood Shades as you will now call us. Keep it to yourself if you want to stay alive. Take a night or two to get used to the idea, then return to me. We'll talk then." My invitation was soft, but firm.

"But Reylan—"

"Brett... goodnight."

Finally, the boy nodded humbly and left. I allowed myself a smile. I liked Brett. He'd do well with the proper care and help. Demetrius glared at me most disapprovingly, from his outstretched position in front of the fire.

"Oh, who asked you?" I sneered, collapsing back into the couch and reaching for the pile of books I'd borrowed. I could barely concentrate as I leafed through the text on werewolves. The other, more curious book, I'd locked safely away in my basement after seeing what it had done to Bakker. The image that had usurped her body, the way he had looked at me, transfixed my memory. The words. *Ryebyenok dyemona...* daemon child.

Now, he was staring at me again from the page.

I stayed on it, breathing steadily, running my fingertips over the image as if to make sure. But there was no mistaking his captionless photograph. The same man.

A loud knocking broke my concentration before I could read more. I cursed under my breath, though far more colourful words came to mind. I was tired and cranky. Visitors, I did not need.

I laboured myself to my feet and forced it open, only to see Jorgas, shivering in the night air. "What are you doing here?"

"Reylan, can I come in?"

I shrugged and let him pass. I wasn't in the mood to fight. "Can you make this quick? Some of us don't do mornings."

"I need to talk to you, and… I wanted to make sure you were all right."

"I'm fine. Just very tired, can't this wait?"

"Not really. Can I spend the day with you then? It's important."

Two in one night? Fine. It was almost dawn, in any case.

I led him back to my room and slid into bed, watching Jorgas nervously shift feet at the end of it like a servant come to the whim of his decadent lord. "You can sleep with me. It's fine." I'd made the invitation before I could reconsider. Was this wise? What was I welcoming back into my bed? To hell with it! I was too tired to be burdened by archaic superstition.

Jorgas slipped off his jacket and pants and climbed into bed, sitting pensively beside me.

"Why'd you do that, Reylan?"

"What did I do?"

"You lied to them."

I raised an eyebrow, looking down at the shaggy mop of brown hair that streamed from Jorgas' head. I hadn't expected this.

He eased himself up and looked at me, his eyes a tempest of sadness, confusion, and anger.

"Yes, I suppose I did."

"Why? Why did you let them think Simon killed those kids?"

I didn't give him an immediate answer. What could I say? That Simon had taken the fall for Jorgas' freedom? Didn't that just make them even? Had I not lied, the boy in my bed would have belonged to Patricia Bakker, possibly for the rest of his life, which might have been quite short, had he not learned to behave himself.

"Because you're the one I chose," I murmured.

Jorgas didn't speak again for a good five minutes. He didn't touch me either. We just sat in silence. The voice of Simon, the confused young werewolf we'd... I'd killed, echoed in my head.

"I'm a murderer, Reylan."

"No, you're not. Your body changes. Your mind changes. You can't control what happens after that."

"Maybe not, but I still remember it."

"I know, and I'm not prepared to judge you." I found myself suddenly unsure of my own feelings, or what kind of answer, if any, Jorgas was hoping for. "Tell me, do you think Simon killed anyone?"

"That one last night, near Fantasy? That had to be him, didn't it?"

The fourth murder, another white lie in the night, forged by Isobel and her police contacts, all to keep the Trust off Jorgas' back. Her way of looking out for me. My dear old friend of dubious morals.

"Yes," I whispered. "It had to be him."

Jorgas relaxed again, turning to face me. I couldn't meet his eyes. "If I tell that nun the truth, she won't believe me, will she? Or she'll kill me."

"You're not going to tell her. What happened tonight's between the three of us. Simon would have killed you, Jorgas.

And he attacked Ross. When he did that, he attacked me. I don't care who else wants to stick their nose in. It's our own bloody business."

Jorgas rested his head on my chest, his arm around me. "You could have saved him."

"Would you rather he lived?" I asked. "He would have told Bakker the truth."

"The point is, now I can't do anything," Jorgas snarled. "I can't even tell her myself. You've forced me to——"

"Forced?" I smiled, bringing my warm hand up to the nape of his neck. "You make me feel all powerful."

"And one night, I'll kill you for it."

My hand caressed the back of his head as his eyes closed, my fingers running through his thick brown hair, his chest heaving against mine as he surrendered to the soft ocean of sleep.

"I know," I whispered.

I held the boy close against me. The comforting warmth of sweet blood glowed from his body as I tightened my embrace. In those few moments, which I spent kissing his forehead, his cheeks and the curve of his neck, I felt as safe and secure as I had ever been. I knew Jorgas would never kill me for protecting him.

Not when there were so many other good reasons.

SINS OF THE SON

Abandoned by his werewolf lover, the only thing Reylan wants is to return to his vampire life of blood and beautiful boys. It's a solid plan, until his first meal as a single man tries to kill him.

Hoping to free his young would-be assassin from the religious zealots that sent him, Reylan enlists the help of Iain Grieg, a charismatic priest with unsettling knowledge of the night's secrets.

Surrounded by conflicting agendas and an army fuelled by hate, Reylan fights to secure his future, if he can only trust the mysterious priest and bury the ghosts of the past.

Also by Christian Baines:

PUPPET BOY

A school in turmoil over its senior play, a sly career as a teenage gigolo, an unpredictable girlfriend with damage of her own, and a dangerous housebreaker tied up downstairs. Any of these would make a great plot for budding filmmaker Eric's first movie. Unfortunately, they're his real life. When Julien, a handsome wannabe actor, transfers to Eric's class, he's a distraction, a rival, and one complication too many. Yet Eric can't stop thinking about him.

Helped by Eric's girlfriend, Mary, they embark on a project that dangerously crosses the line between filmmaking and reality. As the boys become close, Eric soon wants to cross other lines entirely. Does Julien feel the same way, or is Eric being used on the gleefully twisted path to fame?

SKIN

Kyle, a young newcomer to New Orleans, is haunted by the
memory of his first lover, brutally murdered just outside the
French Quarter.

Marc, a young Quarter hustler, is haunted by an eccentric
spirit that shares his dreams, and by the handsome but
vicious lover who shares his bed.

When the barrier between these men comes down, it will
prove thinner than the veil between the living and the
dead…or between justice and revenge.